A VAMPIRE'S SPELL

THE ORDER OF THE BLACK OAK - VAMPIRES

MARIE-CLAUDE BOURQUE

SEA STORM PUBLISHING

This is a work of fiction. Names, characters, businesses, places, events, locales, and incidents are either the products of the author's imagination or used in a fictitious manner. Any resemblance to actual persons, living or dead, or actual events is purely coincidental.

A VAMPIRE'S SPELL
The Order of the Black Oak Series - Vampires
Copyright © 2020 by **Marie-Claude Bourque**
Sea Storm Publishing
P.O. Box 15531, Seattle WA 98115

Edited by Jennifer Bray Weber
Cover Design by Frauke Spanuth
Paperback ISBN: 978-1-956115-02-4

To Logan and Finlay, a little bit of your history

CHAPTER 1

QUICK AUTHOR'S NOTE: If you enjoy A Vampire's Spell, *make sure to go to my website to download your free copy of the prequel* A Vampire's Heart.

Old-Montreal, Québec, Canada
Present Time

*M*aisie Thibodeau silently eyed the tall blonde vampire who was leaning on the stone wall of the *Sanctuaire des Truands.*

"Are you it?" The deadly woman sneered under Maisie's appraisal. The fur collar of her long deerskin coat fluttered in the icy wind. "You're all they sent to contain me?"

The creature pushed herself to her feet and blocked Maisie's path to the curved porch leading into the historical building. Steadying the heels of her thigh-high leather boots on the packed snow of the courtyard, she crossed her arms at her chest with hostility.

Weary, Maisie hiked her travel duffel bag over her plain

down vest. Every inch of her magic legacy soared in her veins as she shot the woman a lethal look.

She would not let Emmeline Dubois rattle her.

Maisie had been chosen to do one job—been sent by the Order of the Black Oak all the way to Montreal from her small New England town of Berwick Hollow for a single purpose—babysit the unstable vampire. And that was what she would do.

Her fists tightened in her fleece mittens as her mind fixated on her charge. Unknown to the Order, she was also dead set on learning as much as she could about the lethal beings inhabiting the city. Only then would her knowledge of the otherworldly be found vast enough to take over the high priestess-hood of her coven from her grandmother when the time came.

She had big shoes to fill and this assignment would finally convince the supernatural council of the Order that despite her social challenges, Maisie was strong enough to carry on the tradition after Nana Thibodeau.

"Where's your leader, hun?" Maisie's tone was as cold as the air surrounding them. She lifted her chin to level with the vampire's pristine blue gaze, unfettered by the beauty's belligerent attitude.

And yes, Emmeline *was* gorgeous. Tall and perfectly proportioned, her body an ideal hourglass in the trendy form-fitting minidress under the pelt coat, her facial features exquisite in their femininity.

But the centuries-old French-Canadian was also a monster. A filthy predator who had a tendency to prey on humans instead of feeding on the synthetic blood offered by the shelter to the cursed ones like her.

And that wretched being was now blocking Maisie's entry to the *Sanctuaire*, an ancient nunnery that was Emmeline's home. Said to have been founded in secret by Saint Marguerite d'Youville in the sixteenth century to help troubled youths, it was now a cleverly disguised haven for newly cursed vampires, the shelter run by none other than Valerian Callan St-Amand, the Mount-Royal Immortal.

Maisie's insides bristled as she searched the courtyard of the sanctuary behind Emmeline, remembering the ancient legacy vampire who'd caught her eye in Berwick Hollow last summer. Valerian St-Amand was nothing like the monster facing Maisie.

"He's got no time for you, *p'tite fille*." Emmeline smirked and took a step forward. A flash of lethal fangs shone beneath the perfectly drawn curve of her lips.

Maisie sighed and cast another anxious look at the entrance, her mouth pursed with apprehension at meeting him again. Then she gripped the handle of her duffel bag tighter. It seemed she would need to deal with her ward before having a chance to meet Valerian to sort out her duties.

"Tell him I'm here," she finally ordered the female vamp, her flat furry boots solidly planted on the icy pavement, her breath leaving tiny crystals of condensation that gleamed under the streetlights illuminating the tortuous empty Old-Montreal street.

"Why?"

"You know perfectly well why, Emmeline Dubois," she spat. "We have an agreement. My nana and Valerian St-Amand. I'm here to watch over you."

The vamp advanced again, her long coat wide open flapping behind her. She was now so close Maisie could smell her expensive perfume and feel the growl that emanated from somewhere inside the creature's belly.

She looked like a fashion model, all right. With her high cheekbones, feline-like features, and her long crystal blonde hair escaping from a luxurious fur hat, no doubt she had ensnared much human prey with that look.

But it was that small cold part of Maisie—that part which made her useless to hold a regular job and unable to read social cues—that made her the perfect guardian for the monster. She would never fall for Emmeline's immense charms.

And of course, Maisie had the magic. As a witch of the White Holly, of those who tethered between sanity and madness, she was fully aware of her abilities to keep the cold beauty in check.

But she really didn't feel like enacting her powers just now.

She reluctantly craned her neck up at the predator and took a resigned step back in a loose defensive pose. Her right hand drew back behind her, her palm prickling with contained energies.

Fighting Emmeline was truly the last thing she wanted to do. She'd had a long bus ride over to Montreal, leaving Berwick Hollow at dawn that morning. It was now past dinnertime; she was hungry and cranky. Her hair felt clammy under the knitted cap, her body stiff from being cramped in a back seat rank with body odor from the overheated vehicle.

She had expected that someone from the sanctuary would be waiting for her at the bus station. If not Valerian himself, then maybe Father Grégoire who ran the shelter with him.

But as she'd stepped off the bus at the busy downtown station, her blood pounding at the anticipation of finally meeting him again, she had realized they had forgotten her.

Her heart crushed, she had quickly understood that her big assignment—her chance to prove that she was more than a political pawn between vampires, warlocks, and witches— was likely inconsequential to the worldly immortal.

"I never wanted you here, *sorcière*." Emmeline's crystalline blue eyes peered down at Maisie with scorn.

"It's not like you have a choice, is it?" Maisie shot back, still disappointed that she'd been forgotten, but ready to show her charge who was boss.

"Go home, you stupid bitch," Emmeline drawled with resentment. "Val doesn't want you here."

Her face was now just above Maisie's. Her eyes sparkled

with hatred. The long hair fanning the vamp's cheeks descended in blonde curtains which brushed Maisie's thick quilted vest.

Maisie inhaled slowly to calm her mind, raging both from the cold trepidation at facing off a vampire and the fury at the creature's words. She may miss social cues, get rattled by busy crowds, and have an unusual aversion for disrupted routines but she was the very opposite of *stupid*.

"I'm not here for Valerian. I'm here for *you*." Maisie narrowed her eyes at her ward—the vampire centuries older than her and who had indirectly created a large portion of the poor cursed souls sheltered in the old nunnery—as she drew the power within her. What had caused the surplus of synapses in her brain, had also enabled her strong ability to channel the magic inside her. "Don't cross me."

"And what will you do about it?" Without warning, the vamp's hand shot straight for Maisie's throat, blocking her airway.

Cripes!

Emmeline clutched Maisie's neck with incredible strength. Her face twisted in a malevolent grimace.

Maisie's duffel bag fell at their feet. Her hands flew to her foe's wrist. She seized it hard, trying in vain to loosen the vicious hold.

A lancing pain hacked through her at the vampire's nails dug deep into her bare skin. The unrelenting grip compressed the thick chain of Maisie's silver pentacle into her flesh.

The undead hung tight. "I told you no one wants you here," she growled. Emmeline's fangs were fully out now, her breath as icy as the frigid wind howling around them.

Maisie's lungs burned, her voice useless for a spell. Her mind slowed, contemplating countless options in a fraction of a second.

"Maybe I'll make a brand-new little bloodsucker out of you," the blonde purred against Maisie's cheek as she lifted her off her feet so that they were face to face.

Maisie's lungs collapsed in lancing agony, her throat a scorching torture. She was looking into two blue pools of pure wrath.

She shut her eyes and closed her body to it all. Detached, as if she was looking down at the scene, she silently summoned the deity of their coven. *Matronae, I call upon your triple essence.*

"And he said you were so strong," the vamp cackled into her ear.

Maisie mentally gathered the energy of the wind around her, the power of her family blood coursing through her flesh, powers long forgotten, passed down from generation and generation, all the way from her very first Acadian ancestor who had set foot in the new world from distant European shores.

Guided by her deity, she gathered it all within her. Felt it roar inside her heart. With her head pounding and pulsing with every ounce of her abilities—taking over any sane thoughts left in her—Maisie mounted the mystical energy into a tight ball of pure raw power.

And she just flung her eyes open.

The magical blast hit the vamp fully in the chest. A pressure wave that forced Emmeline's body to recoil at once.

She released Maisie's throat and stared at her stunned.

"Stryos!" Maisie let her anger bubble to the surface as she shouted another spell, both arms set straight in front of her, palms out.

Emmeline fell back hard to the ice and caught herself, her hands behind her. She shot the witch a look full of fury. *"Non non*, you bitch!"

The monster hissed and snarled, a craving to kill etched deep into her features. Then she leaped. Her body rose up in the air in a tall arc, high above Maisie, and landed right behind her in the deserted street.

Maisie swiveled to face her, her palms burning with contained white fire, ready to strike.

6

"What the hell, Valerian!" Emmeline peered past Maisie to the sanctuary's entrance. "I don't need this."

Valerian? Maisie's heart seized, her limbs froze. With a large gulp, she turned back to the shelter's entryways. Oh flaming hells! It was *him*.

A tall posture in a woolen coat adorned with silver fox fur that fluttered in the cold wind. Dark smoldering eyes in a classic profile with an ever-present undercurrent of darkness, which hummed with magical legacy. All his features joined with the inherited vampirism flowing through his vein to create the man—no the three-hundred-year-old being—who was now casually watching Maisie with a half-smile etched on his full lips.

His hand rested on the head of his hefty black Labrador, who sat on his hind legs by the immortal's side. The dog considered the two women with a calm demeanor, obviously waiting for his master's call to act.

Maisie's core warmed uncontrollably despite the cold, hit by the intense crush that had not left her since she'd first set eyes on him five months ago. She knew she was being silly, that twenty-five-year-olds didn't fall in love with men they barely knew. But she was not a regular girl, was she? And just as she panicked in thick crowds and constantly needed to resettle her racing overactive brain, she had not been able to stop the crazy teenage-like infatuation sweeping her whole.

"Emme, meet Maisie Thibodeau. Your guardian." His voice echoed rich and velvety into the crisp city air as he nodded to Maisie. The tone a deep frequency that settled heavily into her very core.

With her eyes wide, she took him all in. While her heart hammered wildly, she let out a measured breath. She forced her jumbled mind to focus, to calm her intense longing of nestling her weary body right there at his broad chest, her cheek upon the black shirt under the open coat.

Lost in her cravings, she missed the shift in the air.

An unnaturally strong grip seized her from behind. A piercing sting dug into her neck.

Emmeline.

"*Dhio meih ban-dhia!*" Maisie roared her spell into the night.

A surge of protective energy shot straight out through her skin. Blasted the vampire off her.

Searing pain from Emmeline's bite at her neck had scattered through her body. Her pentacle burned red hot at her throat from being so quickly called upon.

She dismissed both and swiveled to face her foe, her arms stiff and ready at her side. Her fingertips brimmed with the last of her harvested magical fuel.

The vamp towered over her, a derisive smirk on her lips, her fangs dripping with Maisie's blood.

Maisie shifted on her heels with slight hesitation. She had learned to fend off wraiths and daevas—those nasty creatures that feed on people's life force—but never a vampire. She was starting to wonder whether she truly had it in her to contain this one.

But she couldn't fail. Not on her first day here.

And oh cripes, not with Valerian watching her.

The hair at the back of her neck stiffened. Emmeline's face was now a mask of hunger. Her eyes blood-shot and feverish, anything that had been beautiful about her had completely vanished. Maisie was facing a raw famished predator angry to get more of her.

Cold fear now trickled inside her as the cool blonde casually strode closer, the sneer still on her face. As if she was toying with her prey, knowing very well that she was taller and stronger than Maisie, that she could snap her like a twig and drain her whole in minutes.

She felt Valerian's presence right behind her. She knew the immortal had magic. Hells, why was he not stopping the cold-blooded killer wanting to end her?

No. Maisie stop. That little voice inside her rose up again.

The tone that could always shut her emotions when things turned overwhelming was now calling, stronger and stronger.

You are a witch of the White Holly. You have ancient powers coursing through you. Your mother, your nana. Your cousins. The Beaudrys and the Thibodeaus. Her full ancestry was shouting to her. Shutting the sweaty fear away. Giving her that last bit of energy she needed to overtake her foe.

"*Fuyrich aloiys lusgadh!*" She thrust one strong arm at the vamp, casting an unseen force that recoiled back into her shoulder, causing her to blink from the strain.

Emmeline screamed. She slumped to the ground and writhed in agony at Maisie's feet while the witch held her invisible grip on her adversary with two steady palms above the perfect body twisting under her command.

"Val!" Emmeline moaned with agony as she shouted to the immortal. Her coat opened wider, revealing the expanse of creamy bare skin of her thigh just below the short skirt.

Maisie glanced at Valerian. Shock hit her to see his aggrieved gaze fall on the monster.

No! He loved her.

The hurt from the revelation shot through her well-guarded emotions, piercing her heart. Shattering the silly hope that she, Maisie, had a chance for the immortal's affection.

"Val!" Emmeline screamed through the pain Maisie was still inflicting. "Stop her."

"Enough," Valerian called out with a short breath before striding by Maisie's side, his Labrador padding loyally behind him.

She shuddered as the immortal's warm scent of spices mixed with masculinity enveloped her whole and stirred enticingly with her insides.

"*Sulahs!*" His spell dispelled Maisie's with ease.

She folded forward on herself. Spent from the strain of using magic, she labored to catch her breath, her palms anchored over her thighs. Her body started to shake from the cold of the night. Her neck lanced from Emmeline's bite.

She had failed. Got attacked by the one creature she had been sent to guard. *Damn*.

"You can't let her do this to me, Val." Emmeline had scrambled to her knees. Her eyes were now beautifully damp from crying, her pouty mouth lush as she pleaded with the immortal. "She's not one of us."

Maisie's heart fell once more to see Val's anguish dig into his even features as he helped Emmeline to her feet.

"She is." Valerian's tone was cutting. He turned to Maisie, his penetrating gaze sending strange flutters right through her chest, further down even, despite the cold air. "Very much so."

She straightened as he handed her a black silk handkerchief for her wound. His full lips curled into a slow wolfish smile while his big dog approached Maisie to sniff her left hand.

"*Mademoiselle* Thibodeau. Maisie. My apologies for not picking you up at the station. Small emergency in the kid vamps' quarters." He cocked an eyebrow at her and a faint hint of amusement crossed his deep brown irises. "Welcome to Montreal."

CHAPTER 2

eigneur! The woman was strong. Just as he remembered when she had taken down that troll in Berwick Hollow this summer. Had he finally found someone, beside himself and his brothers, who was capable to subdue Emme?

Valerian had balked at the idea when the brotherhood of warlocks had wanted to send someone over. He and his siblings had done fine coexisting with humans for centuries. Laying low.

But Mag had put in this thick skull that running the *Serpent Maudit* club was no longer enough to entertain him. He wanted to play with magical artifacts now.

And when the Order had caught wind of that, compounded by the fact that Emme had helped Evan Grant, one of his own cursed pupils, to escape the *Sanctuaire* and mess with one of the warlocks' family, Val and his brothers had had no choice.

A treaty had been brokered between Diesel Stanford of the Order of the Black Oak, High Priestess Thibodeau and The Elder Beaudry from the Witches of the White Holly—the latest coven to join the Order—and himself, Valerian, to represent the Mount-Royal Immortals.

And the first step in their alliance had been to send one of their strongest witches to Montreal as a gesture of faith to keep an eye on Emmeline.

Emme. He gave an inward groan as he glanced back at her lingering in the courtyard. The thorn in his side. The one mistake that would haunt him forever, which had dictated his entire existence.

How many teen vamps did he have to save before he made up for what he had done to her. An infinity. An immortal life, that was how long. He leaned on his heels, the back of his throat tightening.

"You could have helped me." Maisie Thibodeau's modulated voice rose beside him, her tone detached. "You have plenty of magic to stop her."

With a sigh, he watched Emme rearrange her short dress in place before turning to the witch, still marveling at the amount of power in such a slender person. High Priestess Thibodeau had warned him to be careful with her granddaughter, that the girl could be alternately fearless and awkward.

As he looked at her now, a regular twenty-something woman—her elfin body lost in a thick puffy down vest and cream-colored furry boots, strands of poker-straight black hair escaping from a knitted blue hat—she looked harmless. With no hint of the confident spellcaster who had taken down the beast set on her small town, or the woman who had just brought down his blood-thirsty ex-fiancée.

The sharp eyes of jade green now studying him with curiosity betrayed none of the ancestral magical power running through her veins.

She looked very different from the woman he had last admired in the New England forest last summer. She had stood under a full moon with the witches of her coven, clad in a diaphanous foot-length pale dress which quivered in the midsummer breeze, a sleek silver pentacle at her throat and delicate white flowers in her hair. That woman, a key member of the White Holly Coven, had brought deep and unusual cravings right below his belt. As soon as his gaze had rested upon her, the droning of her elders had been meaningless. He had been consumed by the heated pull she had created through his entire body and had to quickly retreat away from her once he'd assured her she would be welcomed in Montreal despite his misgivings about her visit.

"I just wanted to see how you would fare with Emme." He shrugged off the warmth now building at his navel from his recollection, conflicted by her very presence.

In fact, as he'd watched her battle Emme, he had allowed the worse of him to take over. Annoyed at the Black Oak Order's involvement in their lives he'd taken out his resentment on the witch by testing the extent of her power further, gauging how she'd react to Emme's attacks.

But now he was nothing but impressed by her resilience. And his plan to view her as a foe had failed. He still liked her. A lot.

"And…how did I do?" Her brow lifted, her eyes narrowed in concentration. "I hate to call on my pentacle, but I had no choice—"

"You make a great guardian." A surge of protectiveness for Maisie rose within him. He smiled slowly and patted Sasha's head as the dog pushed back against his thigh.

His chest tightened, and he cursed himself from having left the witch fending for herself alone at the bus station. He should have sent a disciple in his place.

"She could have turned me." Maisie shot him a puzzled look. "Why did you do nothing to help?"

"She wouldn't have." Guilt churned his gut at having let it go that far. He had swooped in at the last minute to help her with the troll in Berwick Hollow, but this was different. He knew that while Emme liked to toy with mortals, she wouldn't dare hurt anyone with him right there.

"I was about to," Emme sneered. "I don't need a guardian."

"Yes, you do." Val shot her another aggrieved look. Even

centuries later, the memory of the sweet girl he had turned into a monster dug into his heart. "We don't need another Evan Grant."

"Grant?" Maisie asked.

"The kid used to be so much fun before he became Mag's bodyguard," Emme grumbled.

"I'm not sure if the warlocks told you everything, but Evan Grant is the entire reason for your presence here." Val grabbed Maisie's duffel and sighed. "Let's get in and I'll show you your room. Emme, come on in—you're scaring the tourists."

"It's too cold. No one's around tonight." With a smirk, Emme brushed the snow from her long coat and ambled lazily behind them.

"And this Evan Grant?" Maisie inquired again with purpose. "Is he reformed now?"

Val was reluctant to answer. "So you do know about him. Emme should never have bitten those street kids and fed them her blood last year." The dog at his heels, he led her into the sanctuary. He helped her out from her down vest and hung it above the long wooden bench by the door. "She turned them into vampires. And that's what ultimately led the supernatural council to our existence."

"And to answer your question," he added. "Yes, Evan is fine. He's weaned and on synth blood. He works at my brother's nightclub now."

Maisie took off her sweater and frowned at him as she removed her knitted cap. A cascade of straight black hair fanned against her cheek and down to her chest. The tip of her sleek locks fell over her form fitted t-shirt, which sported a funky space exploration logo right over the swell of her left breast.

He gulped as he noticed her exquisite figure in the tight blue jeans, her plain outfit underscoring too well the gentle curve of her waist.

There she was again. What had been hidden under the

heavy winter garbs was now as enticing as the summer beauty's charms from his memories.

He was about to explain how he'd rehabilitated Evan after months of hard work when he sensed Sasha growling under his hand. Loud noises erupted from the courtyard.

"Val!" Emme's panicked scream pierced the air just outside the door.

He dropped Maisie's sweater and bolted outside to see Emme on the ground in the snow wrestling with three humanoid forms. The assailants' skin was opalescent, their cheekbones sunken.

Val's jaw tightened with a huff. *Rogue vampires. Damn it!*

No one he recognized. Dressed in ill-fitting winter clothing and jeans, dirty hair bare to the snowfall that had turned to sleet, they were struggling to pin Emme down on the cobblestones and losing the fight.

Sasha let out a worried bark, ready to jump into the fray.

"Stay," Val ordered the dog.

In seconds, Val was towering over them, his muscles quivering with fury. He grabbed one by the collar, yanked him off Emme, and flung him at the ancient pillar of the sanctuary's entrance.

The attacker's body smashed into the old stones and thumped hard onto the icy ground. The young vamp gathered on all fours, cast Val a bloodshot look full of fright and scrambled away to the narrow street.

"*Merde*! The fucking thing bit me." Emme's lethal fangs were now fully drawn out as the other two creatures tried to pin her down, wrestling with her frantic limbs.

Val swerved to the biggest one, a grimy young adult clothed in a busted blue hockey jacket. He grabbed the creature's head with both hands and snapped his neck with a swift twist.

The attacker dropped at his feet, motionless.

"*Lruannicth*..." He heard Maisie starting a spell behind him, but her voice was faint. She had to be completely depleted at this point.

"Leave it," he shouted back at her. "We got this."

Effortlessly, he seized Emme's last aggressor by the throat, blocking the teen vampire's airway with a tight grip.

His blood boiled with anger at seeing a scratch mark on his ex-lover's throat. He may no longer be in love with Emme, and she was as vicious as they came, but he would not let any harm come to her.

He hauled the creature completely off her and lifted him in the air.

The vamp's feet, clad in battered work boots, battled the void under him. He gripped Val's wrists, useless. His eyes rolled back in his head.

"Kill him, Val. Come on. Do it. Bastard ruined my favorite dress." Emme brimmed with glee. "Let's use fire."

"No!" Maisie protested as she rushed toward them, her upper body in the small t-shirt shivering in the sub-zero temperature.

"Maisie, go back inside," Val shouted. "It's too cold."

But she just glared at him, rubbing her bare arms as crystallized drizzle dusted her hair.

"You should kill that thing." Emme got to her feet and brushed the snow off her torn dress before pointing at Maisie with anger. "And you, *p'tite fille*, you're supposed to protect me."

"I'm here to protect people *from* you." Maisie's voice rose strong despite her shaking body. "No one in their right mind would attack you."

"She's right." Val dropped the creature to his feet, loosening his grip just enough to let him breathe. He narrowed his eyes at him. "What do you want with Emme? Come on, talk."

The teen vampire opened his mouth and shook his head. Fear rippled through his wretched gaze.

"*Merde*, Val. His tongue's cut out."

"*Diable!*" He saw it now, the gaping hole in the creature's mouth. A series of burn scars and old lacerations were scattered along the vamp's cheeks and neck. Val's anger at his attack on Emme receded. The vampire was just a kid, another blood-cursed victim. "He's been tortured."

"This one too." Maisie stood above the unconscious body of the second vamp. "He's missing a couple of fingers and half his face is burned."

Val trusted his captive to Emme. "Take this one to Father Grégoire," he ordered. "I'll bring in the other one. He might talk when he's reanimated."

The blonde wrinkled her nose at her attacker, who stood meekly defeated, all slumped over himself. She grabbed him by the back of his coat and rolled her eyes with a huff.

"Is he dead?" Maisie asked as she examined the comatose form of the bigger vamp, its neck crooked at an odd angle. Sasha was at her side, sniffing the teen carefully. "He's not breathing or anything."

The witch was crouched in the snow, her long hair brushing her thighs as she gently patted Sasha's flank. A vision of pure freshness, so alive amongst all of them, cursed creatures. His heart went to her and he wanted to sweep away the snowflakes scattered upon her hair, take that slender hand into his to lead her back to the warmth of his home. To safety. Her trembling body was not meant to sustain the cold night.

"No, only fire or decapitation can kill a vampire," he told her. "And sometimes, the sun. Father Grégoire will be able to revive this one so we can figure out why he went after Emme."

Val sighed, once more taking in Maisie's smooth curves, fighting with all his might the rising attraction he felt for the witch. She was too young. Too mortal. He should be trying to find out why Emme was attacked, not pine for the newcomer, no matter how fascinated he was by her.

And now she *had* to stay. To protect Emme.

Sasha returned to his master and Val scratched the back of his dog's ear. He tore his eyes from the witch to look back at Emme dragging her foe across the packed snow on the court-yard with a vicious smirk.

There could be no woman in his life. His love had brought nothing but ruin.

"What's this?" Maisie called. A frown marred her pretty features as she peered at something on the snow bank edging the narrow street.

She picked the object and took it over to Val. A glass hypo-dermic needle was pinched between her fingertips. Were the teen vamps on drugs? Val studied the syringe with care. His heart sank.

"It's blood, fresh blood." And he could smell exactly where it came from. "They weren't biting Emme. They were extracting her blood."

CHAPTER 3

*H*er mind buzzing with too much input and her heart fluttering, Maisie banged her feet on the outside wall by the door to shake away the snow from her furry boots, then rushed inside for warmth.

The place smelled of beeswax, burning candles, and incense. She briefly noticed the chapel at her left and the wooden floor of the entryway, which gleaned with polish under the glow of a refurbished chandelier above her. A small rugged crucifix hung at the wall. So much for that vampire myth.

But she was now much more interested in the syringe in her hand, Emmeline's dark red blood filling half of the glass barrel.

She shuddered and watched Valerian coming in behind her, his friendly dog—Sasha, he called him—not leaving his side. "Does this mean Emmeline is in danger?"

"I have no idea." He yanked the vamp over the doorstep before dropping his captive on the floor. He took the syringe from her and dropped it in the pocket of his long coat. "Maybe this one will tell us when he comes to."

"How can he come back from a broken neck?" She quizzed.

"The bones and nerve system will eventually mend them-selves. Might take a day or two but Father Grégoire has his own ways if we need to hurry."

"Magic?"

"Nah, not like what you witches use. More like ceremonial incantations, alchemy rituals."

"He's human?"

"Yes. A disciple of Nostradamus, ancient protector of immortals." He shot her a half-smile.

"Nostradamus, as in...the astrologer?" Maisie slowly shook her head in disbelief.

"Our dear Father Grégoire." Emmeline snorted as she dragged in her own attacker, who had now completely passed out. She closed the door to the frigid elements behind her. "Val's blood bag."

"Uh?" Alarm caused her spine to snap stiff.

"Oh didn't you know, girl? Val feeds from humans now and again."

"Shut up, Emme."

"Well it's true. You're all high and mighty, thinking you're better than me. Yet you can't survive on synth like I do." She turned to Maisie with a smirk. "He *has* to feed on humans. Otherwise he dies."

"Is she right?" The disclosure cast an ominous shadow in her mind.

Val's expression turned dark, as if he'd shut himself in. "Yes," he finally spat.

Flaming hells! This was shocking news. No one in New England knew about this. If the immortals fed on humans, the Order needed to be told. They had a strict code about human involvement, the least the better. "I'll have to tell Nana," she blurted. "And the warlocks."

"No. You won't." In a blink, he was an inch from her face, his eyes smoldering, his full lips drawn into a thin line. His faint scent of rich spices mixed with the aura of deadly predator folded over her.

"I have to." This was too important. She couldn't hide such a revelation from her elders. Frantic, she reached into her jean pocket for her phone.

"Stop. I'm not one of the bad guys." He sighed as if trying to convince himself and his gaze on her softened. He took a step back and settled a firm hand on his dog's head.

"That's true." Emmeline's pretty features twisted with annoyance. "He's way *too* good if you want my opinion."

"How? Do you really feed from your priest?" Maisie pushed her hair off her face, not sure what to think.

"Yes. I do." Val did not meet her gaze. "I *consume* his blood—I don't feed from him directly. All my brothers participate in the *Rituel du Sang*. And my priest, as you call him, is more than a priest. Father Grégoire is a disciple of the Nostredame Guild. One of his duties is to supply me with his own blood."

"Oh gods." How had she not known this? They'd all happily believed that the St-Amand brothers were content with synthetic or animal blood.

"Once a year," Val said.

"Once?"

"Yes. On the night of the Geminids meteor shower. Always between Samhain and Yule. Like his mentors before him, Father Grégoire is my guardian in this generation. All the way back to Michel de Nostredame who discovered immortals and sought to align with our powers. Nostredame calculated the precise celestial alignment to determine our feeding night."

"And if Father Grégoire can't give you his blood that night?"

"Others in the guild can. They are pledged to us. When we were born, they appeared to our mother, disguised under the church's mantle. She took us to them every year. We've been doing this for centuries."

"And if you skip a yearly feed?" Maisie would eventually need to report back every single detail to her coven.

"I tried… once." He glanced at Emmeline, his voice devoid of emotions.

"The poor *chéri* nearly killed himself out of guilt, didn't you, *mon amour*?"

He flinched. "Don't bring her into our thing, Emme."

Our thing. Maisie felt the words cut deep in her chest, forcing her heart to shrink on itself. Of course, she was the outsider to their three hundred years together. Her twenty-five years of existence were a mere blink to them.

"I want to know." She pushed her shoulders back as she refocused on her true goal for being in Montreal, learning everything she could.

An awkward silence rose as Emmeline and Valerian exchanged a look full of meaning.

"Why shouldn't she know?" The female vampire finally broke the quiet.

"These two need to go to Father Grégoire's lab." Valerian nodded at the fallen teen vamps and ignored the question.

"I need to know," Maisie insisted. A voice in her told her she was being insensitive, but her heart didn't care. She wanted to uncover every secret in Valerian's past. It was her duty to her coven, she reasoned with herself.

But he shook his head and cast her an ominous look. "Don't mention the feeding to your grandmother. It could cause an all-out war between your witches, the warlocks, and my brothers. Black Oak warlocks won't like us meddling with humans. And we've got more to worry about."

"What happens if you don't feed every year?" Maisie said once more, overlooking the dark undercurrent raging across his gaze.

"Nothing," he spat. "Nothing at all."

He hoisted the mute vamp over his shoulder and picked up the other one by his parka before lugging them both down the hall, Sasha at his heels.

Maisie called after him. "But—"

"Emme," he stopped her, "show Maisie where she'll sleep."

He disappeared down the long hallway, his dark curls brushing the fur collar of his coat over the wide shoulders. His steps were precise and strong, emphasizing his resolve to move away from anyone mentioning his past.

"You've done it now." Emmeline picked Maisie's duffel bag and ambled down the hall.

"I don't understand." Maisie hastened behind the blonde.

"He's really pissed."

"But you started it."

"Here's a thing, *p'tite fille*," Emmeline said over her shoulder. "Val will never ever be mad at me."

"And why not? Bless your heart, but you're a real bitch. You know that?" Maisie did not care one iota about her ward's feelings.

"Oh I know. But you see, it was Val who turned me. I don't give a damn. But he does."

"He turned you?" Maisie's brows arched in surprise.

"Yeah. Bit me, fed me his blood, the whole thing. He was so in love. I guess I was, too. But I forgot most of it."

"When was that?"

"On a lovely midsummer night if I recall correctly, 1688," she said, her gaze unfocused. "I had just turned eighteen."

"Accident?" Maisie squinted. She wanted to know everything about Val's past, and exactly how deep his ties to Emmeline truly dwelled.

"Oh no. This was all planned," the female vampire explained as they turned to narrow stairs, the passage illuminated by a few electric wall sconces. "A grand romantic gesture. Both of us, linked for eternity, as immortals. Forever in love."

"And you don't love him now?"

"No. I don't. Val's disciple at the time helped us, but the poor human had no clue about the aftermath of his spell. I lost my soul in the ritual."

"Oh gods. That's awful."

"For me, no. Life's much more fun without these little

moral dilemmas you mortals wrestle with. But Val, he does have his soul, you know. Hurts him like crazy. He stopped feeding as soon as he saw what he did to me."

"And what happened?" Maisie stilled her hastening heart, her throat tightening in empathy at Valerian's fate.

"He wanted to die. But he can't. He just wasted into skin and bones, hidden from all in some crypt somewhere on Mount-Royal. Then after I started to make too many vampires out of boredom, his brother Justin located him. Val had to save the poor idiots, didn't he?" Emmeline clicked the heels of her stiletto boots with annoyance.

"He founded this shelter?" Maisie stepped on the landing above stairs and followed Emmeline along another long corridor dotted with well-worn plank-wooden doors.

"With some nun." Emmeline smirked. Her hand paused on the iron door handle of the room at the end of the hall. "I can't remember. You can say that me feeding on humans and making new baby vamps has, in a way, saved him. We're forever linked, you see. Codependency at its best."

"You're sick." Maisie was floored by how casual the woman was about the tragedy.

"Maybe. But I have to warn you about him." Emmeline nodded at Maisie to follow her in. "I see the signs, *fille*. You have it, too. They all do."

"What?"

"Pining for him. He does that to every woman crossing his path. But their interests are doomed to fail."

"Why?" Maisie's breath hitched with interest. "Can't he love anyone back?"

"Why do you think he's got Sasha by his side? Always calls them Sasha. Since the first one. It was the name of his very first disciple, who died of old age. Val was devastated. He always picks a poor abandoned puppy somewhere. And he grieves each time. I suppose it's easier for him to mourn for a dog than for a woman."

"That's dreadful." Maisie's heart was heavy as she stepped into the small room behind Emmeline.

"This is yours." Emmeline dropped the duffel on a bed covered with a pile of fluffy blankets. The place was small but neat, with the same strong scent of beeswax polish as the entrance. Mismatched Persian rugs were scattered across the wooden floor, and a pretty china washbasin sat atop an old-fashioned dresser under its attached faded mirror. A few fat candles were lit around the room. "Val set it up for you."

"He did?" Maisie brow rose in surprise.

"Stop it." Emmeline's limbs stiffened. Her gaze darkened. "You can't fall for an immortal, girl. For your own sake. Hells, for *his* sake, stay away."

"I'm not here for him." And that was the truth.

"Good." Her lips curled into a genuine smile. "I'm next door. We'll have fun, you and me. You're not a bad witch at all. Quite a lot of power. I respect that."

"Um, thanks. I guess," Maisie said, puzzled by the vampire's sudden change of heart.

"Most of us vamps sleep during the day, but the disciples will be up in the morning. Breakfast downstairs, in the refectory, back of the building."

After Emmeline left, Maisie parsed through her feelings about this whole new world as she sat on the edge of the comfortable bed and dug her electronic tablet from her duffel bag.

Everything she had expected in coming here was completely wrong. Her crush on Valerian had now tripled as she'd learned of his awful dilemma. Only able to care for a dog, for centuries. How incredibly sad.

And the human blood feeding. *Flaming hells!* What should she do with this information?

She recalled the first time she had laid eyes on him in the summer. In the lush forest clearing that was home to the White Holly witches. With its sweet grass tickling the ankles, it was so different than these surroundings of red bricks, iron-work, and ice.

On a hot midsummer night, with his brother Magnovald, he had sat along with Diesel Stanford from the Black Oak Warlocks, Malcolm Dunsmuir, necromancer and King of the Daemon Realm, her Nana Thibodeau and Aunty Beaudry, both elders of the White Holly, and a few more supernatural leaders, to discuss what had to be done now that the Mont-Royal Immortals had chosen to make themselves known to the witches and warlocks.

Maisie remembered very little from the meeting, aside from Valerian. Drawn to him by an unseen attraction, her heart hammering every time he chose to speak, his voice deep and measured, a calm force over them all.

From the outside circle of attending witches, she had watched him, her entire being dying to be near him. An unnatural attraction that she could still not explain.

When it had been decided that Maisie was to go to Mont-real, he had shot her a lazy smile, his smoldering look upon her unreadable. When he'd later found a few minutes to address her alone, she'd had a hard time remaining casual, deeply unsettled by having him so close, and at once elated and fearful that she wouldn't measure up to her task.

And now that she was here, she was torn.

For the first time, she would be hiding something from the woman she cherished and admired most, Nana. The woman who had first seen how miserable she was at school. How much of an outcast her misplaced abilities had made her. She had convinced Mom that Maisie would be better hanging in the back room of the Thibodeau's craft shop and learn on her own instead of being terrorized daily by the bustling hall-ways of the local school.

How could Maisie keep this secret from Nana?

She was not only her grandma but their coven's high priestess. She had to be informed that immortals drank human blood.

But Maisie's heart burst at remembering how Valerian had not killed the mute teen vampire on the spot like Emmeline wanted. She had seen the empathy in his expression. He *had* a soul. A conscience.

She couldn't reveal his secret. Not yet anyway.

She had thought this place with its charming archaic buildings would be just a more urbane and colder version of Berwick Hollow with its verdant forest, inviting even when covered in soft snow.

But here, it was all ice, frigid sharp icicles that clung to doorways, ancient stone walls and dark iron balconies. With architectural features holding centuries-old memories that she could feel in her bones.

Nuns had lived here. As a witch, the thought creeped her out a little. The church had not been good to her kind in New England or elsewhere. How had a nun allied with an immortal to create this place?

Emmeline might not remember, or cared to, but Maisie knew that this nunnery had been built by Marguerite d'Youville herself. As part of the mother superior's mission to save downtrodden souls.

And the dwellings were still used for the same purpose to this day.

A stark wail suddenly pierced her peace, echoing through the walls. Was this some teen vampire in the throes of human blood withdrawals?

She shivered as she undressed.

Her journey weighted heavily upon her. Her first contact with the city had started at the crowded central station and through the dense metro bristling with loud commuters returning home from work. The mix of languages and fast talking had made her dizzy, heightened by strangers jostling past.

She had to rely on years of breathing practice to deal with the onslaught of buzzing emotions rushing through her as she'd made her way to the ancient part of the city.

Somehow, she had thought an assignment in an old nunnery would be in line with her taste for quiet but had forgotten that Montreal was a busy multicultural metropolis.

Her distress at crowds wasn't so severe that she couldn't manage, especially now as an adult where she had more tricks to deal with it, but the short subway journey had taken a toll on her. She had breathed easier only once she was walking down the small street leading to the *Sanctuaire*, the urban sounds muffled by the new snow falling gently around her in the moonless evening.

She hadn't counted on battling her unstable ward upon arrival. Her fight with Emmeline, along with the puzzling teen vamp attack, added to her exhaustion and her eyelids fell heavily.

She snuggled into her flannel pajamas and under the cozy blankets of her bed. She noticed a power outlet by the antique night table, glad that she would be able to charge her tablet. While Nana and Mom still hung to their old grimoires, Maisie and her cousins kept their Book of Shadows online— constantly adding to the files with their latest finds—so they could study their spells at any time, wherever they were.

And study was what Maisie was good at. Her inquisitive mind pushed away all thoughts of Valerian as she logged on to her account using the Internet connection from her cellphone.

She needed to revise and rest to be at her peak. The battle in the sanctuary's courtyard had completely depleted her and both sleep and contemplation was what she required to be ready again.

Magic was where she felt at home. Her anxiety at being surrounded by strangers receded as her fingers scrolled the giant compendium her cousin Jo maintained.

Vampires. Blood. Immortality. The syringe was branded in her mind. Who would want Emmeline's blood?

There was only one way to get closer to Valerian, she

suddenly realized, still unable to let go of her obsession. It was to help Emmeline.

Even her task to contain the rogue vampire was not as expected.

She'd come to prevent Emmeline from hurting others. But it looked like she now had to protect the deadly woman from being attacked herself.

And protecting Emmeline was obviously the only path to Valerian's heart.

CHAPTER 4

"*V*al, brother, we don't want another Emme, do we?"

Valerian peered at Mag through the diffused purple lighting of his overheated club, thinking that for once his brother might be right.

Sasha was resting his head on his thigh, the dog's body stretched on the thick leather bench of Mag's usual corner booth by the bar of the *Serpent Maudit*. Val patted his snoozing dog, who rolled his head to the side with a twitch of his hind leg. "She's not like Emme at all."

"They all are."

"How?"

"Human women." Mag leaned back and stretched his arms on the wood trim behind his shoulders while a waitress placed a whisky tumbler and a clean coaster in front of him. The girl's bare navel was inches from his eyes.

"*Merci*, Sandrine." He flashed the girl a warm smile while sliding his hand on her waist.

She quivered under his touch, her eyes fixed on Val as she served him a frosty beer bottle.

Mag pulled the waitress across his lap, her micro-skirt hiked high to reveal a band of naked thigh above see-through black stockings.

Her figure was ample and perfect, her limbs silky with just enough flesh in all the right places. Her outfit provocative yet classy, like all the employees of the *Serpent Maudit*, from the beautiful waitstaff to the buff barman and professional dancers on the three small stages at the edge of the club. Even Louka and Evan—Mag's bouncers and Val's former pupils—stood at attention leaning along the brick wall, dressed sharply in all black, custom suits, shirts and ties.

This was his brother's home. From the lush dark red velvet seats of the booths surrounding the periphery, the sleek chrome high tables and stools facing the vibrant dance floor, to the polished bar stocked with a vast assortment of liquors shipped from all over the world, everything was touched with sensuality, with a promise that every deep desire would be met here for the right price.

And Mag lorded over it all. His gaze meticulously scanned his domain. His wide shoulders stretched beneath the usual black t-shirt. He kept his hair a little longer than Val's and tended to rake it back when something amused him. He always seemed relaxed, in complete control.

Val smirked as he shook his head. "Do you even need bouncers?"

"Sure, bro. Goes with the image."

"And what is the image, Mag? Big bad vampire? Lord of the underworld?"

"Maybe." He bent his head to whisper something into Sandrine's ear and she giggled. She watched Val with a tantalizing expression and leaned her head back into Mag's shoulder, offering her throat.

"Brother, no," Val protested.

But Mag shot him a bold smile while his incisors slowly elongated against the woman's skin. He slid his hand between the waitress' legs and brushed his lips on her neck while his dark gaze remained glued on his sibling.

Dammit, his brother could be such an ass sometimes. Val swallowed, hit by a surge of intense cravings. A buzz of strong sensations raged inside him. He dug his nails hard into his palms, took a deep breath and let the air out slowly. He reached for Sasha stretched over him and very gently, steadily, rested his hand on his dog's flank.

His hammering heart had slowed when Mag's fangs finally pierced Sandrine's skin. She flinched at the initial prick and slumped back into him, her eyes on Val hazy with surrender.

Dispassionately, Val watched Mag feed a little from his waitress, his hands on her breast, tweaking a nipple that grew taut under the thin white top. After a few seconds which seemed an eternity, Mag withdrew from her neck and licked a little blood from the clean wound. "Want some?"

Letting out another steady breath, Val shook his head silently.

"Want to take her upstairs, then?"

Sandrine's thighs were now parted to let Mag explore her. Her feminine scent mixed with the smell of her blood on his brother's lips reached deep inside Val, fiercely calling the predator that lived just beneath his skin.

"No." Val half smiled.

He'd had centuries of denying himself the feedings. And while he had bedded plenty in the last decades, he knew that once the cravings were assuaged, there was nothing left behind. Nothing but a deep need for real companionship.

Mag lived his immortality differently than Val did. He embraced it fully and masked its loneliness with more drinks, more sex, more shiny nightlights. More experiences. And now with collecting magical artifacts.

Yet, his thrill-seeking brother had never been in love.

Not as Val had been with Emmeline when they first met. With that fierce burning sensation that nothing else mattered. When you couldn't eat, sleep, do anything without the thought of *her* branded in your mind.

He no longer loved Emme. Oh, at first, before she turned, he could think of nothing but her.

He had blamed her first murder on her undead condition. But inch-by-inch, with each of her killings, the love had died. And once he saw she had turned the entire staff of a downtown bordello in one night, his feelings had disappeared entirely.

She was his monster to keep away from others. But the memory of the girl she was had never left him. She'd always had this sweet giggle when he'd come in to her father's shop for tobacco. Serving him with that easy, honest smile she had. Asking about his dad's health, enquiring if his mother had enough supplies for the winter. Emme had always been so generous then.

He could never kill her knowing who she had been.

So he had to persist in teaching her how to live by human rules.

"You shouldn't feed from humans," he finally warned Mag. "That little witch Maisie will go straight to the warlocks if she sees you. She's already freaked by our *Rituel du Sang*."

"I'm not worried about warlocks."

Val sighed. He'd had to battle one of them the year before when he had to retrieve Evan and Emme from Seattle and he did not want to repeat the experience.

Sure, together the immortal brothers could take the warlocks, but there was only Mag, Justin, and himself in town at the moment. And Justin preferred to stay out of supernatural business if he could avoid it, favoring hiding in the comfort of his university life.

"Just slow down—that's all I ask."

"Sandrine likes it. Don't you, *poupée*?" He wrapped both his arms around the human woman's waist and held her tight against his body.

She drew her knees together and nestled further into him before turning her head to kiss him on the cheek. Maybe Val was wrong. Maybe Mag felt as lonely as he did.

Val scratched Sasha's neck under his collar and the animal sighed with a few flaps of his tail, before crawling closer on the leather bench and falling back asleep on his lap.

Val had Sasha and the *Sanctuaire*. Mag had his waitresses. That was their life. No need to dwell on it.

"What about this?" Val nodded at the syringe in the plastic bag on the table between them.

Emmeline was an oddity among them all. Her life immortal but she still needed to feed on blood regularly like the bloodthirsty teens Val had made his mission to save. But why would someone want her blood?

"Right." Mag gave another squeeze at Sandrine's bare waist and whispered something into her ear. She eased herself up and then bent down to him while offering Val a view of her silk-clad perfect bottom under the short leather skirt.

He appreciated her backside, keeping his cravings in check, while Mag unraveled a black bandana from his wrist and gently wrapped it around her neck to cover his bite before kissing her fully on the mouth.

She stood and swiveled to face Val, the jaunty scarf emphasizing her bouncy cleavage in the white glittery top, looking the picture of lush fertility.

Val sighed and clasped his hands together over the bar table. Maybe twenty years ago he would have been tempted. Maybe sex with no ties was what he needed. Perhaps it would take his mind away from a certain black-haired witch with too much power and whose attraction was now getting under his skin.

"The needle," Mag called out to him with a gentle pat on Sandrine's back to send her on her way.

She disappeared with her tray among the crowd of twenty-something trendy patrons who sipped fancy drinks, flirted, and danced under the glitzy pink and purple lights.

He cleared his throat. "Someone wants Emme's blood."

"Why?" Mag straightened his spine, his brow knitted in concentration.

"What do you think?" Val spat, his mind back to business. "There's only one use for vampire's blood."

Mag shrugged. "What?"

"Damn you're dense sometimes, brother."

"Hey."

"You're high from feeding on your waitress."

"Yeah. Maybe." He leaned back into his seat and again stretched wide taking the whole side of his booth.

"Focus."

"You worry too much, bro."

Val patted the plastic bag. "This here could be a problem for Emme."

"She's fine, right? Your old gal's a spitfire," Mag said appreciatively. He'd been amused by Emme's antics ever since she'd turned.

"Of course she's fine. I've got the whole *Sanctuaire* warded so no one can come in. It's not really her I worry about." Val leveled with his brother.

"Ah." Mag sat up straight, as his tone shifted, his lazy demeanor suddenly gone. "You worry someone is trying to make vampires."

"Yep. And who would do that?" *Damn.* The cursed vamp population in Montreal was pretty steady, with Val taking care of rehabilitating them. His pupils knew better than create new ones. No. This wouldn't do. They had to get to the bottom of this before humans get hurt.

"What about a spell to find out for sure, some ritual?" Mag chimed. "What does Grégoire say?"

"He doesn't know. We'll question the vamp that attacked her when he comes back to life."

"Then why are you here?"

"To warn you, man. If someone *is* after vamp's blood, we're as much a target as Emme. And maybe you could ask around if anyone heard about this."

He shrugged. "I'm not worried. I can take on whoever. Plus

Louka and Evan *do* have my back." He nodded at the two cursed vamps standing guard behind him. They were doing great at the *Serpent Maudit*, a testament to Val's rehab's method.

"But sure, I can ask around. Old Morano is due for a visit," Mag said. Checking in with the elusive mob boss who more or less ran the underground crime in town was a good place to start.

"What about Captain Akande?"

"Yeah, her too. I'll ask." Mag liked to keep a pulse on every deal going downtown. On both side of the law. "This looks fancy. People don't use these old glass syringes since the sixties. I should know. We find too many plastic disposables in the back alley. Gotta clean up every night. Kids walk by in the daytime."

"Who would have access to something like that, then?"

"No clue. Wish I'd paid more attention to Mom's lessons. A locator ritual would be handy. But I suck at those."

"Yeah, same." Their mother had tried to teach them as much magic as she could, but they'd been more interested in offensive spells than anything else.

"Griff would be great at this."

Val hadn't seen or been contacted by his brother Griffon for at least six months. "He's offline. Last I heard he was somewhere in Siberia."

"He's got to stop with this obsession of finding our father. It's messed up." The flash of longing permeating Mag's gaze was quickly repressed.

They never talked about their real father. The mysterious ancient vampire had impregnated their mother before she'd set sail to the new world as a *Fille du Roy*, a so-called daughter of the king, one of the hundreds of young women who had come to find a husband amongst the new settlers.

"You could ask your witch to do it," Mag noted.

"Maisie? She's just here as a formality. I had originally planned to let her hang out with Emme in the city for a few days so she could report back to the warlock that she was not a threat."

Although, he realized with a sigh, Maisie would likely report Emme's attack in the courtyard.

"You like her, don't you? And she's hella powerful. Almost as much as Mom."

Val cast him a dark look. "There's no need for Maisie to be involved."

"You *did* notice her during the parlay this summer. Couldn't keep your eyes off her. And I saw you talk to her afterward. She's cute, I give you that. Wouldn't mind her for myself."

"Back off, Mag," he snarled. The thought of Mag's fangs on Maisie's willowy neck brought him jags of anger.

"Whoa, it *is* serious. Sasha, my boy," Mag rose an eyebrow at the dog, "you've been replaced."

"Mag, the needle." Val clenched his jaw.

"Hey man, I really think you should go for the witch. This staying away from women is not good for you. It's unnatural."

"Nothing about us is natural," Val growled.

"I ain't like you, brother. I like what I am. I don't wish to be human. Like freakin' Justin who goes on teaching astronomy, pretending he's one of them." Mag was rubbing the back of his neck, his gaze narrowing on his brother. "Or you, playing saint to atone for some sins you think we committed."

"Emme started all this, creating new vampires who turned more and more. They didn't ask for this," he protested. "They need someone to help."

"Okay, fine. I grant you that. But we, you and I and Justin and our whole family, we were created, just like humans were, just like Sasha here and every other living thing on the planet. Everything we are, from the fangs and enhanced senses, to shifting into bats when we want to, is natural. And we are meant to feed on human blood. That is just the way it is. Stop feeling bad about it."

"I don't. I feed off Father Grégoire's every year."

"Good. The decade you spent without feeding was dumb."

"I shouldn't have tried to make Emme immortal." The guilt gnawing at his gut was a relentless companion.

"Yeah, sure. Now you know." Mag waved his hand in dismissal. "Get on with this girl, won't you? Get it out of your system instead of brooding from afar like you always do. No need to make her immortal. Have her while she's young and fresh. You've bed human women before."

"She's not like others."

"They all are. See Sandrine there?" He nodded at the waitress who swiftly walked among tables, her hips swaying with each step of her red high-heel shoes. "She's as happy as they come. She knows we're having fun."

"Maisie's not like that. She's so... I don't know... real." He sighed. "A bit awkward at first, but with a mind like you wouldn't believe. There's some fragility under all that power."

"Oh, I see."

"No, you don't."

"Oh hells, I do. You like her because of that. You want to protect her. Swoop in just like you did in Berwick Hollow."

"Maybe, I don't know." Val frowned. Was he attracted to the witch because something about him wanted to shield her from harm? It wasn't that simple. "She can protect herself. But magic is not infinite."

"Well these witches of the White Holly are freakin' powerful. Remember Elder Beaudry? The Beaudry line are all hella strong, immortal and all."

"She's not a Beaudry. She gets depleted if she uses it all. She was exhausted after confronting Emme. She's not invincible."

"Right, maybe you *should* stay away from her. Damn, take Sandrine, or Marilou," he added, nodding at the tall dark-skinned waitress who ambled lasciviously on the bar's floor, her full tray steady at the crook of her elbow. "Hells, take both. Just one night. Take the edge off."

"No."

"It might help ease the attraction you have for the witch."

"Maisie." His tone was dark. "Call her Maisie."

"What?"

"Her name is Maisie."

"Fine. Maisie. But careful, brother, we really don't want another Emme. That one is fun and all, but she brought the warlocks on our heels."

"There won't be another Emme. Thankfully Maisie's oblivious to me."

"Are you sure?"

"*Seigneur*, yes. She's all about her craft. She's studying now in her room at the *Sanctuaire*. Emme told me."

"So she *could* locate the owner of the needle if we ask."

"Yeah, probably," Val reluctantly admitted.

"Great. Make her useful then. If the Black Oak warlocks are forcing her on us, might as well use her."

Val bristled. Somehow the thought of *using* Maisie didn't sit right with him. "I suppose I can ask."

"She was sent here to watch Emme."

"Well, it was more about guarding Emme from hurting anyone than actually *protecting* her."

"Still, this is Emme's blood." Mag picked the hypodermic needle inside the plastic bag and looked through it with a frown. "It falls under Maisie's responsibility."

"Right, fine." Val swiped the syringe from his brother and grimly tucked it into his coat. "I'll ask her tomorrow."

CHAPTER 5

a few minutes later, Val was taking Sasha along the back alley of the *Serpent Maudit* back to the *Sanctuaire* just a few blocks away. The dog paused to sniff some small animal tracks in the snow, looked back at Val, and padded ahead again.

With a sigh, Val pondered his brother's advice. Should he have taken him up on his offer to take Sandrine upstairs? He could easily have any of Mag's staff—the waitresses, the dancers. It was so simple. A touch, a compelling look and they were his.

Somehow, he could never enjoy that. Always looking for an emotional connection but finding none. They liked the thrill, the erotic sensations of the bite, but not the man behind it.

Deep down he envied Justin's ability to live his life as a human. His brother had always preferred a life buried in his books instead of running the streets with the lads in their childhood days. He had somehow managed to recreate his Professor St- Amand persona every generation and seemed content with it.

Then, there was their brother Renaud, who had found peace hiding with the Grey Wolves pack in the woodlands of

Domaine-Lasalle in the Mont-Tremblant Park. Ren had chosen to remain closer to his true predator nature than any of the St-Amand brothers had ever done.

Maisie's arrival was now making Val uneasy about his life's purpose. He'd been set on his mission to help the cursed teen vamp ever since he'd turned Emme when they were both eighteen. He'd been so young, entirely naïve and foolish.

More than three hundred years ago. He had created the monster that was Emme. So now the turned creatures she had raised were his responsibility.

He hadn't been able to stop the flow. Once risen, they made more and more. For generations unending. Some went mad and died in the morning sun. Some like Louka and Evan were working for the St-Amands. In fact, Justin employed a handful of reformed vamps to produce the synth blood he had designed to keep them fed.

Like many, Evan had been a hard case at first but, after breaking him and months of intense reformation, he had finally begun his redemption as Mag's bouncer. He'd even visited his human family on the eastern shore once without problems.

But it took work and many, even at this very moment, lingered in the deep recesses of the *Sanctuaire*'s basement, chained and screaming through their hunger until their bodies accepted the synthetic blood and they ultimately agreed to Val's rules.

Had he been right to want to save them all?

And to not kill Emme before she started this?

Heaviness scattered in his limbs. He needed to feed. He was weaker than usual. Questioning himself. That was not good, a sign that the feeding ceremony was upon them. Just another twenty-four hours, Father Grégoire had said.

Val always felt sated after the ritual. The turmoil brought on by the Samhain night assuaged, making him ready to take on the birth of light on Yule a few weeks later with a calm mind.

Seeing his brother feed on Sandrine's blood had rattled him. Had drawn needs and cravings that he was usually able to completely ignore.

An image of Maisie shedding her coat to reveal her body crossed his thoughts and sent shards of desire below his belt. She was so very different from Mag's sophisticated staff, with this power that radiated from her, unexpected with her girl-next-door look.

He was fascinated by how she questioned everything.

He imagined her now sleeping under his roof, in the room once inhabited by the nunnery's mother superior. It was bigger than the others and not so far from his own.

He smiled to himself. He had made sure it was as comfortable and inviting as he could make it. One of the few rooms with a window. Val usually didn't care much about his environment but had recognized that Maisie came from a place where the connection with nature was strong.

He was surprised by his action, considering the undercurrent of resentment he felt that she'd been sent to spy on them.

He had no idea why he was so captivated by her—perhaps from seeing her expertly battle the troll set on her town, her focus so intense during the parlay the next night—but there was no doubt now, he liked her. She had stirred something in him, a deep affection, perhaps something more, he just couldn't pinpoint it.

And letting her wrestle with Emme in the courtyard had come from more than slight resentment of the warlocks. It had been almost as if he'd wanted to see her fail, to lessen the impact she had on him.

Pulling on Sasha's leash to slow the Labrador's pace as they threaded through a patch of unshoveled snow, he shook his head. She hadn't failed. She was indeed everything the witch she'd been promised to be. And not as awkward as her grand-mother High Priestess Thibodeau saw her.

Why not ask her for help? Val suddenly brightened.

He could enjoy her presence for a few more weeks. As

long as he remained at a healthy distance. Maybe he could learn more magic from her. He *was* rusty.

"Right, Sash?" he said out loud.

But the dog had stopped dead in his tracks. His body rigid, a slow growl emerged from his throat.

Another cat. Val gave the leash a patient tug. Sasha was not fond of them. "Come on, boy. Leave the poor kitty alone."

The attack on Val came from nowhere.

A prick at his neck, just above the fur of his thick coat collar, stunned him.

Damn! He slapped a hand on the wound. A steel dart was imbedded deep into his skin.

The predator in him snarled, his fangs bare and ready.

His limbs shook. His vision blurred. The alley turned into a mix of iron stairs and snow banks under the soft glow of a streetlight.

Val searched for a spell, but his mind turned hazy. *What the hell?*

He slumped on his knees. Vaguely, he heard Sasha bark madly at two shapes approaching them.

His gut rose to his throat as a rush of agony suddenly flooded him. He fell over to his side in the snow. His temple hit a patch of ice, blinding him. All he could do was blink hopelessly as he searched the dark sky above for answers.

Sasha burrowed his body beside him and barked louder, the animal trembling with both fear and fury.

"That damn dog," one of the shapes griped.

"I ain't going near it," the other replied.

Val tried to move but was completely immobilized. *Drugged.*

They had fucking drugged him. Just like that!

With all his might, he rolled over Sasha and pulled at the dart in his neck, but it was imbedded deep within his skin.

His nails were now long, his fangs fully extended, his shoulders corded with tension, the beast in him completely out.

Sasha was barking louder and shaking in Val's arms.

"Shut that fucking dog up."

Damn idiots! His heart raced with wrath. They would hurt Sasha if Val didn't do something. Now!

With intense will, he dug into the skin of his neck, gritting his teeth hard to edge the pain away. He couldn't let any more of whatever was in his blood reach his entire body.

Val drew the dart out and plunked it bloody on the snow. He banded every muscle in his limbs to prop himself on all fours.

"It's okay, boy. Don't you worry," he managed to say to Sasha. His anger rose with each breath, fueling his readiness to retaliate against the sick scumbags who had dared attack him.

The dog licked Val's face, his relief obvious at seeing Val recover.

But the attackers were not done. "Get that dog, quick," one said.

"No, we didn't give him enough. Hurry."

Wrath ran like a fiery tide through Val as he finally pushed himself to his feet.

He sneered at his assailants. His lips retracted. Ready to hit back and destroy, sink his fangs and claws into whatever moved. Anything civil in him completely gone.

Another dart pierced his left thigh before he could take a step. The jag burned sizzling hot. The effect was instant, and he fell on his knees again.

"The dog, too."

No! Val's heartbeat pulsed with panic.

Then he heard Sasha whine and the Labrador slumped beside him, his warm muzzle right on Val's cheek.

Bastards. Val's arms twitched, his stomach washed with fury. He was ready to annihilate the both of them.

"Hurry."

"He's still moving. Give him another shot," one cried, frantic above him.

Another searing prick hit the back of his neck. Whatever substance it carried overtook him in a flow of burning pain, numbing any sensation in his spine.

Val laid completely useless, his cheek on the ice, his sharp incisors retracted and one arm over his immobile dog.

"Quick. Before he wakes."

They turned him over and Val's blurry sight made the face of two teenagers. Vampires. Matted hair and maimed features. Cursed ones like the one at the sanctuary. Though no one he recognized.

He cast them a lethal look, hoping to compel them under his glare. He wanted to rip them apart for what they had done to Sasha. But he couldn't focus.

"Shit, man, he's looking at us." The teen vamp blinked rapidly.

"Don't look into his eyes," the other responded. "His sight can draw you under. He's a freakin' immortal!"

"Right."

Unable to move, Val watched his assailant take a large hypodermic needle out of his pocket with shaking hands.

"I can't do this." The undead kid trembled with fear.

"Yes, you can. Just don't look."

"I can't do his neck, I just can't."

"Get his arm, quick." The other teen's tone was wrought with urgency as they both crouched over Val and pushed his wool coat sleeve above his forearm.

"Oh god, no. He's got the mark."

"Mark?"

"La Sorcière des Glaces."

"Oh shut up, that's a kid's story. The Ice Witch never existed."

"No, look."

"Whatever. It means nothing." The teen felt for Val's vein.

Damnation! Another sharp prick hit him.

"How much does he want?"

"Just fill the whole fucking syringe and let's get out of here."

"This will put him out for hours."

"What if we just killed him? His fangs are back in. His eyes look dead." Panic shot through the youth's high-pitched voice. "Then his brothers will be after us."

"Just take the blood. Go."

The blood, they want my blood. Val's stomach sank.

"Does he want us to... finish him, you think?"

"No. He'll be freakin' mad at us if we do." The vamp's voice quivered with dread. "He doesn't want him dead. He wants to be one of them."

Enough of this. With grit, Val gathered all his strength. He managed to move an arm over Sasha and slowly lifted his head up. He had to stop them.

"Fuck, he's moving."

"Dammit!"

Another prick pierced Val's skin and this time his entire body went limp. His head hit back on the ice and his eyes fluttered once.

Like a blizzard in winter, darkness fell over him and everything turned blank.

CHAPTER 6

"Is he okay?" Maisie, hastily dressed in an oversized sweater over her pajamas, gasped as she looked at Valerian's unanimated form, his wide shoulders taking most of the space across his cot in the simple bedroom.

His bare chest above the Native American blanket glistened under the multitude of candles that were positioned throughout the space. What she could see from the rest of his room was basic but neat—a modest antique desk and side table, both covered with well-worn books, a tall century-old wardrobe by the door, and his coat, the fur of its collar dull in the chill air, laying draped over an ancient cane chair by the bed.

"Ah, *Mademoiselle* Thibodeau." An old man in a patched-up black cassock and clerical collar dabbed a cloth upon Valerian's forehead, his kind eyes taking her in as she carefully approached. "May I call you Maisie?"

"Of course, you're Father Grégoire?"

"I am. Sorry to wake you, but you may be of help with this."

"Grégoire, bring him back. Now." A deep voice cut through the darkest part of the room, urgency piercing the anxious tone.

"I do understand your fear, Magnovald," Father Grégoire's statement was calm but steady, "but we don't know what happened to him."

Maisie frowned. Confused, she looked back and forth between the priest and the man she hadn't noticed at first. He leaned against the back wall, his arms crossed at his chest, a deep frown marring his brow. His dark hair was much too long, brushing his broad shoulders under a classy leather jacket. He had an aura of power ready to explode at any moment. "Magnovald St-Amand, Valerian's brother."

He shot her an inscrutable stare. "Why, of course. Little Maisie Thibodeau. I do recall you."

Maisie gulped, realizing she had spoken out loud. "So do I," she replied.

Magnovald had first been a charmer when he'd enter her family's craft store after hours to ask for directions, then later a force to reckoned with at the summer parley when facing the council accusing him to stock magical artifacts for nefarious ambitions.

"She," Magnovald was addressing Father Grégoire, pointing at her while his nostrils flared, "she can bring him back."

"So can I, Magnovald." Father Grégoire's assured him with patience. "Your brother will be fine."

"But he doesn't look fine." Magnovald's tone was full of angst, the immortal visibly distressed by his brother's state.

And so was she.

"What happened?" Her legs restless, she kneeled to Valerian's side and surveyed his body, from the powerful but immobile limbs to the well-defined chest that barely rose and fell with each of his labored breaths. Long lashes rested on the pale skin of his chiseled cheekbones. Strands of his dark hair were plastered on his temples, wet from Father Grégoire's damp cloth.

She frowned at the bandage at his neck.

"Attacked." Magnovald flushed with outrage. "He told me

about Emme's attack, so I had him followed. Evan and Louka found both him and Sasha comatose in a back alley.

"Sasha! Is he..." she wondered with concern for Valerian's fateful friend.

"In the kitchen, with the novices." Father Grégoire nodded at her. "A bit groggy but recovering. Young Ariane is probably spoiling him. She's quite fond of him."

"You've got to bring him back," Magnovald spat at her.

With a sigh, she bowed her chin at Valerian's brother. He was visibly distressed to be ordering her like this. The bond between the brothers had to be very tight. She too was anxious to see Val healed.

With gentle care, she gripped the unconscious immortal's wrist.

His relaxed fingers were slightly calloused, indicating that he didn't avoid working with his hands, but everything else was perfection. Smooth flesh over lean muscles, symmetry of limbs and well-sculpted angles. As heat rose to her chest with longing at the thought of his hands on her own skin, she turned his wrist to find the vein. Her fingers tingled with shock.

The Mark. There, tattooed on the inside of his arm, in black ink only, a complicated set of runes she had only seen in books.

Her eyes widened at the priest, and she turned to Magnovald. "The mark of the *Sorcière des Glaces*. So he *is* a witch."

"We all are." Magnovald smirked with a shrug. He turned his palm at Maisie and showed her the similar mark of the Ice Witch on the inside of his own wrist. "Our mother."

"Your mother is the Ice Witch," Maisie exclaimed. Her grand- mother had mentioned meeting her once but the elusive immortal sorceress always seemed more of a legend to her than someone's parent.

"She is. She lives somewhere down south. Abandoned us all sometime in the seventeenth century."

"An immortal witch." Maisie frowned. How long had the

Sorcière been alive if she was the St-Amand's mother? The immortal witches in her family line were all at risk of madness. "She didn't turn insane?"

"No," he retorted. "A bit of a cow if you want my honest opinion. But very much sane."

She shook her head and felt for Val's life force under the pad of her fingers.

"It's steady," she announced with slight relief. "But his skin his unusually warm. What happened to him?"

"See these gashes?" Father Grégoire lifted the gauze bandage from the immortal's throat, revealing a large laceration right under the strong chin. "I also found another steel dart embedded in the back of his neck. A few more at his thigh."

Her heart skipped a beat at the sight of his injury. "That's a nasty wound."

"Likely gouged it out himself," Magnovald spat.

Maisie shivered in dismay and reached for Valerian's feverish brow.

"I think he was drugged, Maisie." The priest's shoulders slumped, his features flat with grief.

"My bouncers saw two people fleeing the scene."

"And Sasha was hit as well?" Maisie asked.

"Just once. Lucky for whoever did this, Val won't go easy on the scumbag who dared hurt his dog." Magnovald's jaw remained tight as he turned to her. "You can help?"

"Yes, of course." Her soul ached to see the tough immortal so vulnerable. Every parcel of her magical legacy was calling to her to heal him. Her gaze rose to the priest. "May I?"

Father Grégoire nodded, and with care she placed a palm over Valerian's heart, sensing his pulse again, faint but very much like a human, like hers.

He was a sort of vampire, undead. And born this way. Unlike those who sought shelter in these walls, he had never died.

And she felt that strange life force right under her fingers.

The heartbeat running inside her now, through her veins up and in her arm all the way to her own heart.

Matronae, I call upon you. Show me what lay within his blood. She bristled at the closeness she had forced upon them.

Her lips parted with needs. She craved to draw more of his essence within her. There was nothing evil coming from him, nothing malevolent, just pure beautiful darkness.

She breathed in deeper, in unison with his breath. Drew him inside her. "*Roichdadh am muinnshean. Sirona.* Ancestors long gone, reveal what ails this creature."

And the room around them disappeared. Gone were the candles and the priest. Gone was the immortal brother.

There was only she, Maisie Thibodeau, descendent of the Coven of the White Holly, next in line to the High-Priestess-hood, ready to take the place of her elder, Marianne Thibodeau. And there was Valerian St-Amand, Mount-Royal Immortal. Son of the *Sorcière des Glaces.* Both linked in life so that she could survey every single cell of his body, every DNA strand that made him who he was.

She felt everything in him, the power, the excruciating long life, the guilt, the despair and the steadiness of knowing exactly who he was and what consisted of his purpose in this world.

Save the cursed ones. Assist those afflicted by the worse.

She had sensed some of it in Berwick Hollow when she had first laid eyes on him, but this time, it was all there within her. And her heart burst with longing for such a self-less tragic man. Everything in her wanted to take away his burden.

And without the laws that governed their coven, she could have done it. Right here where she dwelt so close to his essence, she had enough powers to remove it all. The memory of Emmeline Dubois's turning, the guilt over it. Temptation to release him from his intense remorse lay just at the edge of her fingers. It would take just a mere few words and he would be free.

Remember who you are, little one. The Thibodeau's ancestors whispered within her. *An ye harm none.*

She bit her lip hard. Pushed her wish away. She would not intervene. She would not alter who he was. No matter how much she wished it.

Deep sadness crept inside her. What was the purpose of her power if she could not shed his burden?

But the witches had laws. She remained bound to them.

"Ketamine," she intoned out loud, now fully aware of the poison in his veins, the knowledge of her family passed on to her. "Animal tranquilizer. And quite concentrated. I'm surprised Sasha is awake if he received a similar dose."

"Val will sleep it off, then," she heard from somewhere behind her. Father Grégoire, Magnovald, she did not know.

"I *can* remove it." She was spent and had not had much time to recover after battling Emmeline. But while she wasn't allowed to alter his consciousness and take away his guilt, she was able to remove every trace of the chemical from his system. That she could do.

She didn't wait for an answer and placed her other hand on Valerian's navel, ignoring the tide of cravings inside her at the hard and defined planes of his stomach. She remained purely focused on her task.

"*Slihnach ayn fhuyl sao...*" A spell she no longer needed to study. A spell designed to flush out any undesirable compound from the body. Never had she used it on a vampire, but she prayed that it would be enough. "*Matronae y Sirona. Slihnach...*"

She sensed the configuration of his vampire's blood, so unlike hers yet so real. Worked at the minute level to rearrange the chemical structures of the compounds that had been forced into his system. Bonds broken and rearranged. Recreated so that they were no longer harmful. "*Slihnach ayn.*"

Sweat beaded at her forehead, her breath turned shallow as she used her own life energy assisted by her deities.

"So mote it be," she claimed out loud in a confident final command.

Her chest buckled forward from the strain and she would have fallen if two strong hands had not caught her.

"Maisie?" Valerian was now sitting upright in his bed, holding her shoulders in a firm grip. "Are you okay?"

She nodded silently, repressing a gag from her lack of energy and hit with a rush of uncontrollable emotions at his hands on her.

His dark gaze connected with hers and something passed between them. Something strong that shattered her heart. He knew.

Knew that she had witnessed the depth of his personal misery.

His expression eased. "Maisie—"

"*Oh mon dieu, mon chéri!*" Emmeline burst into the room in a flash of blonde hair, bare skin, and black sequins. She threw herself at Valerian. "They said you'd died."

Maisie leaned back. Steady on her knees, she brushed her forehead with the back of her hand, breaking Valerian's hold on her.

She nodded silently at him to indicate that she was fine before standing upright.

Emmeline's arms were around his torso, her head against his chest, hair fanning on his lap, her grip intense. A beautiful picture of vulnerable femininity.

Father Grégoire rested a pained look on the female vampire while Magnovald let out a quiet groan.

"I'm fine, Emme." Valerian threw Maisie one last longing gaze before wrapping his arm around Emmeline's half-naked body to bring her closer to him. Propped back on the pillows, he patted her long hair and rested his chin atop her head with a sigh.

Maisie's heart cracked as she gazed upon them both so beautiful, so perfect. Immortals and entirely made for each other.

She tilted her head high and straightened herself as tall as she could with a stiff lip. What fool had she been to think she could connect with Valerian. That he could care for her, even a little. That she could be close to someone like him.

A part of her mind cursed her coven's code. She could have ended this. His guilt, his complex feelings for Emmeline.

But Maisie was soon to be the High Priestess of the White Holly.

Her abilities were needed by her family, her people. She was here to study the undead. Not fall for one of them.

The reasonable part of her finally took over. The senseless teenaged crush gone. Detached, she studied the couple holding each other on the immortal's bed, her heart cold.

There was no one, not even the strong witch she was becoming, that would ever break that unhealthy bond.

CHAPTER 7

*V*al cursed his slow memory. "What the hell happened?" It hit him, and he pushed Emme away. "Where's Sash?" If anyone had hurt Sasha, they were dead.

"He's fine. Milking his ordeal with the young apprentices in the refectory." Father Grégoire smiled, and his expression shifted with unease. "How are you feeling?"

"They drugged me." He rubbed the back of his neck as images from the night returned. "With darts."

"Louka and Evan found you in the alley. You were completely out." His brother's lips curled with relief but his gaze remained dark. "How could something like that happen?"

"You could have actually died." Emme's face was a mask of concern.

"Ketamine." The confident and clear voice echoed through his room. *Maisie.* She was swiping her phone, her attention fixed on what she was reading. "Mixed with Xylazine, the so-called zombie drug. Not so hurtful on animals but deadly to humans."

"You brought me back?" he marveled. She had saved his wretched life.

"Your blood was tainted with this stuff. I had to take it out." She looked up at him, her face etched with strain. He knew how much a spell like that would cost the magic-user. The extent of her power kept surprising him.

"Are you okay?" The people around them seemed to recede despite Emme's heavy perfume and her arms still around his waist. Deeply grateful for the healing, he had eyes only for the witch who had brought him back.

"Just tired." She tucked her cellphone in the pocket of her sweatshirt as she dismissed his worry with a shake of her head. "It had to be done."

He sighed and reached to her, his palm wide open. "Thank you."

The connection between them was real. She had been inside him and he could still feel her light presence in his blood. The spell she had performed within him was as intimate as a lover's touch. He breathed in its gentleness, thankful to have it there while it lasted.

Her lips parted and she softly rested her hand on his. She gave it a soft squeeze. "Anytime."

She meant it only as a polite response, but he suddenly longed to feel more of their bond. So fresh, so lively, like a calm breeze blowing over a lush summer meadow where someone could just rest for a moment.

"How on earth could anyone bring you down, Val?" Emme pushed herself away from him and planted a hand on her hip over the tiny black sequin dress, an accusatory frown on her forehead.

"*Sacrament*, bro. Seeing you like this was scary as hell."

A flush of dread washed over Val at Mag's words, and he released Maisie's hand to turn to Father Grégoire.

"How could something like this happen? It took them just a few seconds to get me down." The randomness of his attack floored him. "A few darts, that's it."

The old man rubbed his chin, his lined features grim. "Drugs, I never thought that possible."

Fully recovered, Val pushed himself off the bed. He paced the length of the creaky wooden floor, going over the assault. "Damn, there were just two of them. Can we be drugged?" he asked to no one in particular.

"I never heard of it," Mag huffed.

"My cousin Jo said it's possible." Maisie was again searching information on her phone.

"Your cousin?"

"I've been gathering as much as I can on vampires and immortals. My family is helping me."

"Oh great," Mag snapped. "Witches looking at ways to kill us."

"We got more worries than that, Mag." Val tilted his head at Maisie. "What did your cousin say?"

"There are only two things that kill vampires, right?" Her eyes were fixed on the small screen of her cellphone as she scrolled through her information.

"Fire or decapitation." Emme smirked. "Or for myself and the young ones, a harsh sunny day."

"Thank you, doll. We know that." Mag was angry now despite the sarcasm. He was fearless and, like Val, had always believed they were pretty much invincible.

Being born this way, the St-Amand brothers were unaffected by the sun. And while Emme had initially feared its ray upon her turning, she now wore an enchanted ring that protected her from the deadly radiations. The Romani artifact had been found by Justin in France three hundred years past, after their mother had hinted to the ring's existence.

"What did your cousin say exactly?" Val was antsy with curiosity.

"There was a pack of immortals in the eighteen hundreds, in the mountains of Austria." Maisie's brows knitted as she focused on her reading. She shook her head. "Mostly hiding from humans, aside from a group of monks, disciples I gather. They were brought down by a certain LeGall, vampire hunter. Looks like he used a different poison, a mix of hemlock, belladonna and rosary peas. All dead. But there was never another documented incident."

"How do we not know this?" Mag was cracking his knuckles, one hand after the other. "Hells, Grégoire, that's your job!"

"I had no idea." The priest let out a slow exhale and avoided eye contact as he carefully gathered the cloth and water bowl together and tidied Val's bedside table.

"Your whole guild, centuries of studies, and you knew none of this." Mag was furious, his chest puffed in frustration. "And a little witch finds out with a cursory internet search?"

"To be fair, Cousin Jo is our crone. She's over a hundred years old." Maisie nodded at her phone. "This is our entire coven's Book of Shadows I'm looking at. And they say it's mostly a legend. No one knows if this LeGall actually existed."

"Damn." Val shivered with horror at the facts. Two teenagers had taken him down. They could have beheaded him, no problem. But they didn't. He racked his brain, trying to remember the attack. "They were talking...they were afraid. Decided not to kill me." He cocked his chin to Mag. "Scared of your retaliation."

"Oh good!" Mag rolled his eyes. "Finally something that make sense."

"But they also said *he* wanted to be one of us."

"He?" Father Grégoire's posture perked up.

"I'm piecing it together now. They took my blood." Val stopped pacing his chamber and turned to Mag. The rest of the room dimmed as he grasped the scope of what had happened. He seized his brother by the shoulders. This was St-Amand business. The blood connection with his brother had suddenly never been stronger.

"Mag." He stared hard into the dark eyes of his sibling. "They took *my blood*," he repeated. "Just like they tried to do with Emme. What would they want with an immortal's blood?" His voice was hoarse, and he saw his own dread now mimicked in his brother's expression. Cold apprehension sank through his gut.

"Fuck me." Mag shook himself out of his trance. He dug into the pocket of his jeans and fished out his cellphone. "I got to tell Justin and Ren."

"They want to make more vamps." Emme was no longer her usual flippant self, her demeanor dead serious.

"No, *ma chère*," Father Grégoire said. "That's not it."

"Then you know what this is about?" Val slowly turned to the priest and his heart sank further to see the distress etched in the elder's expression. His mind raced as he thought this through. "Whoever was behind this, they don't want to kill us all, not like what that LeGall hunter did. They could have done that tonight. Easily."

"No." Father Grégoire set the water bowl down and looked at his hands for a moment. He raised his eyes at Val. "Seems that someone wants to become one of you."

"What do you mean," Emme replied.

"Someone hopes to make themselves just like Valerian," Maisie said. "An immortal."

"She's right," Father Grégoire said.

"How?" Val glared. "And why come after me and not Mag or Justin?"

"I don't know why you specifically." The creased lines in Father Grégoire's face made him appear older than his sixty years of age. "But there exists a ritual to create an immortal. It's a long shot though, no one believes it would actually work."

"And you were aware of this?" Val tilted his head slowly to the side. "Mag, do you hear this?"

But his brother was talking into his cellphone and pacing the floor in animation, ignoring everyone else.

"Can't blame them," Emme interjected. "Who wouldn't want to be like you, *chéri*?"

Dread swept deeper inside him. He didn't have the heart

to reply and looked at the priest with angst. "How hard would it truly be?"

"Honestly, I didn't even know that you could be taken down with modern drugs, Valerian. I came across this as a young apprentice and never thought more on it. You and your brothers have survived for centuries."

"But I fed Emme my blood." His anguish overshadowed the memory. "It did not quite work."

"I don't know." Father Grégoire remained calm, obviously trying to reassure them all. "It's been three hundred years since the ritual that turned Emmeline. Modern science, maybe?"

"What will happen if someone turns like you?" Maisie asked.

Val let out a pained breath. "First, they would need to start consuming human's blood."

"Once a year? Like you do?" She remarked.

Damn, that would be too much to wish for, he thought.

"We have the Nostredame disciples," he told her. "They came to my mother when we were infants. A few days old at the most. That bastard monster might not even know about that."

"They would go on a feeding rampage," Father Grégoire said gloomily.

"Innocent people." Maisie was horrified.

"This is bad," Emme added. "I have my fun now and again. But *that*, is not good at all. We would be out. Everyone would be hunting us. They'd burn this place down."

"So many lives lost," Val said, his tone flat. "Just because of my blood."

Would he ever escape this nightmare? Guilt tightened his throat. This was something he was entirely responsible for. By his single selfish act of turning Emme, he had created the human-turned-vampire population in his city. He had condemned young people to turn into monsters and meet an early death. He was responsible for each and every one of the people lost to this horrible curse.

His chest tightened with the weight of his shame and his angst turned to anger. Someone was trying to create more of him. Why? He, himself, didn't even deserve to be alive.

He felt the sharp tip of his incisive growing. His fists tightened. The fury that someone had the nerve to steal his blood and intervene with the laws of nature had brought out the predator in him. He suddenly wanted nothing more but to rip the thief to shreds.

He was disgusted at himself for having been defeated so easily. His head down, he dug his nails into his palm, corded his forearms and biceps to push his destructive urges back within.

Father Grégoire gripped his shoulder. "Valerian." The priest's stern expression reminded him to take control of himself. The others depended upon it.

"Right." Val stood straight and he exhaled slowly. He surveyed the people around him. Emme, Maisie. Mag who was still on the phone, likely talking to another brother, probably Renaud out in the mountains outside the city.

"We fix this," he asserted with resolve. "We find the bastard, whatever or whoever he is. We destroy him."

"How?" Father Grégoire continued modeling restraint to help Val ease his racing mind. "Do you recall your attackers?"

"It has to be the same punk-ass teen vamp that jumped me. One ran away, remember?" Emme added. "I say we torture the assholes we caught for some information. Are they awake yet?"

"The syringe," Maisie said suddenly. "The one we found when Emmeline was attacked. It had to come from the same person. Twice in one night is too much of a coincidence. Do you still have it?"

"Right." Val could see where she was going. He hastened to his coat and dug out the hypodermic needle from the side pocket. It was still there in its plastic bag.

"I can trace it back." Maisie put her phone away and tugged on her sweatshirt, her chin high.

"A scrying spell," Val said, remembering Mag's suggestion in the club. They would have to call on Maisie for help after all. "You can do this?"

"With a little bit of rest, yes."

"How long would the ritual to turn himself immortal take, Father?" Val was set on action now. The unsettling fury retreated to the back of his skull. "How much time?"

"Let me think. At least twenty-four hours, more maybe. If he has all the components. If I recall, he will need at least a pangolin's heart and some Wagner's viper venom." Father Gregoire rubbed his forehead with an anxious touch. "And don't forget, Valerian, you need feeding soon."

"Never mind that. I'll be fine," Val blew him off despite Father Gregoire's fretful expression. This was far more important than his hunger.

Val considered both his brother and Emme. Mag was even more rusty than he was with magic. Sure they were both the sons of Charlotte Callan, the so-called Ice Witch, but they couldn't do a locator spell now, not without a whole lot of studying.

What they had, though, was a powerful witch in their midst.

He looked at her in her fuzzy pajama pants and his heart quickened, deeply grateful that she had been sent to them. Father Grégoire would probably call it divine intervention.

"So Maisie, what do you think?" He swallowed with trepidation. "A scrying spell. Tomorrow when the moon rises. You and me. We'll do it together."

CHAPTER 8

The next morning, Maisie was contemplating the empty courtyard in front of the sanctuary. The hill of the narrow street ahead was steep, its cobblestones covered in a sheet of ice. She took a cautious step forward and nearly slipped.

"Here, let me." Valerian took her arm and she was suddenly enveloped with warmth. Vampires were supposed to be colder than human, seventy degrees, according to her readings, but all Valerian exuded was an enticing heat, to which she was intensely drawn on this frigid Canadian day.

"Don't you get snow where you're from?" His voice descended deep into her chest and she found herself leaning into him to take another treacherous step.

"We do, but the frost usually melts by daytime. Not like this." She watched Sasha sniff the newly fallen snow carefully before jumping into the fresh fluffy pile with glee. He leaped back out, shook himself and returned to his master's heels, clumps of ice stuck to the fur of his tail.

Valerian clipped the leash to his collar while Maisie looked again at the sleek mirror of frost before her. The shining sun cast the entire city with a bright magical sheen akin to a multitude of tiny pieces of glass. But the breeze was bitter on her skin despite the knitted hat drawn down over her brows and ears.

"This is so cold, I can't even swipe the screen of my phone to find out where to go." She stared at her device with a despondent look.

"You don't need it. I know where the seer's shop is."

" You know her well?"

"I was close to her great-great grandpa." With a twinkle in his eye, he shot her a half-smile and she was taken aback by how truly old he was.

"Cousin Jo said she was the one I needed. I didn't check with Nana."

"Do you always connect with your family?" He offered her his arm and they stepped into the street, Sasha pulling hard on his leash and Maisie holding lightly to the crook of Valerian's elbow over the heavy fur-trimmed coat.

"We're more than a family—we're a wide coven scattered all over New England. We care and look after one another." She glanced up at him and nestled just a little closer for his warmth. "You have magic. Don't you use it?"

"Just what I learned as a kid from my mother. I have Father Grégoire and the Guild if we need more. My brothers do their own thing."

"Your mom was a solitary witch."

"Ah. You didn't rest last night. You researched."

She shrugged. She had done precisely what she did every night, recreating her routine to the best of her ability while away from home. Exactly thirty minutes to review the spells she had used that day to replenish their powers, fifteen minutes to learn something new, then another fifteen in thankful contemplation. Only after could she allow herself to peruse her favorite web comic before calling it a night.

"What did you find?" His smile was amused.

"Not much. But I did read that the *Sorcière des Glaces* was here in the seventeenth century. Another short sighting in the nineteenth century, helping the patriots during the rebellion.

Some even say that she may be the witch responsible for the Black Oak warlocks' power.

"Oh that." He tugged at his fur collar with a smirk.

"Is it true?" Her brows rose. Imagine her coven's reaction if she had discovered the source of the warlocks' magic legacy.

He shrugged. "No idea. It would have been after she left here anyway."

They turned into a wider street. Her furry boots were fine for the winter, but not so great on the ice, she was glad to be holding on to Valerian's steady posture. Steam rose from cars tunneling down the hill, a few people passed them in a hurry—a little old lady in an old-fashioned mink coat, a few young people in neat colorful peacoats and trendy scarves.

Sasha stopped at the corner and pushed his frosted muzzle against her thigh.

"He likes you." Valerian said.

She patted the top of the dog's head. "Aren't you cold, boy?"

Sasha's tail flipped back and forth with vigor as he gazed up at her with trusty chocolate brown eyes.

"He's all recovered." Valerian's eyes shot up to the clear sky as if to give thanks.

"You care deeply about him, don't you?"

"Who wouldn't?" His lips curled into a broad smile as he looked down at his pet with fondness.

"Emmeline told me why you always kept a dog," she uttered without thought.

"Oh." His brows rose but his amused look remained. "And why is that?"

"She said you keep them to make up for the lack of relationship in your life." Her eyes shifted from him for a brief moment and she wondered if she was being too forward. Cripes. She never knew how honest she should be.

He snorted and slowly shook his head. "And she would not be wrong."

"So you haven't had a girlfriend since her." She gazed back up at him, eager to know more.

His body tensed under her arm, and he let out a measured breath. "No."

"And don't you want one?"

"Emmeline and I, that was centuries ago." He stopped and turned to her, his expression filled with unfathomable depth. "We are bonded for sure. By circumstances. She will always be in my life. And me in hers."

"I see." Her heart broke a little at his words.

"Relationships," he said as they started up the hill again. "That's for mortals. Not us. It's for people like you." Her heart broke a little more to see him smile at her with detachment. "Don't you have a young man pining for you in Berwick Hollow?"

She shook her head and tugged at her puffed vest with unease. She hadn't had much luck there. Her awkwardness turned any possible relationship into a basic friendship. And her first, well, that had been a disaster.

"Oh?" He tilted his head at her, inquisitive.

"It's hard for me to connect with people, sometimes. I…"

"It's okay if you don't want to talk about it."

"No, I was young, you see. A teenager. And I had stopped going to school. Nana and Mom just took turns teaching me at home." She was briefly lost in memories. She had actually taught herself. Her computer set-up at the back of the craft store, going through the loose curriculum her mother had put together but mostly studying what interested her, like history and literature. She'd give her mom a hand when the shop was busy.

"It was a courier delivery guy," she suddenly stated.

"Oh."

"He always came to the craft shop. Nice, Mom liked him. He asked me out. So I was really excited. Got my best dress. Borrowed Mom's perfume, Cousin Marla's heels, the whole thing. It was supposed to be romantic. I was a little crazy about him." She shrugged, remembering the confident nine-teen-year-old with the easy smile and spiky hair who liked to joke with her whenever he picked a parcel for delivery.

"He wasn't into you."

"Well, enough to take me out a second time. Ended that night in his car, over the hills. He was my first." She sighed. He hadn't truly forced himself on her that night. No. But they had done the deed and it had been awkward. "Never called after that."

She still shuddered at how cold he'd been to her the next time he came in with deliveries for the store. She'd been so naïve. Believed she had done something wrong.

"I'm sorry."

"Don't be. I guess that's what made me realize that I needed to get out more. Figure out the real world. So I convinced Mom and Nana to let me take college classes on campus in Presque Isle. I was one of the youngest there, but I did make some friends."

He gazed at her in silence with a genuine smile that eased his dark expression.

"There're a lot of different types of people in college." She laughed. "Some just as quirky as I am."

"I don't find you quirky at all." He patted her hand on his arm, his posture relaxed as they ambled farther down the street together.

"You don't?" She tilted her head in surprise. "I can be… awkward, I guess. Missing social cues."

"I think you might be a little scary." His eyebrow lifted. "The way you brought me back. It was… intense."

"Right. Sorry about that." Her face flushed despite the cold. She was a little embarrassed to have invaded his privacy. "There is no other way to do that spell."

"I can still feel you." His tone turned wistful. "In me."

"You can?" She stopped dead in her tracks, staring wide-eyed up at him. "You must have a lot of magic in you then."

He slid his arm around her and urged her forward. "I do.

And it's nice," he remarked as they started walking again, "having a bit of your essence still in me. You have a gentle soul."

She quivered at his words, not quite knowing how to respond, and quickly changed the subject. "How come you don't use your magic more?"

"I guess I should. We're all slightly bitter that our mother left us here at the end of the seventeen-hundreds."

Shaking off the fact that these events had happened centuries ago and that the man beside her had been *alive* then, she nodded to herself at hearing the dismay in his voice. She was so close to her own mother, it was hard imagining her leaving. She smiled inwardly recalling how furious Mom had been at Ryan—the infamous delivery guy—when he'd given Maisie the cold shoulder. Maisie's mom, who used magic for luck and light divinations only, had even managed a spell to turn him impotent for a year, coven rules be damned.

"Do you still talk to your mom?" she asked.

"I do. Easier now that she's just a phone call away. Mag won't have anything to do with her. But I check in with her now and again. She struggles with her immortality. Ever since our St-Amand father died, she's been broken."

"He wasn't immortal?"

"No. He accepted our birth, knowing we were not his. Fell in love with *Maman* as soon as she stepped off the boat that brought her from France."

"A King's Daughter."

"You *have* done your research," he said, impressed. "A *fille du roi*, yes. Seduced by an immortal before boarding the ship. Except she didn't know she carried his children—all six of us, believe it or not—until she reached the shore of *Nouvelle France*. But Antoine St-Amand didn't care. He was smitten. You'd think she would have put a spell on him to save herself the shame, but she didn't need to. They truly loved each other."

"And you?"

"He raised us all as his own children. Six sons in these days, quite an asset. He was a tough but kind man. Treated and loved us like his own. For us, he was our only father. We still miss him."

"And your real father?"

"Somewhere in Europe." Valerian shrugged. "At least that's what my brother Griffon thinks. He's been searching for him for the better part of the last century. A bit of an obsession, if you ask me."

"You don't care to know who he is? Meet him?"

"He used my mother. Kind of what that courier guy did to you." His nostrils flared with disgust. "Why would I want to get to know someone like that?"

"Right," she agreed.

The street turned into a larger artery busy with small shops and eateries—old buildings reconditioned with modern glass and steel. They passed a coffee shop where a few patrons inside animatedly talked with each other or sat snug over steamy mugs of hot drinks.

"Do you ever wish it would have been different?" she asked. "That your birth father could have stayed, so you could learned from him?"

"I don't usually think about things like that." Valerian's voice was flat, tainted with a twinge of sadness. "I have lived for a really long time, Maisie. The only way I can deal with it is not to live in the past but to take each day as they come. Do my best, see who I can help today. Then do it again the next day."

She nodded. There was a tragic thread to his tone but also sturdiness. An aim, a tenacity. Solid and determined. Like he would never hesitate at the course of action to take in any situation.

Her heartbeat pulsed steady and calm, her usually racing mind at ease, as she walked alongside him. He made everything clear around them, filled them with a sense of purpose, something she never truly could find. She found herself

71

noticing the small details of her surrounding as if for the first time. She heard the laughter filled with love from a couple walking hand in hand across the street, admired the cheery refraction of sunlight from an icicle off the eave of a candy shop and watched, mesmerized, the steam from chimneys swirling in the air before softly dissipating.

"And today," he added with a meaningful smile. "I am keen on getting this spell done with you."

And so was she. Not just to help them out, but to spend more time with him.

They stopped in front of an old building, its curved stone steps leading down to a basement shop. *Sortilège*. The French word for spell.

The name of the store was etched onto a large metal plate above a window filled with fairy lights, a collection of dream catchers, and statues of deities from every faith under the moon.

"After you." He motioned her on.

She took a step on the icy stairs and her heel gave under her. "Whoa!"

Valerian swiftly grabbed her from behind. His arms solid around her waist. "Damn old crone," he grumbled. "She could have put out some salt."

His warm breath tickled her cheek and his delicious heat sank within her chest. With his muscles so firm around her like that, it made her heart stop for a moment.

"Are you okay?"

She gulped to slow her adrenaline. "Yes, just missed my footing."

Contemplating the glassy surface in front of her, she gripped tighter on the iron railing as she tried another step down.

"Here, let me." He slid a quick arm under her knees and lifted her from the frozen stones to cradle her closer against his chest.

She gasped and her entire body tingled as her heart

hammered even faster. His intoxicating scent reached deep within her, and she swallowed uneasily as the fox fur of his coat brushed her cheek.

"You don't mind?" His expression on her was amused while Sasha barked with enthusiasm, his tail wagging with glee, thinking this was a new game.

"No." Her breath was short. "Not at all."

She hung on his neck, feeling the corded muscles of his shoulders through her wool mittens as he stepped down the five steps to the entrance.

As he pushed the glass door of the esoteric shop with his back, a tinkle of bells sang into the air. A smell of burnt sage hit her while canned music from a radio echoed from the back.

"*Tiens, tiens*, Valerian St-Amand." The greeting came from a low-pitched voice chiming in the heavy air.

Maisie blinked at the round dark-skinned woman sitting behind the counter of the shop, her dark eyes flat and peering at them. She had to be in her mid-sixties, her hair long and silver, scattered with many braids. Her black leather vest, embroidered in a multitude of pink and silvery threads, hung upon her shoulders over black lace sleeves and her wrists were adorned with many metal bracelets.

Valerian lowered Maisie to the floor. "Madame Ioshta." He dipped his chin in polite respect.

"What can I do for you today, Valerian?" She walked around the counter in a swish of black and shimmering skirts and stopped midstride to stare at Maisie. Her head shifted side to side. "*Mon doux Jesus. Une sorcière blanche.*"

So the indigenous seer knew about Maisie's magic. Nervously, she removed her mittens and shoved them in her pockets. She took a deciding step toward the elder and raised her chin awkwardly at her.

"I'm Maisie Thibodeau. Of the White Holly coven." She wondered if she should offer the woman her hand to shake or bow at her. Instead she stood rigidly in front of the elderly shop owner, quietly wringing her fingers together.

"Of course you are, *ma chère*." She clamped her hands speckled with heavy rings around Maisie's shoulders, and without warning, planted two sturdy kisses on each of Maisie's cheeks.

Maisie bristled as she brushed her lips on the woman's parched skin. Her eyes settled on a series of skulls behind the elder. Human and animal alike, they lined the tall shelves above the counter.

"Are those real?" she asked.

Madame Ioshta breathed a half smile as she pulled back from Maisie. "And why shouldn't they be?"

"You practice dark magic?"

"I practice all magic—tribal, voodoo, white charms, and dark *sortilèges*." She slowly tossed her hair behind her shoulders and her gaze turned to Valerian. "This is not a courtesy visit to discuss traditions between witches, is it?"

"No, we're here for components," Valerian said. Sasha remained at his heels, the dog unusually quiet, his eyes fixed on the old witch.

"Your grandmother hasn't visited me yet." The elder's gaze was dark as she peered at Maisie.

"Should she?" Maisie asked. Aside for Cousin Jo, no one at home had mentioned the shop owner to her.

"Well, you're here now." Her expression eased as she ignored the question. "You're here to study the immortals, aren't you?"

"You are?" Valerian took a step back, surprise breaking his voice.

"How do you know?" Maisie gasped.

"In our world, *ma chère*, we're all connected, aren't we?"

Maisie pursed her lips. How much did this woman actually know about her? She tried to read the wise woman's expression but just couldn't. She decided to drop it for now and focus on their task instead. "We need anvil dust, five railroad spikes, and ground finger bones, for a scrying spell."

"You don't have any of this with you?" The seer quipped.

"I brought very few components in Montreal. Didn't really expect to be conducting ritual magic. And I had to cross the border," Maisie declared, stating the obvious.

"Of course." Madame Ioshta's expression quickly turned to one of a benevolent shopkeeper. "I have all you need. Here, let me get everything packed for you."

She disappeared past beaded curtains behind her wide counter, the surface crowded with many candles, incenses, and small charm bags for any occasion, from lost love to luck at the card table.

"So you're not just here for Emme, you're here to study immortals." His lips flattened and he reached for Sasha, his trusted counterpart.

"Yes, better to see it all in the flesh, isn't it?" Too late, she had blurted out the words, having missed the shift in his voice. "Sorry, I mean—"

"No, I see." His tone was frigid, his hand steady on the top of the dog's head. "It makes sense. The high priestess would want to know everything about as many inhuman creatures as she could, wouldn't she?"

He gave her a brief nod and for the first time since meeting him, she experienced the true distance between them. The immortal vampire, centuries older than she was.

Her face flushed, she offered him a nervous smile.

But he turned away from her and with Sasha at his heels, he slowly ambled to the shop's front window above them. His whole back was now facing her. Ominous and wide, entirely kissed by darkness.

He was *not* a creature. He was a man. A very attractive man. Who moments ago had her in his arms. Had laughed with her.

She cursed her inability to control her habit of saying whatever was on her mind at the wrong time. Ever since she'd met him—had felt his essence inside her—he had been so much more than the vampire she had wanted to study. They had connected.

"Val, I—"

"Here you go, *ma chère*." Madame Ioshta burst out through the curtain, her hands full of small black silk bags tied with silver cords. "No one will hide from you with this."

Maisie shot a last look at Valerian hoping for a reaction. But he remained quiet, standing tall and foreboding in his long coat, his chin held high, Sasha sitting quietly by his feet. His look on Madame Ioshta and Maisie was distant, as if he was not part of their modern world.

She wanted to explain herself but didn't know exactly how. He had turned so cold. Would he ever trust her again?

Dejected, she turned to the shopkeeper. "How much?"

"Nothing." Madame Ioshta nodded back at Valerian. "It's been added to the St-Amand's account."

"Are you sure?" Maisie didn't want to owe anything even though the spell was for him.

The elder didn't answer, apparently deciding that Val would settle up at some point. She packed the spell components in a tidy paper bag marked with the shop's logo of a large crow decorated with a tiny dream catcher. She handed Maisie the bag and seized her wrist in the process.

"How are your Beaudry cousins faring?" the elder quizzed.

Maisie's heart halted to hear the elder asked about her immortal witch cousins. She frowned. "Okay, I think."

"Careful, girl. Don't go mad on us." Madame Ioshta cackled, her rings digging into Maisie's skin. "Like they are."

"I'm not immortal," Maisie told her with a shrug, knowing the seer was referring to her cousins' dark fate, cursed to risk going mentally ill if the undertook the immortality ritual. Like a twisted genetic lottery. A price to pay for their unending life.

"But you could be." The elder's eyes glowed with zeal. "You just need the right ceremony."

Uneasy, Maisie broke the crone's iron grip with a fierce twist of her wrist. "Thank you for the components."

"*Merci, Madame.* We'll be on our way." Valerian had appeared beside Maisie. His gaze on the elder unreadable, his tone flat.

As he laid a light hand on Maisie's back, she felt his protective aura envelop her. His rich voice carved shivers inside her as he added, "We have a spell to cast."

CHAPTER 9

a creature. Val tightened his fist.

She hadn't said the word, *he* had. But he knew that was what witches and warlocks thought of him and his brothers.

And while he couldn't care less about the opinion of others, he was expecting more from her. But no, she was only here to *study* him.

As he grimly stood in the *Sanctuaire*'s chapel, he watched her pour over a giant paper map of the city. She had stretched it over the altar, bordered it with five black candles and speckled the surface with anvil dust mixed with bone powder. A handful of railroad spikes and the hypodermic needle that had pricked Emmeline lay at the center.

His mind was on the witch instead of whoever had been after his blood.

He just couldn't let it go. A future high priestess. Sounded like Marianne Thibodeau had forgotten to mention a few things about her granddaughter.

It shouldn't matter. Really. Already her essence was fading from his veins. The gentle touch a waning memory.

Yet here she stood above the map. Her jet-black hair tied into a loose braid fell over one shoulder, the thick strand ending just at the tip of her breast. The small and high curve was much too defined under the small black t-shirt. The fabric of her top thin enough that he could make the outline of a small push-up bra.

Stop it, diable! Focus on the job. His balled fists and pained breath didn't go unnoticed.

"You need to feed, Valerian." Father Grégoire was right beside him, a heavy hand on his shoulder while his eyes went from Val to Maisie. The priest knew exactly how the immortal felt, the woman drawing both a surge of lust and hunger deep within him. His insides twisting and growling.

"We have time." Val lifted a stiff chin.

"I'd prefer if you did this after the *Rituel du Sang*, " the elderly man said.

Maisie looked up from the altar with furrowed eyebrows. "The feeding is tonight?"

"At precisely one eleven in the morning. You have just about one hour." Father Grégoire clasped his hands together with disquiet. "We should wait until morning."

"I can't. We need the moonlight for this." She nodded apologetically at the faint ray coming through the original stained glass of the chapel. "It needs to be done at midnight and with a clear sky. I suppose we can postpone until tomorrow."

"And let this bastard run free for another night?" Val was angry at the whole situation.

The vamp who'd attacked Emme had been less than help-ful. The tortured kid knew very little. The man Val and Maisie were after was just that. A man. A very bright man, appar-ently. A professor at the university where Justin worked. The teen did not know his name. They called him boss or professor.

But yes, they had guessed right. The scientist planned to use Val's blood to make himself immortal. The vamp had no idea why, and why Val specifically—not Justin. Or even Mag. And like his mute companion, he had been chained to the fiend with potent spells and a promise of regular human blood.

"Let's get this done quickly, then." Father Grégoire took off his cassock.

Her eyes wide, Maisie gasped at the sight of the priest's sinuous arms tattooed with the runes of Nostredame below the sleeve of his plain white t-shirt.

As he approached the altar, the elder's rosary appeared in his hands.

"Not tonight, *mon père*." Val stopped him. "I need you to stay here and keep an eye on Sasha and Emme for me."

Ever since last night, when they were both attacked, Val had realized that his dog was at risk. And for the first time he questioned the moral of his habit in rescuing strays to turn into faithful companions to his loneliness.

"Shouldn't you bring Emmeline with you?" The priest was not convinced.

"Not this time. She's temperamental and might slow us down."

"As you wish, Valerian" Grégoire wrapped his cassock back over his shoulders and crouched down to Sasha's level. "Come on, bud. You're staying with me tonight."

Sasha stared attentively at the priest and turned his deep brown eyes to Val as if wondering what to do.

"Go on, Sash," Val urged him on. "I bet Father Grégoire has some treats for you."

"Let's go, Sasha." The holy man patted his thigh to call the dog to his side. "I have a big soup bone in the kitchen, just for you."

Sasha's tail flapped back and forth at the word "bone" and finally strolled over to the old man with enthusiasm.

Father Grégoire stroked the dog's thick black fur and issued Val a warning. "Be careful."

It was obvious the old priest was still shaken to discover Val could be taken down. And so was he. But now that he knew this was just a mere mortal playing with things he didn't understand, it made Val angry, not fearful. After centuries, fear for himself was not something he experienced.

"I will." Val reassured Father Grégoire with an easy smile.

"And watch after Maisie."

Val followed the priest's fond look to the girl who was now engrossed in a meditative state over the enchanted map. The glow from tall candelabras by the altar's side played over her silky black head.

"I will. I don't need a whole witch coven from New England coming after me," Val jested to combat the growing lust inside him.

"It's more than that," the priest noticed.

"Yeah. It is." Val swallowed.

The girl was his responsibility. But regardless of how strong she may be, every time his gaze fell upon her body, every fiber of his flesh was called to protect her. He could never have her for himself no matter how badly the beast in him now craved for just a taste of her blood, of her spirit. But he would watch over her for as long as she remained in his presence.

"Are we ready?" she said as Father Grégoire and Sasha stepped out of the chapel.

Val strode through the room to stand across from her and offered his hands out above the marble altar, his palms out with his mother's mark glowing under the candlelight.

She placed her delicate hands into his and intoned, "*Matronae y Sirona*. I call upon thee. Assist those who need to see."

"*Ryerath licth tasarah!*" he called after her. A tingle of his own power rose inside his palm as his tattoo burned and glowed. While he witnessed that her powers came from the deities she was calling outside herself, his came from his very own blood.

It always had, for as long as he remembered. Not given by any gods or goddesses but, as far as he understood it, by the creator itself. To the true heir of the *Sorcière des Glaces*.

"*Ryerath...*" Val repeated.

"*Roichdadh fir at bheyl.*" She added the locator spell from her own tradition. Her hands warm and confident in his.

He felt the connection they had together deepen with intensity. Something so strong, it took his breath away.

Where she had been adorably awkward on their trip to the crone, this time she was all business. A master of her magical craft. Admiration rose in him and once more, hunger tested his sanity.

He bit the inside of his mouth, tasting his own blood. He *had* to focus. Had to find the scumbag who thought he could just turn into one of them without any thoughts on what being immortal actually meant. Val still wondered what was this professor's ultimate motive in doing this. And how did he even find out about Val and his brothers?

Maisie's head was bent forward as she mumbled her incantation over and over. Her clean scent of herbs and sandalwood reached his nostrils, and he groaned in agony.

Mist rose from the runes she had drawn around the map. The railroad spikes started to wobble and moved on their own accord.

She was so absolutely focused on her spell that she seemed oblivious to the center spike glowing and crawling steadily across the chart. It stopped and shone pure black, like an obsidian stone.

"Maisie."

She snapped her head up. Still holding his hands, she fixed wide and glassy eyes that went right through him, her pupils the brightest of greens as she continued to whisper the spell. "*Matronae y Sirona, Roichdadh.*"

"Maisie!"

She jerked out of her trance. Her gaze landed on the map. "There," she enunciated slowly. Her lips curled into a satisfied smile. The locator spike now a dull black.

"Interesting," he said. "At the north end of the university campus."

83

"Quick." She dropped his hands, pocketed the railroad spike, and folded the map before heading out of the chapel. "Can you get us there fast?"

"You need a coat." He followed her into the hall and smiled at seeing her rushing urgently in just a t-shirt and socked feet. "And boots."

"I know. Let's go," she called impatiently by the front door and shoved her feet into her furry boots. "I won't need the hypodermic needle anymore. It's all in the spike now."

"We'll take the Jeep." He was handing over her thick sweater. "The campus is just a couple of kilometers from here."

"Hurry. We don't have much time." She slid on her sweater and rubbed the back of her neck, her expression intense.

His mouth was dry, his heart pounding with wonder at seeing her so focused. He helped her into her small puffed vest. "Right, let's go."

CHAPTER 10

*T*en minutes later, Maisie stood in front of one of the oldest buildings of the university, the folded map tucked under her arms, the scrying railroad spike in her jeans pocket.

Her body wasn't one bit drained from the magic. Valerian was so filled with it, the spell they'd performed together had been a breeze. Cripes, to have that much power and not use it to its full potential, that was crazy.

"Chemistry faculty. My brother's office is just two buildings down." Valerian's jaw visibly clenched under the streetlights glow. "I can't believe Justin knows nothing of this."

A lone student crossed the snow-covered university square and disappeared behind a narrow pedestrian street. It was cold and dark, the low hanging moon faintly illuminating the dormant ivy clinging to the brick buildings.

She shivered. Her butt was frozen solid, her coat hitting her just above the hips.

"You're sure it's here?" Val shot her a curt nod, his gaze alert.

"Yes." She hopped up and down on the spot to warm herself. "Just not exactly clear where in the building."

"We should do the spell again."

"I'm freezing." She rubbed her hands together inside her woolen mittens and hugged herself, trembling.

"Here. Let me. That vest of yours is useless with this cold wind." Valerian moved in behind her and pressed his body against her back, their bodies fitting nicely together. He slid his hands over her shoulders and arms with vigor, the entire heat from his body radiating through her skin. "Better?"

"Yes." She turned her head slightly over her shoulder, much too conscious of his breath on her neck. "But I don't know how we can do another locator spell in this weather. I'm not sure I can concentrate."

"Let's get inside." He guided her forward and they both climbed the steps to the thick double doors at the entrance.

She gave them a few shoves, putting in all her weight. "It's locked."

"Not a problem." He barely shook the heavy door and effortlessly broke the lock. He turned to her with a wolfish smile. "See, easy."

"You immortals *are* really strong."

He raised an amused brow, his eyes lit with an inner glow, as he held the door open for her. "Didn't you see that in your research?"

"I guess you truly don't know until you see it for real." Once inside the Chemistry building, her muscles finally relaxed in the warmer air.

"Which is the actual reason you're here," he said, more seriously, following her inside.

"Look. It's not like that. I just..." How could she explain that she'd never seen him as some strange creature to study?

"It's fine." His lips curled into a genuine smile. "Let's hurry and find where that syringe comes from."

"Oh shoot," she gasped. "Your feeding."

"Yep." He drew his mouth in a thin line.

"You really need to feed, don't you?"

"Soon."

"How does it feel?" She wondered if it was like being

parched a whole day without water, or more like missing a meal and having your gut churning.

"Maisie. The map."

"Oh, right." Her mind buzzed with thoughts of what would happen if he missed the *Rituel du Sang*. An entire year to wait. It would be torturous.

His eyes darkened, his gaze fastened onto her. Cold fear seeped into her spine. Could he feed on her? Like Emmeline had tried the night before?

"Focus." He shook his head at her with a smile and the predator in him disappeared. Whatever was inside him, he was controlling it. For now.

"Okay." She unfolded the map over the banister of the lobby. She lay her palms flat over it, ready to do this on her own this time, feeling much better now that she was warm.

She held the locator spike in her hand and called out, "*Roichdadh fir at bheyl.*"

The shadow of the nail zeroed in to the middle of this very building on the map.

She closed her eyes and focused on the artifact in her hand. *Roichdadh.* It all became clear. In her mind, she saw the stairs she knew were just ahead of them, then the multitude of passages underneath the university grounds.

"Do people use tunnels to get around, here?" She didn't wait for Valerian's answer as the railroad spike started to buzz in her hand while the path lay clear under her. She bolted down the stairs, map in hand. "It's down below. I'm sure of it."

He caught up with her, his tall body remaining close as if he wanted to shield her from unseen harm. They proceeded all the way down three flights of stairs.

With each level, the surroundings turned less and less modern, the steel banister replaced by wood carved with the patina from centuries of students now long gone.

The last steps took them to a small tidy landing leading to three tunnels. All of which lit with an overhead glitchy fluorescent tube. The concrete floors were mainly clear of litter, obviously used by students and faculty to get around campus during the colder days.

"Can you still see it?" Valerian urged.

"I sense that there *is* something, not sure. It's west of me, I think."

"West?" He frowned at her. "How do I know which way west is?"

"Here." She took the map and studied the orientation of the building with respect to the rose compass, as well as the twists and turns they had followed down the staircases. The underground tunnel ran northeast under the east-facing building. "This way," she pointed with confidence.

They ambled forward through the long narrow tunnel and then she stopped. Her eyes closed. She waved her hand up and down, the spike in her palm having turned burning hot. "It has to be in there."

A tiny passageway lay to their right. Blocked with a tall, rusted grate, the area beyond was filled with junk and spiderwebs.

"No one goes there," Val told her.

"Ugh..." She shuddered, peering at the heavy old padlock guarding the gate. "That's it."

"Are you sure?" He rattled the gateway and the creaking echoed many times over along the walls.

"Yeah." An eerie feeling of malevolence crept through her bones. While the plain tunnel was bathed with the aura of busy students, the forbidden area was shrouded with an obvious evil presence. Her lips thinned. "The needle came from here."

"Okay." He grabbed the padlock with powerful fingers and, without strain, crushed it within his grip. He discarded the metal pieces and pulled the gate open. "After you."

She squinted, trying to make out the artifacts dotting the hall. "It's pitch black in there."

"Of course, I forgot you can't see in the dark. Here you go." His cellphone flashlight lit up for her.

"I know there is something here, ahead of us." The magical buzzing in her ear was getting louder, as if the syringe's essence now in the object in her hand wanted to get back to its owner, or its rightful place.

"You're right," Val said. "Someone is using this corridor. The spiderwebs are not as thick."

He lowered his light and they both saw footprints on the dusty floor.

She searched the darkness again and a musty smell, tainted with strange chemicals, rose to her nostrils. A slow rattling clang rumbled through the passageway.

"Valerian, I don't like this." She edged closer to him, the evil pressing in on her.

"You're hearing it, too?" He wrapped his arm around her, but it did little to calm her apprehension. Suddenly, her sixth sense prickled and all she wanted was to be away from this place.

But no. She recalled Valerian's inert body at the *Sanctuaire*. They had to find who had attacked him. She had to press on. The muscles in her back tightened in readiness.

I can take it, I can face anything in here, she repeated to herself over and over like a mantra. She would have to bring her courage way up if she was to step into Nana Thibodeau's footsteps. One hand on her pentacle, the other on the spike guiding her, she swallowed. She nodded at Valerian and felt braver. No doubt that with him there, she felt safer.

"A few feet forward," she said.

"There's an entrance over here." The light of his phone illuminated a wooden door, a century old and barred with iron.

"The sound is coming from behind. I hear moaning." Valerian's hearing was obviously more sensitive than Maisie's. "And whispered prayers."

They trudged toward the blocked door, her heart battling

like crazy within her chest. The railroad spike trembled madly and she nearly dropped it.

"Yes, there is something here. No doubt." She slipped the nail into her jeans, the pain from its heat now too hot for her to bear.

"Will I?" He indicated the door.

"We have no choice." She dug out her own phone and checked the time. "Val, you only have thirty minutes before the ritual!"

"We have time. Let's just see what this is about. Five minutes and then we'll drive back to the sanctuary." His sturdy tone was filled with calm. "Sound good?"

She nodded.

He placed two steady hands in the middle of the heavily barricaded door and with a slight shove, it gave up in a shatter of wood splints and broken metal. The door scraped as he pushed it open a couple of inches. In the silence that followed, a chain rattled.

Alarm seized her throat and she forced herself to shake off her apprehension. She really *had* to see what was on the other side. Someone had attacked Val. Had drugged poor Sasha. She recalled his warm muzzle on her thigh and his happy jumps in the fresh snow. Anger rose in her at knowing someone could hurt the innocent dog.

And dammit, someone had also assaulted Emmeline. Even though she should hate the female vamp, she was her responsibility. This was her job. No turning back.

While shielding her body, Valerian fully opened the door. The whole place was pitch black.

"*Luxmier!*" Valerian called out as they stepped through the threshold, illuminating a series of gas lamps that he had likely detected with his sensitive vision. "No one here."

He was wrong.

A terrifying shriek echoed loudly in Maisie's ears.

Two disembodied and glowing red eyes froze her on the spot.

"Watch out!" Val's arm was right at her chest, protecting her.

"*Lruannicth tùth...*" Maisie took one step back, one hand facing forward, the other behind her, ready to strike. Her heart hammering, she watched the creature loom tall over Valerian.

A wraith. The hideous monster stared down at them, skeletal teeth in fleshless emaciated features. The body insubstantial in flowing rotten cloths, half-spirit and half-alive, a true evil from the beyond.

"Don't move," she told Valerian.

But the immortal's fangs were already out, his body bristling with contained power, barring the monster from touching Maisie.

"*Daúscayrl hyenthx,*" she intoned. She had to dissolve it quickly before it could touch them.

The wraith took one swipe at Valerian with a skeletal but powerful arm.

Valerian blocked it and grabbed the monster by the throat. He struggled with the creature. Tattered clothing shook caustic dust all over them.

"I can't crush it!" He flung the beast across the room. The wraith bounced off the far wall and rebounded right in front of her.

"Maisie!" Valerian's panicked voice roared and he unshielded two daggers from under his coat.

"*Daúscayrl,*" she repeated. Her back pressed against the damp stone wall behind her, both hands out facing forward.

Her palms seared with heat as she tried to block the apparition from getting near her with the unseen shield she had risen to protect them. She had fought wraiths before and while Valerian seemed unaffected by them, one touch by the foul being would be deadly to a witch.

Valerian appeared behind it, raised his arm to stab the beast in the back, but the monster was faster and swerved a bony limb at him. It knocked the dagger out of his hand and shoved its horrific head back at Maisie.

Sweat beaded at her forehead, her arms tensed with strain at holding the shield.

The wraith's putrid face was now just a few inches from hers. She craned her chin up and caught the look of pure evil in its red eyes. She gulped once, her hands at her chest, and shouted, "*Stryos!*"

Power erupted in one big tide, washing over the wraith. Rippling through its body, from its gruesome limbs to its cavernous ribcage all the way to its misshapen head.

"Valerian, watch out!"

The wretched being's body exploded in a blast of splintered rotten bones and musty linen.

"Holy hells!" he shouted.

She breathed out and wiped her brow. *Nasty creatures.*

Valerian was right at her side. He sheathed his dagger back inside his coat. "Are you okay?"

"Yes. Lucky it's only one. Looks like your professor has found some pretty dark grimoires." She blinked with dismay. "Summoning a wraith like this."

"I have never seen anything like it." He shook his head and picked back his other knife from the stone floor. "Daevas, yes. Rogue werewolves. Plenty of ghosts. But not this."

"Well, he definitely has something to hide." She took in her surroundings—tall wooden benches all around, empty dirty glass cabinets, and hooks everywhere. "What is this place?"

"A laboratory." Valerian's pursed his lips with a frown. "An abandoned one by the look of it."

"This is where the syringe came from." She grabbed an unused needle from a small pile on the worktable. "No doubt."

Valerian nodded grimly. "Whoever was here has packed up and gone."

"The wraith had to be guarding something."

A heavy clang of chains rang from the back. A slow moan followed right after.

"Oh gods, what's that?" She froze, her breath short. "More wraiths?"

"Over there." Val strode to an alcove partly hidden behind a sturdy metal cabinet. "Oh hells no. The poor souls."

"What is it?" She wasn't sure she really wanted to know. Maisie peered around the cabinet. On the other side, floor-to-ceiling iron bars enclosed a small dank antechamber.

Valerian's eyes were dark with anger, his lips razor thin as he turned a bleak look at her. "Dying vampires."

"Helllp..." The chilling word dug straight through her bones.

She flashed her phone into the small room. The horrific sight broke her heart. Three emaciated bodies were chained to the wall, kids really. Half-naked, their chests covered in burns and open wounds. Only one was conscious, his eyes fluttering madly at her blinding light.

"Vampires?" She gulped with pain at their obvious suffering. "Cursed ones? Like those at the sanctuary?"

"Yes. He obviously experimented on them."

"That's despicable." She cringed at the pleading look crossing the eyes of the tortured teen.

"We can't leave them here." Valerian's expression was haunted. "We've got to bring them back to the *Sanctuaire*."

"All of them?" She rubbed her damp forehead under her knit cap.

"I'll call the shelter." He retrieved his cellphone from his pocket but suddenly buckled over.

The phone dropped to the flagstone floor; its screen shattered.

"Valerian?"

"*Diable!*" He let out a low moan, bent over himself, both arms seizing his stomach.

"Val!" She blurted his nickname before putting a slow

hand at his back, her insides churning with worry. "What's happening to you?"

"Stay away," he ordered, his voice chilled.

She jerked her hand back, puzzled by the frosty command. "Val?" she asked cautiously.

"Helllp..." The vamp's creepy plea reverberated through the stone chamber, but Maisie had eyes only for Valerian.

He was now shuffling away from her, one hand on the tall metal cabinet, the other wrapped over his stomach. His face was hidden, his dark hair fanning over his pale features. A low animalistic growl resonated through him and scattered through the entire lab.

"Maisie, go away." He slowly enunciated the last words as he finally lifted his head and faced her. A chill ran deep along her veins and shot through every single nerve in her body.

His fangs were fully out, his lips retracted in a snarl. His skin sallow and gaunt, his eyes dark and feverish.

The ritual! The realization hit her like a bout of vertigo.

"Is it too late?" Her heart pounded up to her throat as she slowly stepped away from him. Her mind ran through every defensive spell she knew, and she carefully drew her palm back, ready to cast an incantation.

She did not want to have to defend herself against Val. Not after dissolving a full wraith. She no longer had her entire strength. This was not just a strong vampire to take on as Emmeline was, but an immortal and the son of the Ice Witch.

She took hold of her body, which was quivering like a leaf, trying to calm herself. She had to talk him down from wherever hell he was.

"You need to feed, Val." While she kept her distance, she drew one hand out in offering, as if to appease a deadly beast. The ritual was due to start in minutes. "We have to go."

He took another step toward her and she saw the starvation in his eyes. In mere seconds, he had turned from her fierce protector to a dangerous predator. The hair on her forearms lifted from her prickly skin.

"Valerian!" She hoped there was at least a trickle of her essence still within him. "It's me, Maisie."

And just then, a flash of recognition crossed his eyes. He stood to his full height and swept the lapels of his coat over his tortured body.

She froze in anticipation and swallowed hard.

"*Shirax.*" His voice reverberated eerily against the brick.

A bright light blinded her, and she stood mesmerized to see a large bat flapping its dark and veiny wings in the dank air, where seconds ago Valerian had stood.

Flaming hells!

The creature flew straight past her, the tip of its bony thumb catching a few strands of her hair on its way to the entrance of the lab.

She swiveled in time to see it disappeared in the corridor, leaving her alone with his broken phone at her feet and a pack of dying vampires chained to the wall.

And with fifteen minutes left before her only chance at witnessing an immortal's *Rituel du Sang*.

CHAPTER 11

"*E*mmeline, you have to help me." Her cellphone glued to her ear, Maisie was leaning against Val's car in the freezing night, cursing that she had no key to open it, start it and get a bit of warmth. And she *had* to get to that feeding ritual.

When Emmeline had swapped phone numbers with her earlier, she hadn't expected that this would be why she'd needed to call the vamp. She knew the blonde had no love for her but hoped she could rally her with their common care for Valerian.

"Aren't you attending the *Rituel du Sang*?" she added. "I worry about him. He was in pain. And he shifted into a bat. What if he doesn't make it? I have to check on him."

"Oh that dull thing," Emmeline drawled. "Been there too many times."

"Please, where is it?"

"Outside a dank little crypt at the top of Mount Royal. The cemetery of the damned, or something like that."

"Cripes, I can't get there on my own. I'll never make it on time."

"Oh fine, I'll take you. I was getting bored anyway. All the disciples are gone, nothing but Sasha and a couple of lowlifes screaming down the cells. Where are you?"

Maisie quickly filled her in, while huddling within her small puffed vest. If she were to stay in Montreal any longer, she'd need to get proper winter gear.

Impatient and tapping her foot with angst, she watched the slim moon disappear behind unseen clouds. She checked her phone again. Emmeline could be here in five minutes if she hurried.

But would she? She was so unpredictable that Maisie had no idea.

She shuddered at remembering the dark look on Val's face. He had wanted to drain her blood. She knew this at a visceral level. For a minute there, her entire being had wanted to flee. Her hands shook and she reeled at recalling his hungering look.

He was a predator. No denying it now. A human-like being that had changed into a giant flying animal before her very eyes.

She blinked as the image of the large bat he'd shifted into crossed her mind. She could still hear the flap of its wing and feel the pull at the strand of her hair as he flew past. She shook herself, still awed by the vision. She fought revenants and daevas, wraiths. But she'd never seen anything like this.

Yet an hour earlier Val had been her partner. Doing magic with her like any other male witch she knew. They had connected at such a deep level, the feeling creating a large expanse of her chest.

Running down the hall and exploring the condemned lab, he had been just as human as she was. With powers yes, but still a man. A man who cared for his dog and for saving the innocents who'd been tortured and left behind to waste.

The look he had given the poor creatures had been haunted, filled with the urgency to take them away from their misery.

And there, her crush for him had returned fully. So much

deeper than when they had connected in Berwick Hollow. This time strengthened with the knowledge of his inherent altruism.

But he knew her only as the witch who'd come to Montreal to study him. Learn more about his kind. Like a weird inhuman creature.

And she supposed that was *actually* what she was here to do.

She bit her bottom lip and looked down at her mittens. Her goal sounded so crass now. Did she want to see more of him because of her relentless attraction or because she needed to show her wisdom of the world to her coven, so that they would trust her with replacing Nana.

She shook her head, leaning farther on the frigid car.

And what about this ritual? Her grandmother would be disappointed to hear that Maisie had missed it once she would tell her about it.

And could she *truly* tell her coven? Reveal Val's secret?

Her loyalty suddenly felt divided.

It was surprising that even Cousin Jo didn't know about this. She hadn't even mentioned the possibility.

Right now, Maisie was sitting with this incredible piece of information, a secret that, as a high priestess, she would have to tell the coven members. She would have to tell Nana.

She would have to betray *him*.

No! A heaviness sheathed her heart.

Could she do that? It would create a war between the warlocks and the immortals if they knew Val and his brothers survived on human blood and human blood only.

Would the warlocks come here in force, calling the Seattle branch, the Huntsmen, and even the Guardians of the Daemon Realm who had allied with them? Would they come and try kill Val and his siblings?

A tide of dread seeped into her at the immense dilemma this knowledge gave her. The immortals unchecked *were* dangerous, though.

Emmeline's attack on her had been vicious. And Val would have taken her down just now, drank from her, had he not controlled himself.

But he had. Warmth descended inside her. He had reined in his primal urge, called out for her to run. He had transformed before her eyes and fled the lab to prevent attacking her.

He had not harmed her. Not at all.

And this was a close call. They had pushed it too far. No doubt the magic they had performed had not helped by draining part of his essence and precipitating his hunger. Next time, they wouldn't let this happen.

She smirked. Next time? Why was she thinking of next time? Was she even considering being here for the next feeding? Next year?

She was nuts. And why would he even want her here?

She recalled the look he had given her in Madame Ioshta's shop when she had revealed her intention to study him. She had hurt him.

He had feelings, not cold-blooded predator instinct, but human feelings.

Maybe he did want to be as human as she was. Did he not mention his brother Justin lived as one?

A lump swelled into her throat. Should she really impose on this private ritual? Was it her place?

Her mind a swirl of confusing thoughts, she reached for her pentacle, fingered the smooth surface through her mittens and let out a slow controlled breath. She dug her boot in the packed snow of the university's tiny parking lot. She was a witch of the White Holly. She would soon leave this city and the vampires to lead her coven amongst this magical world that was getting wilder and wilder. She barely knew about the wolf-shifters that haunted the Domaine-Lassalle Forest and the banshees who lived across the country. So much to learn. So much politics to unravel, so many potential threats to be on the lookout for.

She had to be informed. No choice, she had to see the extent of this ritual. It was her responsibility to her people.

An angry screech of wheels on the pavement dragged her out of her thoughts, followed by an impatient horn.

Emmeline. Her blonde head peered out from behind the slanted windshield of a metallic rose gold Porsche, which gleamed of luxury under the streetlights.

Maisie pushed herself from Val's Jeep and hastened to the car. The heat from the cabin hit her with blessed warmth as she opened the passenger's door. "Oh gods, thank you."

With a raised brow, Emmeline shook her perfect head of hair while Maisie took off her mittens and rubbed her numb hands together. Sasha, standing on the back seat, pushed his damp muzzle on her frozen cheek as a welcome.

"You won't survive the ritual dressed like this." Emmeline jerked her chin to the back of the car. "I brought you a warm cloak."

Surprised at the uncharacteristically kind gesture, Maisie reached with gratefulness to the cozy wool fabric trimmed with soft synthetic fur. "So you'll take me. Won't they mind?"

"Oh, they won't mind," the vampire said. "Because they won't see you. Val would kill me for bringing you there."

MOMENTS LATER, just past 1:11 in the morning, Maisie was crouched behind a bush of evergreen in the middle of the forest on Mont Royal next to Emmeline, who held onto Sasha by the collar. The dog was quiet and looking back from Maisie to Emmeline, as if accusing them of spying on his master.

Maisie gawked at an ancient stone altar rising from the fresh snow, which covered a clearing surrounded by dormant oak and birch trees. With each gust of icy wind, the branches creaked in the crisp air. Their limbs created an ominous skeletal canopy over the attendants of the *Rituel du Sang*.

Tall torches burned bright and high to illuminate the three men—no, the immortals—who waited bowed and still behind the altar.

Naked from the waist up, the three legacy undeads were immobile despite the frigid wind and portentous chant from the hooded figures surrounding them.

The immortals were so similar in looks—with their dark hair, chiseled jaws and wide well-defined shoulders—that at first Maisie thought they were identical. But she soon recognized Val's stiff posture in the middle of his two brothers. And while Magnovald leaned back with an unconcerned expression over the assembly and the other brother sporting horn-rim glasses and neatly-trimmed hair—most likely Justin —stood at quiet attention, Val appeared jittery, his fists steady at his side, his lips a thin slit.

Her whole heart went out to him. He had to be in terrible agony by now.

"*Immortels du Mont-Royal*," a clear voice echoed in the night, "*en cette nuit du douze décembre*, and on this day of the peak of the Geminids shower, from the celestial body now known as Three Thousand Two Hundred Phaethon, we the disciples of Nostredame Guild, offer you our blood."

A hooded figure stepped forward and removed his head covering. *Father Grégoire.* Maisie gasped at his solemn expression.

Emmeline tightened her grip on her wrist. "Shh," she whispered into her ear. She was so close, Maisie could smell her perfume over the heavy incense coming from the ritual.

Sasha's breath came out ragged, as he strained against his collar in an attempt to join the immortals and their disciples.

"Do you accept our gift?" Father Grégoire added, and the rest of the congregation bent before the St-Amand brothers.

Maisie rubbed her cold fingers together in the thin mittens while staring in awe. Val's dark locks brushed over his tense forehead and the plane of his chest glistened under the light from the torches.

Warmth descended from her heart down to her navel as she recalled her hand on that skin, remembered their connection as his essence penetrated her core while she'd hunted to fix his blood from the poison in his vein.

She yearned to touch him again. To feel him so close she could shroud his consciousness with her own, feel every fiber of her being merged with his.

And she died to rest her lips on the alabaster chest in the valley where his pectoral muscles met his sternum. Her nails dug to her palm unconsciously and she let out a low groan.

Emmeline seized her wrist tighter. "Quiet."

Maisie glanced at the vamp's moonlit features and saw the fever in her eyes.

Oh hells. Why hadn't she thought of that? The feeding would likely trigger Emmeline's own constant blood thirst.

Maisie slowly pulled back from the vampire but Emmeline turned a dark look on her with a tighter grip, and then let her go to point back to the circle.

She shrugged deeper into the fur cloak Emmeline had given her, her throat well hidden from the female and, with a defensive spell at the cusp of her mind, she shifted her gaze back on the ritual.

"Brother Cyrille," Father Grégoire called.

One of the men approached the altar and shed his coat to reveal a torso inked with a multitude of magical runes, not unlike those she had seen on Father Grégoire's skin earlier.

The disciple trusted out his wrist right above the first chalice.

Father Grégoire retrieved a long white knife from his belt and in one swoop, slashed Brother Cyrille's forearm. The young man yelped in pain but kept his arm steady over the receptacle that was placed just in front of Magnovald.

Cringing, Maisie saw Val leaned back with restrained urges as the blood dripped into the cup, but he remained behind the altar watching the disciples carefully.

"Sister Ariane." Another figured approached, this time a

female with long red hair cascading down her bare torso, the same tattoos adorning her skin. She gracefully drew her arm over the chalice in front of Justin who smiled at her fondly.

She didn't utter a single a word when Father Grégoire sliced into her flesh but kept her head high and steady, her breasts taut in the cold wind. Maisie wondered if she'd been drugged. The female disciple didn't seem to notice the weather at all while Maisie continue to bury herself into the fur cloak and pressed her body onto Sasha to stay warm.

"Immortals, we give our blood so that you can survive, as it has been done for centuries." Father Grégoire now shed his cloak—his sinuous body gaunt in the night—and slowly slit into his own forearm. He placed his arm above the middle chalice casually, showing he had conducted this ritual countless times. With devotion and sincerity, he spoke to the man before him. "It will be over soon, Valerian."

Val remained silent but with his jaw stiff, he nodded at his old friend.

An incantation rose amongst the attendants as blood from the disciples dripped into the cups, their multiple voices interfering into a modulated chant intoned in a tongue Maisie did not know, while the three immortals waited solemnly for the offering.

"Yanis!" Father Grégoire called out to an attendant who rushed to each donor with pristine white cloths covered in sigils.

They wrapped their wounded arms tight in the sacred linens and then Cyrille and Ariane stepped back from the altar. Their cloaks were returned to them.

"We offer you our blood," Father Grégoire called. "Will you please accept and henceforth protect our guild?"

Maisie was mentally cataloging every detail of the ceremony with precision. She wished she could snap a few pictures for her coven's Book of Shadows, but didn't dare get her phone out with Emmeline there.

Her heart fluttering, she watched the three St-Amand brothers step forward.

"We do and we will," they called out in unison before each seizing a cup from the altar.

"Know that we are grateful." Justin bowed his head to the small crowd of disciples.

Magnovald tossed a worried look at his brother. "Go on," he urged Val.

Val's fingers gripped his vessel which he brought feverishly to his lips.

Mesmerized, Maisie hoped his torment eased.

Sasha suddenly bolted up, escaping Emmeline's grip on his collar. He ran forward to his master with a loud bark.

"Oh *merde!*" the blonde vampire cursed.

"Emmeline," Justin shouted, the blood chalice poised at his lips. He surveyed the darkness. "Is that you?"

Sasha shot straight to Val, his tail frisky with glee as he jumped around him wanting to play.

Val lowered his cup, blood dripping from his chin. He smiled at his dog. "Hey, boy, you shouldn't be here."

"Is that Maisie with you?" Magnovald shouted at the dark. "What the hell?"

The entire community turned to look at Maisie and Emmeline as they rose from behind the bushes.

Maisie caught Father Grégoire's stunned look but she avoided Val's gaze. Her heart hammered and she suddenly felt faint.

"Is this Val's witch?" Justin was clearly peeved. "What is she doing here?"

Emmeline dragged Maisie to the center of the ritual. "Shut up, Justin," she quieted him with a deadly look. "It's fine. She was worried about Val. That's all."

Magnovald gulped the rest of his blood offering, "I think she wanted to report this to Marianne Thibodeau and her coven," he said, casting Maisie an amused expression.

But Maisie was wishing she could hide from everyone,

keenly aware of Val's gaze on her but too awkward to look directly back at him. She jammed her hands into her pockets and looked down at her toes digging in the snow.

"Are you okay?" Emmeline rushed to Val's side. "Maisie told me."

As Maisie finally dared to look in Val's direction, she saw the female vampire's hand resting upon the middle of his naked chest.

"A close call again?" Emmeline asked.

Maisie's heart crumbled at the two immortals' connection. They kept saying that they didn't love each other but their bond was undeniable.

Val sipped the remainder of the blood, wiped his chin with a clean cloth offered by a disciple and pushed Emmeline gently aside to walk over to Maisie, his dog at his heels. His smoldering look dug straight to her core.

"I'm sorry." He reached out to tuck a wayward strand of hair under her wool hat. "About earlier, in the tunnel. I must have scared you."

"You didn't hurt me," she said. "I knew you wouldn't."

"I never would." The pad of his finger lingered on her cold cheek. Warmth connected deep inside her and she leaned lightly toward him.

"I wanted your blood." He closed his eyes for a second. "I really did."

"But you didn't hurt me."

"No." He licked his bottom lip and she suddenly was hit with a tide of cravings. A moan lay repressed at the depth of her throat. "A part of you had to be left inside me. Something told me I shouldn't."

She peered into his gaze and it was as if the entire congregation vanished. As if they were alone, together in the crescent moonlit night, both with a slew of unexpressed feelings.

Maisie lifted a hesitant finger and caught a tiny speck of blood from his lip. "Are you better?"

"I am." He captured her hand in his and drew it to his

naked chest. Right there at the center, where Emmeline had touched him. And where Maisie had wanted to trace the contour of his defined muscles.

"You must be cold," she said.

"I might be soon," he quipped, with an amused curve of his lip.

"Yanis," Father Grégoire called and Val's familiar coat was draped over his naked torso, the fur touching his cheek, a curl of his hair caught by the collar.

Suddenly, all Maisie wanted was to bury herself against his broad chest, feel his strength, his everything.

The coven, her job and all that was gone, and she was left with only one thought, one desire. Him.

On her, over and around her. Now.

Their gaze connected deeper and she witnessed the same craving in his eyes suddenly chased by a deep sorrow. He grasped her hand in both his and gently pushed her away.

As he released her, her heart shattered whole.

He turned away from her and the cold of the air sank straight to her soul.

"Well, brothers," he called out to his siblings. The moon had disappeared and the snow started to fall around them, his noble profile decisive and showing none of the debilitating hunger she had seen before. "Time to hunt the one who dare make himself one of us."

iable, how Val would have liked to gather her body trembling with cold into his arms as he had the previous night in the university courtyard. Instead, he paced the hall looking at the poor souls who had been brought along from the campus' tunnels, Father Grégoire besides him, Sasha darting back and forth between the open cells and sniffing the thresholds with caution.

His fingers tingled with the need to feel her skin again. While trying to focus on his task, he still couldn't get her out of his head. He had felt her want to be closer, had felt their souls connect in that one gaze they shared. The feedings always made him so much more aware, made everything so clear.

He stopped by one of the cells and stared at the cursed vampire huddled on the ground. His body looked emaciated in the clean jeans and sweatshirt provided by the shelter, his skin cleaner now but marred with misshapen scars.

"It's a shame we need to keep them chained like this." He turned to Father Grégoire. "They all look so miserable."

"I'm afraid there's no choice." The priest shot Val an empty stare. "We don't know how far they're gone."

"Right." Val nodded and snatched a blood bag from the

tall fridge set against the stone wall a few feet from the open cell's door. He crouched down at the young vampire's level while Sasha took a careful sniff at him and retreated back to Father Grégoire. The dog was always weary around teen vamps.

The wretched creature on the floor glared with feverish eyes. With great effort, he managed to hiss at Val before his head dropped down to his chest.

Father Grégoire pointed to the bare arms covered in pricks. "Whoever did this is a fan of injection."

"Come on, bud." Val seized the teen vamp by the back of his head. "You got to eat."

He held the bag in his hand, his blood hunger completely gone now. The ritual had assuaged any craving he'd felt earlier. And he cursed the fact that he had very much been ready to bite Maisie.

The physical attraction he felt for her had intensified his blood lust to a dangerous level and he truly could have killed her. Hells, he'd been so careless! His chest tightened with guilt. He could have drained her dry. And then what? Make another Emme? Or send her dead body to High Priestess Thibodeau.

Damnation. He rubbed the back of his neck. When was the last time his lust for fresh blood had been mixed with a profound desire to be with the person he craved? Not since Emmeline was just a young girl he courted.

And look at what had happened to their love. Destroyed. Turn into something else. A monster she was now. How could Val ever take the risk of letting himself fall for someone again? Another innocent life ruined.

He had done so well in keeping this sort of thing in check over the centuries. Worked with monks and shamans to control his hunger, spent nights only with the females he knew he could step away from and who also sought the thrills of one-night encounters.

But Maisie, she was different. And for one, she was

nothing like the young Emmeline of their youth. She was a fully-fledged witch, strong and fearless, just as was his own mother.

"He won't feed," Father Grégoire said above Val. "I'm afraid this one is lost. You can't save him."

"Can't have that." Val gritted his teeth together. His anger grew tenfold at the mysterious foe who dared mistreating these kids like this.

"*Koir idash!*" he spat, knowing that with his restored life force, magic would not drain him as dearly.

The vamp's eyes opened, and he craned his neck back at Val, the kid's long matted hair barely covering the multitude of pricks at his scrawny throat.

"Drink." Val shoved the rubber tube to the teen's lips.

The vamp turned his head away, wrinkling his nose and closing his eyes, as if he thought the blood would hurt him.

Val grabbed the back of his head with force. "Drink, dammit!" He held the kid steady with his immortal gaze, a compelling look that very few could escape.

The teen finally stilled. Now completely under Val's power of persuasion.

"Go on," Val ordered again. "You'll feel better."

The vamp opened his lips in compliance, and sipped on the ruby red liquid, slowly at first, and then frantically as if he hadn't fed for months.

Val tucked the bag on the teen's lap and stood. "Well that's a start."

"We have two more," Father Grégoire said.

"Yeah." Val stared at the rows of open cells. Sasha pushed his body against him, and he patted the dog absentmindedly.

The teens would have to be fully fed for a few more days before they could place them in more comfortable dwellings.

"You're restored?" Father Grégoire tilted his head with concern.

"I am."

"You won't need Maisie anymore."

"No. I won't," he stated. However, the truth was that he could still use her abilities. Her magic was stronger than his, even now that he was back.

There were complex spells that would take him hours to study, things he may not even know. She had been fully trained, her whole life. And while Val's mother was likely more powerful than any of the witches of the White Holly, he hadn't been interested in absorbing the full depth of her knowledge for himself.

"I wish we could send her back," Father Grégoire said.

"Not possible," Val stated. "The Black Oak warlocks want someone here to watch Emme."

"She's a risk to us all. She has already witnessed the *Rituel du Sang*. How much more do you want her involved?"

Val sighed, assaulted by a score of mixed feelings. How much more did he want her near him was the question. He could still smell her blood, feel some of her spirit in him.

He kneeled by the next vamp and cringed. This one had bruises all over his face. One of his eyes was black and blue and completely shut. *Bastard!*

"Maybe we can keep her focused on Emmeline," Father Grégoire mused.

"You do like her, don't you, Father?" Val gently examined the vamp's cheek and noticed what looked like a broken jaw.

The teen barely moved; his sallow eyes fixed into nothingness.

"She did bring you back." Father Grégoire passed Val another blood bag, human blood for now, taken from a local clinic. They rarely used human blood, but they needed the real thing to bring the poor kids back.

"You could have done that, too," Val replied as he pushed the container into the teen's curled fingers.

"Maybe. But she identified the substance in you right away."

"Wake up, kid!" With a flick of the hand and a quick spell, Val drew the young vampire's attention out of his catatonic state. The teen's eyes widened in terror. "It's okay, bud. I got you."

Val brought the feeding tube to the vamp's lips and the youth began to drink madly, his body hunched toward the wall as tight as he could.

"We got to find the son of a bitch." His breath grew heavier. "He's using these guys to experiment on them."

"You *could* use Maisie's aid, then." Father Grégoire was still chewing over the issue. "Keep her here. Keep you at peace with the warlocks and witches. Help with the madman."

Val stood and scratched Sasha between the ears. He let out a deep breath. The priest had no idea of the true turmoil in his heart. Val was falling hard for Maisie. And for that reason, he had to convince her to go away, far from here.

He breathed out another sigh. "I think I'll send Emme to Renaud in the mountains for a while. Maisie will want to go with her. I don't want her to report everything we do here. Hells, she will love checking in on the wolves over there."

Father Grégoire nodded, recognizing Val's frustration. "How are you going to break the news to Emmeline?"

"What news?" The clear voice of Val's ex-girlfriend echoed down the underground hallway. "Making decision for me again, *chéri*."

"Emme." Val's soul sank to see her walking down the corridor followed by Maisie. The witch wore her usual jeans, and her fitted t-shirt featured a gaming company logo this time. The sight of her long hair, loose and following her every curve, strummed Val's heart.

"Oh gods." Maisie's gazed upon the kid vamp feeding in the corner of his cell. "Are these—"

"Yeah. They were brought in from the lab last night."

"Will you return them back to life?" She lifted her brows at him.

"Of course, that's what I do."

"I see." She frowned, as if wrestling with thoughts, crouched down to the vamp and rose a hesitant hand at him.

The kid was still slurping the blood from his bag, not paying attention to anyone.

"Careful, Maisie." Val couldn't help himself from stepping closer to her, but Sasha beat him to it and sat by her side, his furry body edged between her and the cursed teen.

"Hey, boy." She wrapped her arms around Sasha and the dog's ear lifted. He gave her hand an affectionate lick.

Val's heart swelled. Sasha seemed taken with her, too.

"So what was that you wanted to tell me?" Emme sidled next to him, her perfume, as always, a little too strong.

"I think you two should go to Domaine-Lassalle."

"Are you fucking kidding me?" The female vampire flinched back, her nostrils flaring. "In the backwoods?"

"Why?" Maisie turned a questioning look to him, and his heart dropped to have to push her away. He thinned his lips and tried his best to remain as distant as he could as she added, "This was not what the council agreed on."

"Safer." Val gave her a slow shake of his head, still conflicted. "With whoever tortured these vamp, Emme's not safe. She needs to be away from here."

"What are you talking about, Val?" Emme protested. "If I'm not safe, neither are you or, god forbid, Justin at the university."

"She could meet the wolf-shifters," Val insisted. "Isn't that what you are truly doing here, Maisie?" He grimly forced himself to remember her true intentions in being here to study supernatural creatures.

"Yes, but"—she stopped to gather her words—these kids… shouldn't I help?"

"No need." He strode to the next cell. "We got this."

"But Val…" Emmeline caught up with him, and he shot her the darkest look.

He felt her flinch. As her maker, technically he could force her to do whatever he wanted. He rarely used his dominance, but this was one of those times where he should. He needed Maisie away from Montreal. Safe. And once she'd visit with his brother in the mountains, and Val had taken care of the madman, she could be on her way back to Berwick Hollow and become the high priestess she was meant to be.

"Win-win," he mumbled to himself grimly, hiding his gloom to see her go.

"Fine." Emme rolled her eyes but understood he would not be swayed. "But not until we nip over to the *Serpent Maudit*."

"Why?"

"Mag called. Check your voicemail. Apparently, Captain Akande's got something to report that might help with this lunatic. She'll be there tonight. And Mag wants you with him."

CHAPTER 13

$\mathcal{A}$n hour later, Maisie was sitting in Emmeline's Porsche as the female vamp maneuvered to park over a snow bank right in front of the *Serpent Maudit* club. It was a Saturday night and a long line was forming at the entrance, starting at the colossal black marble pillars graced with a multitude of swirling iron snakes, and ending all the way by the century-old bank at the street corner.

Maisie had wondered why she had let Emmeline convince her to dress up, but a look at the people in line told her that the club's patron liked it fancy. Many high heels dug in the snowed-in sidewalk, tiny leather jackets did very little to fend the cold, but everyone's face was bright with animation in anticipation of a fun night out.

Maisie had only one top that was not a t-shirt—a little black lacy affair that revealed her navel—and Emmeline had found it as she'd dug through her clothes in the armoire of Maisie's room. The female vamp had declared it the cutest thing ever. She had then pulled Maisie's hair up in a flirty ponytail and lined her eyes with heavy black liner.

Maisie had protested, reminding her that they were looking for clues about her and Val's attacker, but Emmeline was adamant. She wanted fun, and fixing Maisie up was her idea of fun.

Thank goodness Maisie had managed to slide on her hoodie over the small tank top and even with the fur cloak over it all, she was shivering with cold.

"Let's go, Maize." Emmeline shot Maisie a bright smile. "You know, in all these years, I never had a girlfriend."

"Centuries and no friends?" Maisie gulped and again reminded herself that Emmeline was still an evil predator and that she had to make sure she was ready to take her on if the vampire's mood changed.

But the female's loneliness made her a little sad. Aside from the brothers—and those ties were steeped in dysfunctional history—Emmeline really had no one.

Maisie followed her out of the car and they walked straight ahead of the line of patrons.

"Raphael." Emmeline nodded at the bouncer, a tall and muscular twenty-something man of Asian ancestry.

"*Mademoiselle* Dubois." Raphael's smile was both warm and respectful as he unhooked the red cord to let them pass.

"One of mine." Emmeline grinned as they reached the coat check counter.

"What do you mean?" Maisie shed her fur cloak and, hit with a sweltering heat, took off her hoodie. She tied the sleeves around her waist.

A quick look at the thick crowd reinforced that this was the last place where she wanted to be tonight. She shuddered with anxiety at having to mix with so many people.

"I made him," Emmeline explained, passing on her heavy deerskin coat to the girl behind the counter. "Didn't mean to but couldn't stop myself from draining him. Sadly, he doesn't have that much longer to live."

"How so?"

"Most of these baby vamps won't make it past thirty."

"What, they just die?"

"Yes. Something about the human body not being strong

enough." The blonde frowned, apparently not thrilled by the bouncer's unfair fate. "No pain. Just fade away one night in their sleep."

"But not you?"

"Nope," Emme smirked. "I get to live. Forever and ever."

As Maisie took in the information, more questions rose in her mind. "Did Val take care of Raphael when he turned?"

"Raphael, yep. And Louka and Evan, Mag's bodyguards." She nodded; a grave expression darkened her striking features. "Did you know Val has convinced Justin to try and find a cure? Maybe not to immortality but at least for a human life."

"Really?"

"I don't know why he bothers, but he feels he needs to save them all."

Maisie's heart went to Val. He had taken on the whole burden of the cursed teen vamps, almost as if they were his own children.

"Come." Emmeline's eyes lightened and she pulled on Maisie's arm as they entered the club itself. "Let's get you a drink."

The music pounded through the flooring. A scent of rich perfumes mixed with heated skin rose to meet Maisie's nostrils. She gulped and took a deep, mindful breath. She could do this. "I thought we were supposed to join Val and his brother."

"They're here somewhere. But let's have a little fun first." Emmeline pushed through the crowd while Maisie continued to practice her breathing. "Remember they're packing us up for the woods tomorrow."

They reached the bar and Emmeline ordered two drinks from the bartender—a lean but muscular man in a tight tank top, his sleek bare arms covered in snake tattoos that reflected the decor etched everywhere on the walls.

"Right." Maisie wasn't sure how she felt about this change of plan.

But she was here to watch Emmeline. She had witnessed the *Rituel du Sang* and now had a chance to see real lycanthropes, *loup-garous*, Val had called them.

The witches in Berwick Hollow would have to agree to her ascension now after she reported what she had experienced. The trip meant that she would also meet the recluse Renaud St-Amand.

Her excitement at the new discoveries sank as she acknowledged that she would have to leave Montreal. An overall feeling of numbness flooded her limbs. She would leave Val. And again she was torn. Between her feelings and responsibility. Her heart ached at the thought of being away from him.

Maisie would have to insist on coming back to Montreal once the threat was eliminated. She hated running away from danger like this. But Val had been oddly adamant. And Maisie *was* supposed to stick with Emmeline.

Thoughts continued to war in her mind when a purr echoed in her ear.

"*Bonsoir, ma p'tite sorcière.*"

Maisie turned toward the voice; her heart tumbled in surprise. *Madame Ioshta!*

"Did you catch your immortal yet?" The seer bellied up to the bar beside Maisie. Her long shimmering skirt grazed the floor, and she wore the same embroidered leather vest as before.

"What do you mean?"

"Your feelings are strong. I could sense them from across my shop."

Maisie clenched her jaw. "There are no feelings."

"He cares for you, you know."

Maisie eyed her. "It doesn't matter."

"What are you doing here, bitch?" Emmeline passed Maisie a small shot glass filled with neon pink liquid and then wedged herself right beside her, almost as if she wanted to shield her from the seer.

"Hello, Emmeline." The elder curled her lips back at the female vampire. "Still eating humans, I presume?"

"What do you care?" The tension between them was like ice.

"I don't." A dark current pass through the old witch's gaze. "As long as you stay well away from my people."

"You two know each other?" Maisie examined both of them in turn.

"For too long." Madame Ioshta was smiling now.

Emmeline was silent and had slightly retracted her lips to show a tiny edge of her razor-sharp incisors "Get out of here," she finally said.

"I'm not here for you, vampire." She extracted a small card from a long, fringed leather handbag and turned to Maisie with a look pregnant with meaning. "It's immortality you *do* want."

"No, never," she countered. It was just not something the witches in her immediate family would ever think of doing.

"Nonsense." She took Maisie's hand and tucked the business card in her palm. "I can help you. Call me."

And with that, she swiveled and disappeared into the crowd.

"I don't know why Val insists on dealing with her." Emmeline downed her small shot glass in a single gulp. "The old crone gives me the creep."

Maisie remained silent and tucked the card into her jean pocket, her mind full of questions, planning to email and ask Cousin Jo what she knew about the seer in Montreal as soon as she was back at the nunnery.

Emmeline took a seat at the bar and as Maisie leaned back next to her, two guys approached them. Medium size, pressed jeans and button-down shirts opened at the neck. One had tiny crystal earrings at his ears, and the other's hair was trendily spiked at the top. Both completely human.

"What are two beautiful girls like you do in a dump like

this?" The tallest of the two—the one with the earrings—wore an appreciative cocky grin.

Maisie gulped her drink and set her empty shot glass on the bar. A little dizzy, she looked at them silently.

"Why?" Emmeline eased back on the bar's railing. "You want to take us somewhere else?"

"Emmeline," Maisie warned.

"I got this, Maize. Chill." The blonde leaned into the newcomers, her blue eyes suddenly filled with lust.

"Maybe," the man with the earrings said. "I know the best places in town."

His friend with the neat haircut flashed Maisie an apologetic smile.

Emmeline thrust her chest forward, her breasts pushing against the gold fabric of her tiny top. "You could start by buying us another drink." She licked her lips and rested her hand on his chest, just below the collar of his shirt.

"I'm Adam," the shortest guy introduced himself to Maisie. "He's Zach. What will you have?"

Maisie flicked a look at Emmeline and recognized the signs in the female vamp's feverish eyes. She no doubt wanted these guys for more than a drink.

"You're a big one, aren't you?" Emmeline traced the muscles of his chest, taking him in.

"You like that, don't you?" He placed his hand over hers and gave it a squeeze before calling out to the bartender with an authoritative hand in the air. "A round of whatever they're having."

"It's okay. We should really go." Maisie didn't like the vibes she was picking up between Emmeline and Zach. The man was completely entranced by her.

He leaned forward into her, trapping the blonde with his arms on the bar. She was reclining back in offering, a perfect vision of female surrender, slowly licking the top of her plump lips.

"Emmeline." Maisie tugged at the vampire's arm. She

knew exactly what the blonde was thinking. And she did not want to use magic to stop her.

Adam grabbed one of the shot glasses the bartender had prepared and offered it to her. He took one for himself.

"To you." He nodded at her and downed his drink. "That's a real cute top you got on." Adam was harmless. But she had no time for this. Still keeping an eye out for Val and his brother, she wished the two men would just go away.

"Look, Adam, you're really nice but I'm waiting for someone," she said.

"A boyfriend?" He sounded disappointed.

She smiled inwardly. As if she could call Val a boyfriend. He was anything but. Still she said, "Something like that." She threw back another shot.

"That's really too bad." He nodded toward Zach and Emmeline. "Those two are really getting on."

Maisie sighed to see the blonde now intertwined with Zach on her stool. They were kissing each other fiercely, his hand seizing her hair, his thick body forcing his way between her legs while Emmeline took hold of the back of his neck.

"Emmeline." Maisie poked at her with annoyance.

The vamp turned her head to Maisie, her cheek resting on Zach's shoulders as his hand explored her breasts over the corseted strapless top. Her gaze was hazy, the tiny point of her fang poking out from under the blood-red lipstick. *Flaming Hells.* Her mouth was much too close to the guy's neck.

She shot Emmeline a warning look, but the blonde smiled idly back at Maisie. "I think me and this beefcake need a little time in the back alley. What do you think, big boy?"

"Hell yeah, gorgeous." Zach slammed a possessive arm around Emmeline's shoulders and leaned to his friend. "You're fine, right Adam? Just want a little time with the lady."

"Um, sure, I guess." Adam cleared his throat.

Maisie scanned the room. No Val or Mag in sight. Where

the heck were they? She huffed. Well this was why she was here, wasn't she? To protect humans from Emme.

She gripped her pentacle between her fingers, brought it to her lips, and whispered, "*Unnsinn smychd...*" Her gaze was fixed on Zach. "*Unnsinn!*"

His arm abruptly fell away from Emmeline, and the vampire tottered on her vertiginous heels.

"What the hell?" Emme flung her head back with a huff.

But Maisie's eyes were on the human. "Don't you have an early call tomorrow?"

Zach frowned, then blinked rapidly. "Yeah, maybe?"

"You should be home. Right now." She reached out for Adam and patted his arm with a meaningful stare, casting another suggestion spell upon him as well. "Take your buddy with you."

Zach took a puzzled look at Emmeline and turned to his pal. "Shit, Adam, I forgot. Big meeting in the morning. We should go."

"On Sunday?" Adam glared at his friend, then at Maisie, confused.

"Thanks for the drinks," Maisie said, nodding with vigor.

"Sure. I think." He glanced around the room in confusion, his posture loosened. "Hey, Zach, it's late."

But Zach was already halfway across the club. Lost into the crowd.

"I should go...with him, I think." Adam was fumbling with his words.

"You do that," Maisie encouraged, and Adam ambled away after his friend.

"Bitch, what was that for?" Emmeline glowered at Maisie and sat back in her stool with a pout.

"You wanted to drink from him." Maisie shot her a flat look.

"Yeah, and why did you stop us?" Emmeline shrugged lazily. "I just wanted a little bit. I wouldn't have killed him."

"Drinking from humans is wrong, Emmeline."

"Oh, and how do you make that rule, Maisie?" Emmeline leaned back on the bar and reached for her drink. "You're a baby. You know nothing. I'm three centuries older than you."

Maisie took one step closer and grabbed the vampire by her bare arm. "Emmeline," she snapped, her jaw tight. "I may be twenty-five to your three hundred years—"

"Three hundred and twenty-one," Emmeline corrected, dropping the shot glass on the bar.

"Whatever." Maisie squeezed her upper arm tighter, ignoring the deadly look suddenly rushing through the blonde's eyes. "I was sent here from the Black Oak council. The warlocks *and* the White Holly witches. Together we are a huge coven. If you step out of line, I have to report it. And Val and his brothers will be history."

Emme huffed but remained silent.

"The only reason Diesel Stanford did not send the whole order after you is because his childhood friend Malcolm Dunsmuir convinced him not to, "Maisie pointed out. "Don't you remember Malcolm? They told me you met."

"Right. The Daemon King. And his consort, Harper Grant. Evan's sister." She looked down at her feet with a sullen look. "I remember."

"Do you want a bunch of warlocks and witches coming down on you?" Maisie insisted. "They'll try to kill Val. And Magnovald and Justin. They'll hunt all of you down until no one is left."

"They can't hurt us." She shot Maisie a daring look. "The St-Amands will summon their mom back. The freakin' Ice Witch. Renaud would bring the wolves. And I bet Madame Ioshta and her clan would ally with the Immortals if she has to choose."

"Oh they can hurt you, and they will," Maisie said with force. She noticed how her nails had dug into her palm. She had expressed her exact fear, that a war would break between them all. That Val would be hunted, his teen vamps burned. Father Grégoire and his human disciples caught in the middle. Everyone she was starting to care about destroyed.

Emmeline slumped back in her stool, her eyes downcast for a moment.

"Do you need to feed?" Maisie let go of her arm. "Synth blood?"

"Nah." Emmeline's shoulders dropped. "Give me booze."

Maisie signaled the barman for another round, wondering why they had come here. Val and Magnovald were probably having their own secret meeting and hadn't wanted them around.

"Here." She passed another alcohol shot to Emmeline. "Last one and we go."

"We need to wait for Val," Emmeline whined.

"He's not even here." Maisie was now fully taking charge, her jaw set with purpose.

"Bottoms up." Emmeline's sassy mood returned as she winked at Maisie before downing her glass.

Maisie had no choice but follow suit again. She gulped her own tiny glass—something like her third so far—full of a potent mix of hard liquor and sweet syrup. She shook a little. She had been tiptoeing around Emmeline since she'd called her for help at the university, but she couldn't do that again.

Emmeline slammed her empty glass down and nabbed Maisie's arm.

Now what?

"Come on." She dragged Maisie toward the dance floor.

As she stepped forward, a wave of dizziness washed through her. She'd had way too much to drink. But the beat thumping under her feet was enticing. Usually she would have avoided such a crowded space, but the alcohol had taken root and numbed her inhibitions.

The smell of ozone from the smoke at their feet mixed with opulent perfumes and the scent of growing lust. Girls in micro-skirts showing a lot of bare skin whirled around them on the dance floor as if the small microcosm of warmth knew nothing about the freezing weather outside. A man in a tight undershirt seized his partner by the waist as she swayed against his crotch, while two women were intertwined in a lavish kiss nearby.

"Come on, Maize. This is our last night here, before we disappear to the woods." Emmeline swiveled her hips and lifted her arms in the air.

A small group of dancers pumped their fists, cheering her on. She was obviously a popular figure in the club. She moved from one to the other, kissing lips, seizing waists, and patting butts indiscriminatingly.

When she swayed back to her, Maisie leaned in so she could hear her over the loud music. "Are these vamps or humans?"

"Can't you tell?"

Maisie pulled her by the shoulder to holler in her ear. "I don't want to have to use magic here again." She worried that Emmeline would want to bite someone once more.

"Oh, stop being so boring, just let go." Emmeline shimmied her body alongside her.

The beat thrummed in her center, her vision slightly blurred by the flash of the strobe light. The music filled her, and she started moving.

She did love dancing. Mostly on her own in her car, or while cleaning her mom's shop after hours.

She flipped her hips side to side, and from nowhere she smiled at the sensation of swaying to the beat.

"There." Emmeline grabbed her waist and dragged her to the center of the floor, where flashing lights bathed the crowd in a series of blood red hues.

Her body continued to undulate and for a moment, Maisie was lost in it, forgetting it all, the people around them, the unrelenting cold of the city, the poor vamp victims, the wraith she fought. She let go, falling into the thumping music, the luxurious atmosphere and buzz from the alcohol. She welcomed the sweltering heat of the air, of the sexy bodies all around them, and warmed at the cheers and claps of the dancers forming a tight circle around her and Emmeline.

She lost sense of time, and with her eyes closed, untied her ponytail to let her hair drop down her back in soft strands at her bare skin above her jeans. Sweat beaded at her forehead and the back of her neck. She slowly lifted her arms to push back the heavy mane of her hair in order to cool a little. An easy smile fell on her lips as she let go and reveled into moving freely to the music. Her chest filled with a bliss that descended all the way down to her core.

The usual frantic little voice in her head had been completely quieted by the alcohol and lavish dancing. Casually, she opened her eyes into slits to survey the bar far behind the dance floor.

She almost froze. Her mouth gaped as she caught *it*.

His gaze.

Oh hells. Val was watching her.

His smoldering dark eyes were pinning her to the spot, and again, despite the distance between them, she felt their connection.

Val motioned her to him with the crook of his finger.

She didn't know if this was the mythical vampire compelling power or just her intense desire for him, but her insides summersaulted at his call.

While the rest of the people gyrated around her, completely oblivious to her turmoil, she could do nothing but stare at him, her heart filled with bottomless longing.

CHAPTER 14

*H*ells, *the girl is hot.* Val had tuned out Captain Akande as soon as he saw Maisie being dragged by Emme to the center of the dance floor.

The female undead was her usual self, all lavish curves and crystal blonde hair, ensnaring everyone around her under the strobe lights. Everyone, except him. Because, despite the slew of sexy women scattered in the club, he had eyes only for Maisie.

In a short lacy top above the hoodie tied at her waist, and which bared her perfect midriff and emphasized the gentle curve of her small breasts, Maisie had swayed to the beat with surprising wildness.

That band of naked skin at her navel was haunting him. He could not stop staring at it. And the animal in him just wanted to seize that small waist and see her arch her back just for him. He was dying to sink himself within that subtle body. His feeding had brought control, yes, but the hunger for her remained. Different now, with the carnal thirst intensified.

He growled inside as he continued to hold her in his haunted gaze.

She broke eye contact and disappeared behind two dancers.

He reined himself in, jealous that they were all so close to her, close enough to touch her skin and inhale her sweet herbal scent.

Oh seigneur, what was wrong with him?

"Focus, brother." Mag nudged him in the rib.

They were seated at a tall table near the bar to hear what Captain Akande of the Sureté du Québec provincial police had to tell them.

"Bodies ripped open, you said?" Val tore his eyes from the dance floor with difficulty to concentrate on the police captain's words.

The sturdy forty-something black woman wore a plain navy pantsuit, white blouse, with a small gold cross pendant at her neck that matched the thick gold hoops at her ears. The well-cut fabric fit just right over her heavy but muscular limbs.

"A rise of what looks like wild animal attacks." She nodded with her no-nonsense expression as she handed them her phone to show them images of the crime scenes.

"Two bodies discovered on the frozen river, one more on Mont Royal. We can't explain it. Bears don't come this close. Wolves are rare."

Val cringed at the pictures—no one he knew, but the teens wore misshapen winter clothes and secondhand boots. Much like his recent detainees he had hoped to rehabilitate. Throats that had been ripped open. Their young lives snuffed too quickly.

"They were vampires,' Captain Akande said, her tone accusatory.

Mag barely lifted an eyebrow. "How do you know?"

"Incisors were fully out in death. You two promised there would be no more." Captain Akande's voice remained icy.

Val raised his palm. "Not by us. I can assure you."

"And truly dead vamps would have been decapitated, or burnt to a crisp," Mag added.

"He's right." Val looked at the pictures some more while rubbing the kinks out of his neck. "What are all these marks?"

"They've been tortured. One had deep cuts, another was covered with blisters in a strategic pattern. All had older scars and pricks over their entire bodies." Captain Akande looked at him directly in the eye. "I've seen drug addicts. This was not it."

"Test subjects." The very idea pained Val. They had been turned, tested upon, somehow killed, and then dumped back in the city.

"What do you mean?" Her well-defined brows knitted.

Val filled her in on what he had found with Maisie in the university tunnels.

"Someone is experimenting on homeless kids?" Her features paled.

"Looks like it," Val said. "We rescued three with very similar conditions."

"But alive," Mag added.

"Barely."

Captain Akande leveled Val a flat expression. "You found more vampires?"

"I have them at the sanctuary."

"Don't go sending more vamps into the city," she warned him.

"They're a long way from going anywhere."

She shook her head. "I don't like this."

"Val's method works. Look around you." Mag waved a hand toward the club patrons. "I bet you can't tell who is a vampire and who is human."

The police officer narrowed her eyes and then slowly surveyed the club. "Well there's Emmeline. Of course," she snorted. "What about that little thing next to her. Long dark hair. Black top, jeans."

Her gaze had stopped at Maisie who was trying to catch Emme's attention by tapping her repetitively over the shoulder. Val's fist tightened with annoyance. He wanted to shield Maisie from Akande's curiosity.

"Just a witch," Mag said despite Val's warning look.

"A witch." Captain Akande's dead cop stare flinched for a fraction of a second. "Dang it."

"She's Emme's guardian," Mag explained.

"Maisie Thibodeau. From New England," Val said, his voice hoarse. "Just let her be."

"Sensitive topic?" Captain Akande had become amused as she asked Mag with a cocked brow.

"Oh hell yes," Mag said.

"Right. " Captain Akande smirked and pocketed her phone. " What about the dead kids? Why dump them in plain sight?"

"No idea." Mag shrugged.

Val searched for Maisie again but she and Emme had disappeared from the dance floor. Disappointed, he shook his head to ponder the dead teenagers who'd obviously been attacked by their mystery madman.

Suddenly, he was struck with insight. "He wants us to see it."

"Who?" Captain Akande asked.

"You're right, bro," Mag said. "I think he wants to show us what he can do. He turned them or captured them somehow. He studies then kills them. Not sure how though."

"Some chemical compound lethal to vamps." Val's hands were folded together on the club's table, his body still. "Some crazy person is trying to become immortal, like us. He used the zombie drug on me. He's well versed in chemistry."

"A fuckin' deranged doctor," Mag spat.

"Did you ask your brother Justin about it?" Captain Akande asked.

"He knows nothing about this," Mag said. "But he's keeping an eye out on campus."

"Zombie drug, you say. I'll have to check with forensics. Get a record of the chemicals the university orders. Who bought what and the likes." She tilted her chin to Mag. "I texted you both the pics. You should ask around."

Mag gave the police officer a solemn nod. "I will."

"Look, you two. As long as things are quiet," she added with a steady look, "I'm happy to overlook a few things."

"Like what?" Mag said, with a half curl of his lip.

"I know you feed on the staff, Magnovald. And you, Valerian, it would be much easier to make these vamps completely disappear than try to rehabilitate them." Her mouth turned into a grim twist. "I'm not prepared to carry on a full immortals hunt in the city."

"You couldn't kill us all." Mag's voice dropped an entire octave, his tone swelling with foreboding.

"No. But some of your friends could die." She looked back at the dance floor and Val followed her gaze.

Emme and Maisie had reappeared and were in intense conversation, Emme with her hand right at Maisie's bare waist, trying to convince her of something.

"Emmeline would be the first to go," Akande added. "The witch could be hurt."

Protective feeling surged into Val. His right hand clenched into a fist.

He wasn't that bothered by putting himself and Emmeline in danger. But Father Grégoire and Sasha were a different story. And the thought of Maisie being caught in the crossfire by the madman after him shook him with dread.

He slowly turned to the captain. "The scumbag is already dead."

"Good. But I won't stand for vigilante justice," she told him. "I want him alive. If he killed teenagers, vampires or not, the authorities will make him pay for it."

"We'll see," Val said, his tone dark, still watching Maisie. He was not prepared to make a promise he couldn't keep, not sure that he could stop himself from enacting his own justice.

"I'll follow you out." Mag pushed away from the table and got to his feet.

Captain Akande stood and straightened her jacket. She curtly nodded at Val and headed for the exit. Mag ambled after her, a casual but protective hand on the woman's back.

Maisie was talking to Emme with animation, pointing back toward him. But his ex was intertwined with some man, her hands all over him, as she always did.

Val clasped his hands tight together, turning his knuckles white. The fact that Maisie could be hurt from the current threat brought a slew of feelings inside him.

He needed her now. Needed to feel her alive near him.

And it was more than the predator hunger in him that wanted her. It was his heart. Beating steadily at the thought of her gentle spirit within him.

He finally caught her gaze and for a moment, he wanted to truly compel her. Force her to come to him and serve every single of his cravings.

Mag would have no issues doing just that to a woman. And as his brother had done with Sandrine the night before, Val could do the same with Maisie. Sink his teeth in her fresh flesh. Capture her slender waist, bring her upstairs and do things to her, with her, that would both leave them weak with desire.

She shot him a helpless little smile and he lost it, his heart in complete turmoil.

He lifted a hand and curled his finger to motion her to him again. Was he compelling her? Swallowed by his need, he couldn't really tell.

But what mattered was that she had now fallen deep into his gaze. And, as if ignoring everything around her except for him—like in a trance—she took a few steps in his direction. Her black hair fell gracefully on her shoulders, almost all the way to her bare midriff. Her lips were parted. Her eyes, heavily lined, were fixed on him.

And she was all his now.

CHAPTER 15

*O*h *cripes!* She was drunk.

A scorching tide of cravings filled her as Val called her toward him. Was he using some spell on her? Perhaps that well-known vampire look that could compel one to do anything the predator wanted.

No. It was the alcohol. Or the dancing, which had awakened her senses.

All she knew was that she was keenly drawn by an insane desire to be near Val's calm strong presence and far away from everyone crowding her on the dance floor.

Forget Emmeline. Maisie had been curious to meet with the police captain but in the time she had tried unsuccessfully to convince the vamp to follow her, the officer had left with Magnovald.

Unable to tear her eyes from him, Maisie now ambled over to the tall table where Val sat alone. As she stood right in front of him, his gaze trailed over her entire body and she felt herself ignite from the inside.

"Nice shirt." He raised one eyebrow at her.

She shook her head awkwardly and pulled down on her lacy top. "Emmeline said I had to dress the part."

"You fit right in," he said. She wasn't sure if it was in approval or not.

"You found out more about the man who hurt those teens we discovered?" She drank him all in—the wide shoulders under the crisp black button-down shirt, the alabaster skin exposed at the throat, the *Sorcière* mark below the rolled-up sleeve.

"I did." He hooked two fingers into the belt loop of her jeans and pulled her closer. She tottered into him, and his scent intoxicated her further. This was much too close for comfort.

"What did the captain say?" She felt compelled to continue talking about their common foe to mask her thirst of him.

"They discovered three dead vampires, victims." Val tugged some more and she found herself lodged between his sturdy thighs. "Don't worry. You're safe with me."

She gulped and licked her bottom lip. "Vampires? Dead? But that's impossible."

She tried to stay on topic, but the man before her was nothing like the cool and distant philanthropist she knew. This now was the very enticing male who had carried her over Madame Ioshta's icy threshold, the one who had looked at her with haunted hunger in the tunnels, ready to sample every bit of her while holding himself back with immense self-control.

Except this time, the hunger was not for her blood. But for something entirely different.

Her body could not ignore the mix of danger and sexiness he exuded. And the crush she held for him flushed all over her. Every fiber of her body yearned for the totality of his essence.

She edged closer to him with a tentative hand on his shoulder, wanting to confess her mounting feelings for him. "Val, I—"

"*Ma belle.*" Something heavy passed between them. His cheek brushed hers as he whispered against her ear. "I know."

He slid a hand on the bare skin of her back and her knees buckled at the electrifying touch. She would have fallen if his thighs hadn't trapped her deliciously against him.

His breath was on her temple, his arms around her waist, his broad chest gently brushed against hers. "You smell so good," he said. "Like the spring rain."

As he inhaled deeply against her earlobe, a thousand sensations scattered through her.

She anchored the crook of her arm behind his corded neck. Her free palm splayed wide to settle on his chest between the two of them, just there at the swell of his taut muscles.

He pulled her in closer and she fell into his embrace, tilting her head back at him. "*Mon ange*," he groaned slowly against her cheek.

Her heart hammered wildly, her chest searing with pent-up cravings as she turned her mouth against his and gently brushed his lips with hers.

"*Seigneur*," he cursed.

Then, as if it was all he needed to act, he responded with a powerful kiss, his passion released in a broken dam of cravings.

His mouth forced hers open, his tongue searched her own with intense longing.

She lifted herself on her toes to meet his insistence, her mind lost in a buzz of yearnings, of wants, for the seductive immortal in her arms. The bustle of conversation around them faded as the thumping beat of the loud music hastened in tune with her beating heart.

She was hot, pliable and ready, to take all of him, her tongue exploring his, her nails digging into the back of his neck, her hand gripping the fabric of his shirt and pulling him closer toward her.

His arm at her waist descended lower, seizing her butt to anchor her firmly against him, while he slid a hand under her top and let his finger trail up her spine.

Her breath eased as delicious shivers scattered along her

skin and she sank farther into him. She broke their kiss to breathe against his lips, "Val."

"You're so perfect." His whisper was in stark contrast with his demanding embrace.

She craned her head back to look into his eyes and sensed it again—their deep heartfelt connection. That bond they had shared since she had probed into his core to cure him.

No, she corrected herself. It was the link she'd felt when he had scooped her out of harm's way when she was battling the troll set on Berwick Hollow last summer and how he had later stood his own in front of the supernatural council. Where he had stood, tall and strong, with all the marks of a leader, as he defended his brother's rights to own magical artifacts.

His desire of her now was an unyielding fever etched deep in his eyes. Pure and true. It was nothing like the blood lust she'd witnessed in the university's tunnels earlier. No, his gaze now was soft and loving and full of a thirst for closeness.

She let go of his shirt to touch her bottom lip. Her index finger lingered on the swollen skin he had just kissed, still throbbing with the traces of his claim.

The corner of his lips lifted into a crooked smile. "Oh Maisie," he groaned.

Without warning, he kissed her again and pulled her in closer.

Her taut breasts pushed tight against his solid torso, leaving her breathless and weak. While she gripped his hair fully between her fingers, his touch found her bare belly and she moaned against his lips with lust.

He edged her away by a mere inch, just so that his hand could slide upward over her bra to capture her breast in his whole palm. He tweaked her nipple tenderly between his thumb and forefinger.

His wide body shielded her from the people in the bar. The combination of his touch and the alcohol made none of them matter. Their connection blocking everything that wasn't just the two of them.

Flaming hells! She was hit with a wave of cravings that mounted straight from the depth of her core to crawl down between her legs. Nothing had ever felt quite like it. As if he knew just how to play her to make her melt in his arms, with just enough force, but edged with a hint of tenderness.

Again she would have fallen if it hadn't been for his steady arm securing her waist. The muscles of his thighs were so forceful around her body that she was going nowhere.

"You're gorgeous," he said, taking a measured breath and sliding his palm slowly over her erected nipple. "Why do you have to be so sweet."

Through the shards of craving hitting her relentlessly, she detected the pain in his voice.

"Kiss me again," she ordered. This, them, was right. It had to be. Everything fitted just perfectly.

"Non, c'est impossible." His tone was hoarse as he shook his head and released her.

She frowned at him, confused.

He let out another long exhale and rearranged her top in place around her torso.

"Maisie." He rested his hands on her hips over the jeans, holding her lightly at arm's length.

She gulped, her throat suddenly dry. "Val, this was good, right?"

She reached out to trace his temple, trying to pick out any verbal cue that would let her decipher his thoughts.

"It is." He took her hand in his and held it captive. His gaze was impenetrable, his dark eyes stormy, indicating nothing that would give her hope, or a clue at what their kiss had meant to him.

"Then why—"

"I could do this all night," he said.

She raised an eyebrow, not knowing what to do now, or what to think.

He shot her a small smile. "I could kiss you all night. More even, I could take you upstairs in one of Mag's bedrooms and make love to you with everything I got."

Her stomach fluttered. That, there, was all she wanted. "Let's do it."

"Hells, Maisie," he growled, his voice distressed. "I can't do that."

"I don't understand." The world around her seemed to slow down. He was rejecting her.

He brushed her hair from her forehead, let his finger linger on a single strand before letting it go with a sigh. "It's complicated."

"I don't see why. You enjoyed that kiss, I felt it." His erection had been very evident against her navel. "Why not more?"

He pulled her toward him with a groan and rested his lips on her brow before softly pushing her away.

She was a torrent of confusing feelings, her heart hammering wildly with hurt.

"Madame Ioshta said you have immortal cousins," he said.

"I do. The Beaudrys. What about them?"

"Why aren't the Thibodeaus?"

"Immortal?"

He nodded and an insight hit her.

"It's because I'm not immortal, isn't it?"

His lips leveled into a thin slit and he remained silent.

"I'm not Emmeline," she said, her voice flat. How could she explain that things would be different? That she wouldn't be a careless burden.

"Oh no, definitely." His tense expression eased. "But you are mortal."

"You don't want to see someone get old." She lifted her hand toward him and then lowered it uneasily. She *would* get old and die. Just like his beloved dogs.

"I wouldn't see you get old," he insisted. "I would turn you. I know myself. I couldn't see you die."

His words brought her a small comfort. Her heavy chest eased. He did care enough to want her by his side for eternity.

But she remembered what Emmeline had said about Sasha. He couldn't have a normal relationship with a mortal woman. Yet she was not entirely human.

"My cousins are immortal," she informed him, "but they all risked insanity when they went through the ceremony."

But some had not gone insane, she suddenly reasoned. The Elder Beaudry was perfectly fine and thriving. There was a risk, yes, but there could be very good reasons to undergo the ritual.

"Some have died from the madness," she mused, repeating her nana's words. "So our family has decided that the dangers weren't worth it."

"And they are right, it's not." He traced her temple, his finger a searing but gentle touch. It lingered on her lip. "I would never want you to risk anything for someone like me. It's not worth it."

"What if *you* are worth it?"

He snorted. "Sweetheart, you're so young."

"I may be young to you." She eyed him hard. "But I'm *not* condescending."

"Maisie." He reclined back against his stool and lowered his hands to her hips. "I've lived for over three hundred years. I've seen so many relationships begin and end. Love *is* fleeting."

"Love?" Her heart fluttered with a surge of euphoria. He had actually used the word out loud.

"Call it what you want." He shrugged. "I feel something, you feel it too, this connection we have. Maybe it's your spell to bring me back, maybe it's more, but you and me, it's there. I don't know what else to call it."

"Love?" She repeated the word before biting her lower lip, wishing suddenly that she was better at expressing the many emotions warring inside her.

"I don't know." His hands were steady over the fabric of

her tied-up hoodie while he considered her. "But whatever I feel for you, I shouldn't have acted on it."

"I can handle it," she said. "Even if it doesn't go beyond tonight." She was eager, acting on impulse. She wanted more of him, even if just for one night.

"But what if *I* can't?"

She swallowed. For once realizing that maybe she had misjudged what he felt for her. She thought of Sasha and how he always had a dog by his side. She thought of his loneliness.

"I truly could make myself immortal," she blurted, surprised by the intense feelings consuming her whole. "For you."

"*Mon ange.*" He shook his head slowly. "Even if you survived it, you don't want to live forever. It's a curse. I am not worthy of this kind of sacrifice."

He captured her hand in his and hopped from the bar stool, forcing her to crane her neck even farther to try to catch his tortured expression.

"I really could go through the ceremony," she insisted. "Become immortal."

She was absolutely certain that he was worth all the risks. Knew in the depth of her heart that he was *the one*. She wanted him. Wanted to be everything with him, do everything with him. Wanted to ease his loneliness.

She didn't want to be so easily pushed aside like some other random mortal girl when they both knew they were something special together.

His lips thinned again and he reached toward her face. She tilted her head in anticipation, but he held back, his hand poised in the air before he dropped it by his side.

"You would go insane."

"Not necessarily." She was muddy on the subject and realized it was something they rarely talked about in their family. Taking her cue from her mother, she hadn't pursued any research on it. All she recalled from the family's stories was that two of her young cousins were already insane, that a few had even taken their own lives in the depth of despair, and that it was a line she would never be allowed to cross. It would be a betrayal of all Nana had taught her.

Val breathed heavily and finally laid a heavy hand on her shoulder. "This is not meant to be." His face was an impenetrable mask. "I'm sorry."

Her heart broke in half. A dull pain settled right at the center of her body and she shot him one more hopeful look.

But he let go of her and took a step back. "It's just not meant to be, Maisie."

And with a heavy sigh, he grabbed his coat and swiveled away from her to leave her behind, alone by the bar table.

As the throbbing music cut heavily through her, she watched his wide back and imposing figure part the crowd. Patrons carefully stepped out of his way with what looked to her like longing as he passed them by.

Despite the sweltering heat, she was left with nothing. No feelings at all, except for a deep emptiness carved inside her, the loss as frigid as a Montreal winter night.

CHAPTER 16

*H*e could still smell her on his skin. His gut churned at how he had pushed her away, how her face had fallen just before he had turned from her.

No. He hadn't wanted to do that to her.

He still felt her lips on his, her nails digging passionately in his neck.

Seigneur. He wanted to go back, hold her, feel her body against his. Now.

Both his heart and soul ached to sweep her up her feet. Take her away from the crowd and make her his.

His blood had boiled over to see her smile at the man who had bought her a drink earlier. Of course he'd been jealous. And he had kissed her. For what? To prove to himself that she could be his? For a few minutes? For a night? More? His throat tightened in pain.

Once his lips had locked with hers, when her svelte body had nestled against his chest, he'd realized he wanted her for an eternity. So she could be by his side. Forever.

He pushed the exit door to the back alley with fury. Angry at the situation. Livid at himself. Why the hell did he have to kiss her? Now all he wanted was to bite her, drain her. Feed her his blood, make her like he was. Another Emmeline.

No! His entire being rebelled at the idea.

He stopped and slid into his coat. Then leaned back on the old stone wall of the *Serpent Maudit*. One of the original buildings of the city, it was almost as old as he was.

He took a slow breath and peered at the dark sky, trying to make out a few stars despite the bright lights blocking their glimmer.

Music pulsed through the club's back door. As well as clinks of glass and animated conversation, laughter, life.

He instinctively reached by his side for Sasha to help steady himself but realized he had left him home with Father Grégoire. The dog wasn't fond of the *Serpent*'s Saturday night busy crowd. There were times he wasn't either.

The ache at his chest spread and he let it flood him, let the pain diffuse into his entire body.

This *was* his life. Alone aside for his brothers and Emme. With the disciples at the sanctuary. With one mission. To do good, to help. To keep the peace in his city. To make it so that those young vampires did not run amok and kill and terrorize humans. To restore a bit of life into what they had lost.

He recalled the poor souls he had found in the tunnel, the pictures of those Captain Akande had showed him, burnt, tortured, killed. He had no idea if those vamps had hunted anyone before finding their ends at the hand of a madman, but the cruelty of it bothered him deeply.

Who could have done something like this? As Emme had been the first maker of the poor creatures, Val was ultimately the cause of their fate. It was his responsibility to find the bastard who did this.

He should not be distracted by a pretty witch.

He snorted. *Face it, Val. Maisie is so much more than a pretty witch.*

She was not Emme. Nothing like the shopkeeper's daughter who had needed a man to protect her.

Maisie didn't need anyone. She stood strong on her own two feet. Had battled Emme, when very few could, had restored Val's health in minutes when it should have taken days, even with Father Grégoire's ancient rituals. She had brought down a wraith by herself. Even Mag respected her and that took a lot.

Why couldn't Val have someone like her at his side. The future high priestess of the White Holly coven. *Oh diable,* what a partnership that would be?

She could help him here with his cursed pupils. He hadn't missed her compassion upon seeing them chained in his basement.

Could he follow her to Berwick Hollow? An enchanted thought crossed his mind, a dream of embracing Maisie in the clearing of the woods, taking her on a hot summer night surrounded by the dainty lights of fireflies and the cozy songs of frogs calling out to each other.

He kicked the snow at his feet. That was wishful thinking. An illusion. Maisie was wanted by her coven just as he was needed here.

There was no world where they could be together. No world where she could be by his side for eternity. Most of her cousins had lost their sanity at immortality. Even his own mother had turned strange after living for so long and she had left them so as to not tarnish their relationship. The St-Amand brothers somehow endured with a clear mind, but it was not natural.

Not a risk he was willing to take by someone he cared deeply about.

And no doubt he cared about Maisie. A lot.

She had a place in his heart. Would always.

And he vowed right there that he would do the hard thing. The right thing.

Val would take the high road to work with her, keep her in his life as the priestess leader she would soon be, but restrain himself, never letting his feelings show. She would eventually get over him.

He bent down to scoop a pack of snow, shaped it into a

snowball between his hands, the cold a welcoming sensation, numbing what he truly felt and containing the searing hot need he had of her.

Her hurt, confused expression as he left her alone in the bar was still on his mind.

That wouldn't do.

He would go back to her, right now. Apologize for the terrible way he had deserted her. Then he would tell her everything Captain Akande had told him. Show her the images the officer had texted him. See if with her talented mind she could help find some clues, a spell maybe that would lead them to the crazy scientist.

It was what he should have done in the first place, instead of acting upon his feelings.

Soon she and Emme would go to the safety of his brother Renaud in the mountains. That would put a stop to his insane infatuation.

After patting the snowball once more, he threw it across the back alley. It landed with a splat between two narrow windows above the bakery across the street, the brick wall speckled with crystalline white snowflakes.

Val would find something to distract himself. Back to the boxing ring. He'd been complacent in the last century. His old friend Remy Viaux had passed, but his son still maintained the old haunt. Yes, punching a few bags and letting out steam was what Val needed.

With one last look at the empty back alley, he returned to the bar.

The heat and scent of lust hit him again, clogging his brain. All that had been cleared outside was now confusing him. He focused on one thought—find Maisie. Apologize. Not for the kiss, no. He could never apologize for something so precious, but for leaving her like that, alone, without much of an explanation.

Someone tugged at his coat. "*Monsieur* St-Amand?"

Val shrugged off, ignoring the call, anxious to reach Maisie. Others could wait.

But the grip wouldn't let go. "Valerian?"

Annoyed, Val stopped his pace and turned to a man, medium in height with a slightly receding hairline, in a tweed blazer over jeans.

"Don't you remember me?" the stranger asked, an eager expression on his face.

Val shook his head. "No, sorry." He tried to move on, but the man seized his arm again.

"Ethan," the stranger said as he pulled Val toward him. "Dr. Ethan Collins. I was a kid when we met, you probably don't recall." His tone shifted and Val detected a hint of frost.

"Sorry, man." Val scorned at the hand holding his forearm. "Can we do this later? I really got to find someone."

"The witch?" Collins sneered. "Maisie Thibodeau? She left."

Val froze. The man let go and slid his hand back over his skull. His peculiar gaze was fixated on Val.

A trickle of alarm slivered inside Val. "What do you know about Maisie Thibodeau?"

"I know everything." Collins tilted his head to the side with a strange smile that caused Val to scrutinize him deeper.

Middle-aged, forty maybe. A little old for his brother's club crowd. The tweed blazer was ratty with patches at the elbows. The button-down white shirt collar was a little yellowish. A deep frown was etched at Collins forehead while his faded blue eyes peered from behind outdated black-rimmed glasses.

"Ethan, is it?"

The defiant crease left the man's features and he brightened. "Yes! You do remember."

"Refresh my memory." Val's tone was steady as he surveyed Collins further. There was something strongly off about him.

"You cured my dad."

"Your father?"

"Joey Collins. Yeah. My father. Don't you even remember?" His last words were said with a twinge of resentment.

"When was that?" Val shook his head. "I'm sorry I've been doing this for a while."

"You flippin' don't remember us." Collins took an outraged step toward him.

Val put his hand out at the odd man while leaning back on his heels. The stranger seemed angry, but Val did not want to hurt him. Or cause any ruckus in his brother's club. This was not the first time this type of thing happened. He had similar encounters before.

But Collins would not be stopped. He surged forward and grabbed the lapels of Val's coat. "You have to remember me." His breath reminded Val of the lingering scent in the hospitals he sometimes scoured in search for cursed teen vamps. And the man's strength was incredible.

Val narrowed his gaze upon him. "You're a vampire." He braced himself, his arms stiff at his side, but set on not harming the man. "Did your dad turn you?"

"No, he didn't." Collins finally let go of Val with a huff. "I'm not quite there, but I will soon be just like you."

"What do you mean?" The back of Val's neck prickled with foreboding. Something wasn't right. He studied the man further, noticing the injection mark at his throat and a myriad of scars along the carotid artery. "*Who* are you?"

"Valerian, my friend," Collins stepped in closer, "I am, will be, one of you. A vampire just like you are. You saved my dad. Well, you saved *me*, actually. From him. Once he got turned and stayed with you, my family's life was perfect. No more beatings, no more yelling. When he came back to my mom and me, he held a job, provided for us. Darn it, he even took me to hockey games at the old forum. But he eventually had to die."

Val frowned at the spew of words, searched his mind to remember who this man was. A kid with a teen-turned-vamp as a dad? How long ago would that be? Thirty, thirty-five years ago? What was Val doing then?

"I don't want to die, you see. I want to live forever." Collins' eyes were now glossy, feverish. "I want to be like you."

Oh hells no! Realization hit Val like ice water to the face. His muscles constricted, ready to take down the crazy bastard.

Forget Mag's peace, the one responsible for the attacks was right here. And he wasn't going anywhere.

"I *want* to help you." The senseless man's face was animated. "I want to get all the deadbeats, chain them to a wall, and change them. Like you do."

"The tunnels, under the university—"

"So lucky to have discovered that empty space, wasn't I?" Collins shrugged and flicked a finger back and forth between them. "We can do this together, you see. And I got much better than synth blood. I know you kept my dad alive with it, but I'm a chemist. I found ways to keep them alive without synth. Or kill them if I want. You'll be amazed at what I can do with vamps."

Collins turned his palm out and pushed up his sleeve to reveal more of the scars as he added, "Darn, even with myself."

"What *have* you done?" Val's gut tightened.

Collins let out an odd cackle that sent a chill to Val's spine. "I turned myself. Just like that. No sucking, no burying. Just vampire blood."

"Mine." Horror pushed bile to Val's throat.

"Oh no. Yours is so I can become an immortal, just like you. I wanted to ask you for your blood, but I wanted to make sure it would work first."

"You started with Emme's blood."

"Your fiancée, yes. One of my guys managed to bring her blood back to me." Collins' brow softened as a dreamy look crossed his face. "I remembered her from way back. So beautiful. Like a princess she was to me, then. You and her, oh my. You came into my life and just like a pair of guardian angels, you made it all better. And you never aged. So perfect. So..."

He licked his lips in a nervous tick before adding, "It's when I got diagnosed with cancer that it all came to me."

"What came to you?" Val needed to know the full extent of Collins' madness.

"The plan. If I just turn like my dad, I'll die within the year. I'm too old. But as an immortal, I'll be here forever. I have so much medical research left ahead of me. So many I can help."

"You can't do this." Val crossed his arms at his chest, his feet firmly planted on the ground. This was not the first time something similar had come up.

Now and again, a disciple would question their fate, wonder if they too could be immortals. But the few that had begged Emme to turn them had died within a few months of the change. Older bodies were simply unable to sustain the toll of vampirism, which needed the constant cell regeneration found in young people.

It was why most didn't last into their thirties. Emme was likely still alive because Val himself with his legacy immortality had turned her.

"It will work. I'm sure. I just came to ask for more of your blood." Collins was nodding to himself, his lips in a rictus of trepidation. He let out a nervous laugh. "Oh gosh, I did it. I was finally brave enough to come and ask you for it."

Val exhaled slowly. "I can't let you do that. Look, I'm sorry about your illness. I could help you, find better doctors, private clinics. But you'll lose your soul if you use my blood."

"I won't. I started the process already. With the blood I took from you." Collins' eyes were bright with glee. "And once I have all I need from you, I will find Maisie Thibodeau. Who would have thought, a real honest-to-god New England witch, right here, in town. Her magic legacy in my own veins."

Cold spread through Val's limbs while a surge of protectiveness rose inside him. The calm man he aimed to be had been usurped by the predator coiled for retaliation.

He snatched the scientist by the collar of his tweed jacket and lifted him from the floor. With his face an inch from Collins', he growled, "you will *not* go near Maisie."

The madman's body tensed, and he seized Val's arms again in an inhuman grip. Hells, whatever he had done to himself, the man was strong.

"Right, well, I'm sorry. I fear I may have upset you." He almost sounded normal, jutting his hands up in surrender. "I mean no harm, I swear."

Val set him back down and took a half-step back, Collins' coat collar still in his hands.

"Where do you do these experiments," he asked evenly, struggling to not rip the man's throat out on the spot. Together with Mag and Justin, they would shut the whole place down tonight. He hoped there were no more tortured vamps for him to rescue.

"Funny you say that." Collins lifted the corner of his mouth with a quiver. "In fact, I was wishing you would come with me. It's all set up so I can extract enough blood from you. For my turning ceremony. In just a few hours."

"You know I won't do that. Look around you. Vampires everywhere." Val nodded to Mag who was back in his familiar booth, surveying his domain with a satisfied and lethal expression. "You know of my brother."

"Yeah. I know. Magnovald. He does scare me a little. But once I'm like you, he will have to accept me. I'm sure Justin will love me. A scientist, just as he is."

"This *won't* happen." Val glared at him, ready to compel the scumbag to take him to his lair.

"Whoa there, wait." Collins blocked his hand in front of his eyes. "The famous vampire stare. I don't think you want to do that. See I have something of yours. Something you care about very much."

Val frowned, the hair at his nape stiffened. "Go on."

"I'm not dumb. I wouldn't have come to you without insurance that you and your brothers wouldn't hurt me. If I don't come back, my gang of vampires are just going to kill them."

"Them?" Val did not like the sound of this.

"Sorry, may I?" He lowered his hand from his eyes and motioned to his inside pocket.

Val grumbled with an irked scowl.

The scientist took his phone out, swiped the screen a few times. "Here," he said shoving the device under Val's nose. "There's a good one."

A hard thud hit Val's chest. The image showed Father Grégoire kneeling on concrete, his neck tied up with rope, his mouth taped up, his face fierce with anger. Sasha, leashed and muzzled, lay at the priest's feet.

Val lost sense of his surrounding as wrath swallowed him. A low growl rumbled at the bottom of his gut and his fangs lengthened against his lip.

He breathed out with care and forced himself to study the image further. His old friend and furry companion were surrounded by a pack of teen vamps. They were in some empty warehouse, lit by a lone industrial spotlight.

Barely containing his fury, Val slowly raised his gaze to Collins, his eyes as dead as a vampire's soul.

"I'm sorry, friend. " The scientist pursed his lips while Val raged to snap his scrawny neck. "But I had no choice. I really need that blood of yours."

CHAPTER 17

*W*hy did she let Valerian St-Amand affect her like this?

Maisie peered at her reflection in the wide mirror above the sink in the club's bathroom. Two girls were leaning by the door waiting for their turn, chitchatting loudly in French, their hands moving wildly in the air.

A waitress strode in. Tall and confident, she wore a small waitstaff apron over her micro leather skirt. She checked her eyelashes in the mirror and turned to Maisie. "You okay, *fille*?"

"I'm good, thanks." Maisie nodded and then studied her face closer as the girl left, the heavy wooden door slamming behind her. Her eyes were red, mascara running, her hair a mess.

He had done that. His hands had dug into her locks as they kissed. An ache was lodged at the back of her throat as she tried with difficulty to swallow.

No doubt now. She *did* have a full crush on him.

And he wanted nothing to do with her.

No, she corrected herself. He wanted nothing to do with relationships. Which was dumb. What was it they said, it was better to have loved and lost than never to have loved. Something like that.

Had she fallen in love with Valerian? Possibly. What she knew was that she hadn't wanted that kiss to end. That when he'd pushed her away from him, she'd felt empty. Like a part of her had been torn away.

She had yearned to have him take her into his arm, to have each other rip off their clothes and see where their passion would lead.

And even now, she wanted him by her side. To feel his strong presence, a soothing balm quenching the buzzing in her head brought on from too many people in the bar.

She shook her head grimly, entirely sober now.

She had no idea how Emmeline had managed to convince her to dance. She shuddered, the pounding of the loud music on the other side of the bathroom door now a menace. She didn't want to go back there, with the sweaty bodies, heavy scents, and dizzying lights.

She touched her lips, remembering how his own had sampled them.

She *had* to get out of here. She'd been hiding in the stalls for the last ten minutes. They would be looking for her. And Emmeline might be trying to feed on some innocent human if Maisie was not around.

Come on, girl, snap out of it!

She turned on the tap and let the water run until it was as cold as ice. She splashed some on her face, rubbed her damp hand on her neck, and used paper towels to wipe her face and the traces of mascara under her eyes.

Feeling a little refreshed, she zipped her hoodie back over her torso and slid her palms over her jeans.

She had to put the last half hour out of her mind completely and focus on what was ahead. Get Emmeline, force her out of the club, with magic if needed, and drive them both back to the *Sanctuaire*.

Forget Val for now.

She tightened her fist as she checked herself in the mirror again. Yes, she *was* the future high priestess of the White

Holly coven. Her skin was clear, her green eyes steady, and her chin proud.

But yet she knew better. She looked the part, a powerful witch with self-assurance and fortitude. But her chest still quivered at the bare thought of *him*.

What would she do the next time she saw him? Ignore what had happened between them? Remain calm and all business? Avoid him all together until she and Emmeline were shipped to the mountains?

Oh cripes, no! She no longer wanted to go to Domaine-Lassalle. No matter how she had wanted to meet the *loup-garous* wolf-shifters. She did not want to be away from Val.

She *could* turn immortal. The thought rose fierce and ruthless in her mind.

She actually could.

Not all Beaudry witches became insane. Some were perfectly fine. In fact, those who were mentally sound were also extremely powerful, like Agatha Beaudry. She must be what now, over a hundred and fifty years old? She was strong enough to act as some eternal watcher for High Priestess Thibodeau, just has Maisie's favorite cousin Ava Beaudry was destined to do when Maisie rose to power. The Beaudrys had fought hard against the Black Oak Order's summon. The immortality gave them an unconventional perspective that enhanced each spell on a space-time continuum different than what their mere mortal counterparts could cast.

Yet it was a possibility that was forbidden to her own family. Nana would never let her entertain the thought. She was dead set against it after seeing her elder sister turn so mad from it, she eventually committed suicide.

It was after the tragedy that the Thibodeau family had decreed that they would no longer partake in the immortal tradition.

But Maisie was not in Berwick Hollow anymore. She was surrounded by vampires. Had defeated a wraith by herself just twenty-four hours earlier. Shouldn't the new high priestess be immortal?

Madame Ioshta could do it. Now, tonight, if Maisie wanted.

She fished the elder's business card from the front pocket of her jeans. Looked at the embossed lettering with the tiny dream catcher logo in the corner.

Yes, the seer had hinted that she could perform the ritual.

Maisie would be like the Beaudrys, like the *Sorcière des Glaces*. Charlotte Callan. Val's mother. How would he react to her if she were immortal? Could he not have a relationship with her then? She would still retain her soul. Nothing like Emmeline.

The Elder Beaudry and the others who were now immortal still had their souls. Witches ritual had nothing to do with whatever Val and his disciples had concocted for Emmeline.

There was no chance of her going on a killing rampage. No, she just would be stronger. Have more powers. Live forever.

A small smile curled her lips as the possibility crossed her mind, and a rosy future lay ahead. She really *could* do this.

Val and her. With Sasha. Warmth rose inside her to think she could be a doggy mom to the good-natured pet. She'd have to warm the coven to Val's presence but no doubt Nana would welcome the alliance. Politically it would be good for them, it would tamper the Black Oak Warlocks' influence on their coven to have a St-Amand Immortal in the family.

She pushed the bathroom door open and was assaulted by the club bustling ambience. Her rosy dream crashed around her.

Was she truly thinking of taking the risk of insanity to capture the heart of a man? She shook her head grimly. Even for Val—and he *was* everything she had ever dreamed of, her soul unable to let go of him—she couldn't do that.

If she fell into madness, aside from the fact that she could take her own life or be a burden to her family, the coven leadership would have to go to her cousin Davena. She was only twelve. And more interested in her skateboard than spells.

No, she just couldn't let her people down.

Her back muscles tightened with readiness. She *would* follow her destiny. Go study the wolf-shifters while keeping an eye on Emmeline and then return to Berwick Hollow to take over the coven.

Maisie sighed with sadness. Leaving Montreal for the mountains now would be for the best. She would persuade Emmeline to leave as early as possible tomorrow. Let Val and his brothers take care of the madman threat.

She rose to her tiptoes to catch a sight of the blonde vampire above the club's patrons and finally saw her near the bar. Emmeline was frantically scanning the crowd, her even features unusually bunched up with alarm.

Something seemed dead wrong.

Emmeline's gaze caught Maisie's, and the female vamp bolted straight to her, pushing people out of the way. "Oh *merde*, Maisie. Where were you?" Her voice was filled with angst, her face flushed. "I just saw Val take off with some random guy. And he looked mad as hell."

CHAPTER 18

*V*al glared at Collins as the scientist drove his small gray Prius out of the downtown area, a strained expression pasted on his pale face. The image of Sasha slouched at Father Grégoire's knees haunted him.

The priest could hold his own with his ceremonial magic, but he was getting on in age. Val had tried countless times to convince him to retire now. And Sasha, well, his dog didn't deserve to be a pawn in all this. A victim for the second time.

"Faster," Val ordered Collins, his jaw set.

The professor glared at Val as they skidded a corner on the icy road. "You have no right to stop me, you know."

As soon as he'd seen the photos of his kidnapped companions, Val had been done tiptoeing around the lunatic. He had yanked him by the collar and with one deep look, compelled him to do his bidding.

Collins had no choice but to do as ordered, no matter whether he wanted to or not. Val may have helped Collins when he was a kid, but now he was a grown adult fully responsible for his actions.

"I have every right," Val barked.

Collins flashed him a hurt look but didn't protest.

"How much farther?" Val would only know peace when

he felt Father Grégoire's holy touch at his shoulder and saw Sasha's happy frisky tail.

He felt cramped in the small car, the space too confined for his tall form. The snow had started to fall more heavily, and the wipers of the Prius swooshed back and forth across the windshield.

"I only want to be like you—you don't understand. I want to do good." Collins was breathless with anguish, his fingers drumming on the steering wheel. "And I can do it better than you. I know what it's like to be human."

Val's fists were balls of anger. He let out a slow breath to keep his control, wanting no emotions to cloud his actions in getting his friends back.

Ethan Collins was nothing like Val. Who would harm a dog or an elderly man? Hells, even Emme had never been that cruel.

"Drive," Val spat at him.

Acknowledging Val's taut posture and the steady gaze controlling him, he sneered, "You'll see."

Val didn't give him the satisfaction of a response and the rest of the drive was quiet. The scientist gripped the wheel tight as his car sped along the highway leading out to an industrial park in the suburb.

Five minutes later, Collins forced his tires over the snow in a deserted parking lot beside an empty warehouse a few miles north of the city.

He turned off the ignition. "It's here." He nodded at the boarded-up building in front of them.

"Car keys." Val held his palm out. "Then get out."

Collins passed his keys over to Val and exited his car.

Val followed, right by his side. Annoyed at Collins' slow pace, he grabbed the back of his coat and pushed him forward. "Move."

"Up there," Collins said, more or less compliant, his tone meek.

With Val's hand tight on his tweed jacket, Collins punched

a code on the security panel by the heavy metal door of the warehouse.

The door clicked to let them in and together, they stepped into the dark.

The attack came from nowhere.

A sharp slicing pain hit Val deep in the shoulder.

Collins struggled under his grip, but Val held on to the madman with a grit of his teeth. He shoved them both back into the door as it closed on them.

"*Vahrasth!*" he called to the darkness, blasting out whatever creature had attacked him. "What the hell was that?"

As his sight adjusted, Collins pivoted against him. "My sentinels," the professor snarled.

There were more than one. Damn. His heart pounding, shoulder in agony from the gash, he held Collins against his body to use him as a shield. If anyone were after Val, they would get him, too.

"Call them back," Val ordered.

"I can't. They defend the lair, not me." His tone has shifted and his body trembled against Val.

And that was when Val saw them. The eyes. Multiple pairs of red eyes, disembodied moldy cloths floating and surrounding them in the dark. *Wraiths.* The one that attacked him was crouching low, licking its lips. Talons drawn out, ready to slice more into his flesh.

"How many?"

"Five."

Diable. How on earth would he blast out five wraiths while controlling Collins? He suddenly wished Maisie were here.

"Told you, you couldn't stop me," Collins jeered.

"You conjured them," Val growled. "Call them back."

"I can't. They can be... unpredictable."

"Fucking dumbass." His lips pulled back into a sneer. "Dealing in things you know nothing about."

"Not true," Collins objected. "I am as strong as you and soon I'll live as long as you."

Damn, had Collins no idea that the wraiths could choose to eat their summoner if they became restless?

The beasts' growls grew louder and made Val antsy to get to Sasha and his priest. "If these things go anywhere near my friends, I will end you." His rage at the reckless human now held no bounds and he let it fuel the magic in his veins.

"They're fine. Look, I didn't hurt them. I just wanted you here." He sounded eager, like a kid who wanted to show his dad some misshaped art he just made.

Seigneur! Val had to end this madness now. "Sasha, Grégoire," he called out.

A faint whimper replied in the dark.

"Sash!" Thanks the heavens, his dog was still alive. But he had no idea how the priest fared.

He eyed the wraiths, gagging on their putrid stench. *Oh hells, let's just get this over with.*

He grabbed Collins with both hands and shoved him hard into the mass of monsters. The crazy man tumbled forward. He knocked over one of the beasts with his fall.

Val gathered as much energy as he could for a spell, calling forth the essence of his mother. "*Koir idash sinnsearachd...*" The tattoo at the inside of his wrist burned white hot as he felt her presence within him.

"*Annehyentx!*" He thrust both arms forward and blasted the evil horde with pure frigid power in a halo of blue energy.

A shriek of pain echoed against the concrete walls of the empty warehouse. Two of the wraiths were hit.

Val reached inside his coat and grabbed the two ancient daggers always sheathed against his body. One for each hand.

Poised, he waited for the remaining wraiths to come at him when he noticed Collins crawl on his hands and feet to the safety of the stairwell.

Fucking coward. Immortality would not be kind to a

164

weakling like Collins. When the hunger struck, he'd have no control over himself.

Val had to stop him.

And this time, he was no longer anemic from being minutes from a much needed feeding. He had his full strength.

Fangs fully out, he dived into the pack of snarling beasts.

It took mere seconds.

He lashed and sliced at the wretched horde, jabbed a chest, bit a neck, stabbed a heart. Nasty creatures that breathed icily on him, skeletal limbs attempting to trap him.

As one dug its vicious talon into his thigh, Val leaped at the ceiling. He held on to the dangling industrial pendant light, which hung midway down into the massive atrium. He waited for the three of them to gather below him and then dropped down upon them.

He slit a throat clean, sheathed his daggers to snap one wraith's neck before tearing into the last one's flesh. He gouged deep, his fangs shredding tendons and arteries. Spitting the monster's foul blood to the cement floor.

Soon he was surrounded by the corpses of his vanquished enemies.

"Sasha," he called out.

He heard his dog's whine again and searched his surroundings. A light switch laid by the stairwell. Not caring one bit if Collins' minions find him, he flicked it on.

A diffuse light from high above turned on, showing the tall atrium enclosed by three levels bordered with metal railings.

There was no sight of Collins. The damn son of a bitch. Val's anger at the psychopath hadn't lessened.

"That's it, boy," Val called again. "Tell me where you are."

His dog's whimper reverberated across the open space warehouse.

"Again, Sash. I'm coming for you, bud!"

Sasha whined once more and this time his location was clear, two stories high, to Val's left.

Val jumped to the second floor over the banister, caught his footing, and there they were.

Father Grégoire was very much alive, duct tape across his mouth, kneeling by a pile of metal boxes in the corner of the wide dimly lit room, Sasha with his legs tied two by two at the priest's feet.

Val dashed to their side. "Sorry, old man," he muttered to his friend, as he ripped the tape off his face.

"He's mad, Val." Father Grégoire's was adamant. "Forget us, you *have* to get him."

"Not until I have both of you out."

Val freed the priest with one of his blades and then bent down to Sasha. He removed the leather muzzle and cut the rope holding the dog's paws.

Sasha lapped his hand with vigor and shook out his whole body.

"That's it, buddy." Val patted his flanks to check that he was unarmed while the dog jumped up and around before pushing his nose at his palm.

"You're okay, boy. I'm taking you home." Val stroked his dog's head as Sasha finally settled down.

"We have to stop him, Val. He has the ceremonial spell."

"What spell?"

"The incantation he needs. To make himself into one of you." Father Grégoire rubbed his wrists, his expression filled with anguish. "An immortal."

"He won't. He doesn't have enough of my blood."

"You and your brothers must stop him," Father Grégoire insisted.

"I know." Val stood to his full height, his palm on Sasha's head.

"No, you don't. He has all the spell components. And he knows summoning spells that even *I* can't practice."

"I need you both out of here first. His car is below. I have the keys." Val patted the pocket of his pants.

"The monsters guarding the door?"

"All dead."

Father Grégoire finally smiled. "I should have known you could take them."

Val wrapped an arm around the priest's frail shoulders as the old man fished his cell phone out from under his cassock. "There was no way I'd leave you both here for a moment longer."

"This is your problem right there, Valerian St-Amand." The nasty voice resounded loud and clear from the shadow.

"*Oh doux Jesus.*" Father Grégoire flinched and turned on the flashlight of his electronic device to illuminate the back wall.

Collins stood before them, his jacket askew, his eyes even paler in the unnatural light. The madman was surrounded by teen vamps.

But worse, he had summoned a pack of horrible creatures —thick, stone gray, and almost as tall as the high ceiling.

Seigneur. Val's stomach dropped with dread. Collins had gone too far.

"Golems," Father Grégoire gasped.

Sasha barked madly at them, his fear shaking his flanks.

Val seized the back of the dog's collar and stood perfectly still as he considered the monsters, not daring to breathe.

Golems. Damn. The towers of sentient mud were invincible. How the hell was he supposed to fight that? How would he get Father Grégoire and Sasha to safety?

"You keep thinking you and your brothers are the strongest supernaturals in this city," Collins sneered. "I think I've got you beaten."

Overcome with hatred, Val let his fury wash over him. This bastard had tortured and killed teen vampires, kidnapped and bound his friend and pet, had assailed him and Emme, and threatened to use Maisie. Val wanted nothing more than to rip Collins' head from his neck.

He eased the keys over to Father Grégoire. "Run," he said under his breath.

"But Val—"

"Take Sasha. Run. To the sanctuary. Get Mag and Justin."

Val's heartbeat hammered senselessly as he assessed his opponents. Reaching to the ceiling, the monsters had massive chests and no neck. Arms like stone pillars and hands so big they could easily crush a human neck between their thumb and forefinger.

For the very first time in his entire life, he doubted his abilities.

Nine golems faced him. His magic was dried up from blasting the wraiths. He had fangs, claws, and strength. Also speed. Those were his only ammunitions to prevent them from going after Father Grégoire and Sasha.

"Go!"

Sasha stared back at him, his expression hurt as he looked at the golems and back at his master. But Father Grégoire pulled hard on his collar and they finally both disappeared behind the stairwell.

Val had barely a second to turn to the golems before his entire world turned to darkness. An acrid scent of decaying mud clogged his nostrils and he collapsed under the weight of them.

And with his lungs drained of precious air, his brain screamed the true horror of being buried alive.

CHAPTER 19

"*I* got him." Magnovald stormed into his office, cell phone face up in his palm. "It's not good."

He raked his long hair back, his jaw tense. The quick look he shot Maisie was raw with despair and she trembled with apprehension at Val's fate.

He'd been gone without a word to anyone for more than an hour. Emmeline and Mag had texted and called everyone they knew without success while Maisie waited, frantic, on Mag's sofa in the back room of the *Serpent Maudit*, wondering if she should perform a scrying spell.

Without further explanation, Mag dialed and put his cell to his ear. He eyed Emmeline and Maisie. "You two go back to the *Sanctuaire* to meet up with Father Grégoire. I'm calling Justin and Renaud."

"Got it." Emmeline spoke without protest at being ordered around, sensing the urgency of the moment.

"What happened?" Maisie asked.

Mag shot her a brief look. "Val's been taken. Hurry."

Taken? Maisie bolted from the couch and her knees turned weak with fear.

"*Merde!*" Emmeline's voice rose with alarm. Her lip trembled. "By whom?"

"That crazy professor. He had Grégoire and Sasha. They're fine now." Mag turned away to bark at his brother Renaud on the phone.

"How?" Maisie insisted.

Mag waved at her with impatience. "Go. Grégoire will meet you there."

Emmeline tugged urgently upon Maisie "Let's go."

"But what happened?" Heart hammering, her mind raced through all the spells she knew. "How can I help?"

"Maisie," the female vamp insisted. ""Let's get out of here. Mag's got this."

Maisie turned to the club owner and his eyes were so dark, his presence so tainted with deep-seated wrath, that she didn't dare to ask again.

She shuddered as she rushed behind Emmeline through the busy bar, pushing patrons out of their way.

Val. Taken. No. Images of the chained tortured vamps at the university filled her with horror. She caught up with Emmeline as the blonde grabbed their coats from the lobby. "We *have* to help him. Go get him now."

The female vamp zoomed pass Raphael without a single word and pushed the door to the freezing outdoors. "Maybe," she told Maisie. "Let's get in the car first."

The madman had wanted Val's blood. He'd had Sasha and Father Grégoire. Maisie tried to piece the tiny bits of information she had. Her hand shook on the cold door handle of the Porsche. She couldn't find her mittens.

The snow fell in thick heavy flakes, but she was oblivious to the weather. All she could think about was the poor mutilated vampires they had rescued. She feared Val would be next.

What would happen when the crazy man no longer needed Val?

And how could Val be taken so easily? Had he just followed the stranger on his own? Why?

Drugged. It had to be drugs. Or wraiths.

Emmeline slid into her vehicle and Maisie took the passenger seat beside her. "I can fight wraiths," Maisie announced.

The blonde frowned. "What do you mean?"

"I fought a wraith in the tunnels of the university. It was guarding the teen vamp prisoners. We can go get him."

Emmeline scrolled through her phone. How could she be so damned calm?

"Emme!" Maisie shouted. It was the first time she'd used her nickname.

The female vampire looked up from her screen. "Oh lord, you do love him, don't you?"

"Yes," Maisie blurted out. And there it was, in the open. "And he's in danger."

"You two are meant for each other," the undead said, her expression unreadable.

Maisie had no idea whether Emme was hurt or if she cared. But it didn't matter. What mattered was that Maisie was connected to Val and that she would do anything to save him.

"Here it is. Father Grégoire texted us all. Val's held in an industrial park. I have the location here. The lunatic, Collins he's called, lured Val by kidnapping Father Grégoire and Sasha. They are both fine, "she added at Maisie's yelp. "They were waiting for Val but were chased away by some guards."

A ping echoed from Emme's phone. She read the new text and looked back at Maisie. "Mag and Justin are going to get him. They're waiting for Renaud who's driving down from Domaine-Lassalle. At least another thirty minutes. Boy, it has to be bad for Mag to wait for Ren."

"Oh gods." Maisie was hit with dizziness at the news.

"Father Grégoire says he doesn't expect he'll kill Val yet. He wants his blood."

"Oh flaming hells! No!" Maisie had a vision of Val drained slowly, like an animal waiting to be butchered.

She seized the female vamp's arm. "Emme, we *can't* wait. We have to rescue him."

"What, like you and me?"

"Yes. We can take him."

"No. If Mag says we need to wait, I say we wait. We'll have the three immortals and Father Grégoire's ritual magic. He's got loads of old books full of spells at the *Sanctuaire*."

"I have spells—remember what I am." Maisie's was stern, her lips pressed together.

Emme's expression softened. "I know you're scared for him. I am too. But Val wouldn't want you to do this. He wouldn't want you hurt."

"He wouldn't want to be in some crazy guy's lair being bled to death," Maisie countered.

"He can hold on for a little longer. He's been through worse. Look, Maisie, he cares for you, a lot. I know him well and see the signs. I was wrong. You're different. He's really into you. I won't have you come to harm."

"I can fight all of this." Maisie set her shoulders back with resolve, her heart fast and steady. "Save him."

They shouldn't wait for the St-Amand brothers. She had never been so sure of anything in her life. She had been brought here to watch Emmeline and had intended to study Val and his kind, but yes, she had fallen for him instead. Those extra thirty minutes could mean his life.

And she *would* rescue him.

"The son of a bitch has raised golems," Emme spat, turning the key in the ignition. The car started and the heater blasted noisily in the cold cabin.

"Golems?" she gasped.

"Yeah. Father Grégoire said Val managed to beat the wraiths guarding the lair but was overtaken by golems keepers."

"Shit." Maisie slammed her head back on the headrest, swamped by helplessness. She held her breath for a few seconds. *Golems*. The huge monsters might be made of mud

172

and not very bright, but they were impossible to kill. A simple squeeze from a golem's grip would kill you. They were that strong. At least, that was what Cousin Jo had said.

"We wait for the St-Amand brothers."

"I could take golems." Maisie's hands balled into fists and tingled with pent-up magic and confidence. She knew just how.

"Maize, no..."

"Have you ever seen golems?" she glowered at Emme.

"No, but—"

"Have Mag or Justin or any other immortal ever fought golems?"

"Not that I know of."

She dug into the front pocket of her jeans. "Listen, Emme. Right now, there is only one person in Montreal who can fight golems." There was no time to ponder—her decision was made.

"And who is that?" Emme's fear was reflected in the edgy tone of her voice.

But Maisie had no fear.

Her heart steady, her will filled with purpose, she pulled out the little card from her pocket and stared at the vampire. "An immortal witch."

CHAPTER 20

*A*fter treading carefully on the icy steps to the basement shop and with Emme right behind her, Maisie flung open the purple door of *Sortilège*, the overhead bell responding with a clang.

Madame Ioshta looked up from her newspaper. The elder was waiting for them after Maisie had woken her from sleep when she'd called urgently with her single-minded request.

"I knew you'd call."

An understanding passed between them. Maisie wasn't sure if the crone could read her thoughts, but it was clear to both of them what their meeting was about.

"*Merde!* If this turns sour, I had no part in it."

"Emmeline Dubois," the old witch acknowledged the blonde vampire with a raise of an eyebrow. "There is always a risk. Looks like she is ready to take it."

"If she dies, you know Val will come after you." With a harsh squint, Emme poked her pointed finger at the seer.

"She won't die." Madame Ioshta slowly tilted her head back.

"She might go insane," Emme retorted. "I know all about that."

Maisie frowned at Emme's palpable concern. Who knew the unpredictable vampire actually cared about her fate.

She cocked her chin at them. "Can you both stop talking like I'm not here and let's get on with it."

"Of course," the elder said.

"Valerian has been taken and I have to free him."

"Taken?" Madame Ioshta winced. "*Quel dommage.*"

"A crazy doc who likes to experiment on vamps. Know anything about that?" Emme's voice was frosty.

"I heard things."

"The ritual." Maisie waved her hand in the air with impatience. "Quickly."

"*Bien sur,*" the seer said. "A pity the yard is frozen. But we'll make do."

"You have everything?"

"I do." Her calm composure was driving Maisie nuts.

They had to do this now. Maisie had reviewed the Beaudry section of the coven's Book of Shadows on the way over. She knew it could be done. The risks were still there but smaller. With her tribal tradition, Madame Ioshta had a conduit to the earth that the White Holly witches could not access.

"You have a familiar?"

"Indeed." The elder called out to the back of the room. "Onatah." A large crow flew out of the dark corner to perch upon her shoulder.

"She won't like the cold." She picked up her heavy skirts, slid off her stool, and ambled over a crooked stack of books, where she plucked a thick tome bounded in faded brown leather.

"Please hurry." Maisie was impatient. Every moment passed could be a moment of suffering. "Val is being drained of his blood. He's hurting."

"What you should really worry about is the consequence of having his blood used in the worse possible way." The elder blew on the top of the book and a cloud of dust floated down to their feet.

"I know." Maisie clenched her jaw. But for now, all that was important to her was Val.

"The asshole wants to be an Immortal," Emmeline spat. "Freakin' lunatic."

Madame Ioshta brushed the grimoire and flipped through its ancient pages. "Everyone wants to be something they are not."

"Not me."

"Yes, we know, Miss Dubois." The elder shot the vamp an enigmatic smile. "I will need you tonight."

"Me, why?"

"Something immortal. It will speed up the ritual since time is ticking."

"Emme." Maisie fidgeted with her pentacle as she peered at the blonde. "Please, for Val."

"Yeah, sure." Emmeline shrugged. "You need blood or something?"

"No. I will just hold on to you to tap into your own immortality." The elder rummaged through one of the wooden drawers encased into the wall and brought out what looked like a crystal ball the size of a summer squash. She looked back at Emme and Maisie with a satisfied smile. "Let's begin, shall we?"

Moments later, they were standing in the private yard behind the shop at the edge of a frozen koi pond surrounded by white statues of female deities. The small garden was dotted with tall creaky birch trees and encircled by a dense dormant cedar hedge. The snow had stopped falling and the city's lights were dim in the background, the sliver of moon now bright above them.

"We need this whole area thawed out," Madame Ioshta mumbled to herself.

Maisie reached at the back of her neck for her pentacle's clasp. "Want me to—"

"No, keep your strength."

With the grimoire tucked under one arm, the elder swept her free hand into a wide arc in front of her. "Let the spring return, but for a time. *Printemps du jour, printemps de la nuit. Pour cette cérémonie, viens à moi aujourd'hui.*"

The packed snow at their feet dissolved to be replaced by fresh grown grass. The tree buds blossomed into tender green leaves. The ice melted into a clear water pond where large goldfish could be seen frisking around.

Emme's mouth popped open as she witnessed the change in weather.

"This here is the foundation of my power." Madame Ioshta nodded to the sizable pentagram etched with small stones into the ground. All lines pointed to a large flat boulder at the center of the pond.

With a curt nod, she handed the crystal ball to Maisie, who knew what she had to do.

Her fingers on the sphere were tense with trepidation. Her mouth was dry, all her senses heightened as she found herself at the cusp of taking on this new destiny.

"*Scìreadh lan adhyr!*" Maisie held onto the magical globe as she slowly ascended a few feet in the air. She crossed over the clear water, which rippled in the mystical warm breeze blowing over the garden, and she landed on the bolder at the center.

"You won't hurt her?" Emme's voice was unusually fearful but Maisie was beyond worry.

This was her path. Her choice.

"No," Madame Ioshta assured her. "She will only be what she was always meant to be."

"*Matronae*, shield me from harm, *shyatch mieh!*" Maisie prayed to herself, blocking out the vampire and the seer. She was ready to take on the mantle of immortality.

"Aradia, Aradia, I call thee. Morag of the many faces, witch of old, witch among us, show her the way." Madame Ioshta stood at the edge of the water, her grimoire in the crook of her arm, her familiar at her shoulder, and held on to Emmeline, whose apprehension was twisting her pretty features.

A mist rose languidly from the pond. The ball in Maisie's hands grew warmer, and swirls of greens curled and eddied inside the glass. Without warning, the colors burst out of the crystal itself to enclose her, merging with the rising fog that was now so thick, it obscured the starless sky above the crone's garden.

"My dear child." A clear and compassionate voice spoke to Maisie.

"Aradia?"

"No." The disembodied female voice broke into a crystalline laughter and her image emerged from the white and green mist. The woman wore a simple long black dress and a quartz pentacle dangled from her neck. Her dark hair fell in loose waves over her shoulders. Her brown irises considered Maisie with detached interest.

"I am Charlotte Callan. The one you call *La Sorcière des Glaces*. My essence is bound to this land."

"How are you here?" Maisie was awestruck.

"I was summoned. By Laketa Ioshta. Back to my true home."

"You're Valerian's mother," Maisie said, noticing the resemblance in the dark eyes and noble curve of the forehead.

"And Magnovald, Cassiodore, Renaud, Justinien, Griffon, my sons, yes."

"You left them." The words were the first thought that had come to mind.

Cripes. Her heart skipped a beat and she cursed her lack of filter, hoping she didn't offend the legendary witch.

"I did. I joined my kind in Louisiana. It was time." She tilted her head to the side. "So you seek an immortal life."

"I seek more power." She paused, organizing the request in her mind. "To rescue Valerian."

"I see."

179

"Val is in danger. I must save him."

"And you don't think his brothers can do this without you?"

"I don't know." She searched her brain to see if there was any other reason for her to become immortal and betray her family's wishes. "But I have to do this. I love him."

"Yes." Val's mother smiled knowingly. "A witch of the White Holly. You may wonder why you two are connected."

"I healed him."

"It's more than this."

"It is?" Maisie's skin tingled. What did the witch mean by more?

"Morag," Charlotte called out, and the mist dissolved. "My sister."

Maisie gasped as an imposing svelte woman of unknown age materialized before them. Her hair shone fiery red, her fingers covered in many pewter rings. Swirls of greens and gold mist hovered at her feet.

"Maisie Thibodeau," the new apparition said with a tilt of her head.

Maisie stared at both women, one after the other. She had heard of Charlotte Callan, the name of the Ice Witch filling them with awe as children, but the new priestess was something else. A being as old as earth itself which made Maisie both want to sink to her feet in reverence or hug the lady forever.

"Are you a goddess?" she asked the apparition.

"No." Her lips curled into an unfathomable smile. "Why aren't you immortal as your Beaudry sisters?"

"Who are you?" Maisie's knees trembled with uneasiness.

"I am Lady Morag Callan, High Priestess of the Callanish Coven." She swept a hand back to a tall, crooked stone that had appeared behind her. "Your ancestor. The first."

"Witch?"

"Aye. Most from our coven perished in times so ancient I sometimes struggle to remember," the red-headed lady continued, "but the children I had with my consort Iain have scattered around the world and made more and more descendants. You. A soul reborn..."

"The First Witch." Maisie gaped at her, shook her head and pointed at the Ice Witch. "You two are related." A shard of ice found its way to her heart at the revelation. "Valerian and I—"

"Are not blood relations. Charlotte is my magical coven sister reincarnated. Died with the others on the coast of the Celtic Isles to be returned in Gaul during the Iron Age."

"Your magic connects you, *ma chère*," Charlotte Callan said. "Valerian and you. From the very first coven."

"I must rescue him." Relieved that they were not related, Maisie's single-minded thought had returned. While she found her origins interesting, there was only one thing that mattered at that moment. *Valerian.*

Both ladies nodded and the First Witch spoke, "And for that you want more power."

"I do."

"Immortality."

"It is not the long life I seek. Just the means to help him."

"Very well."

"You know the risk?" Val's mother's voice was tinged with compassion.

"I may go insane."

"Magic always has a price." Morag's voice broke a little. "I trust your mind will be strong enough to withstand it."

"It will." Her voice was firm, despite the small flutter in her stomach. There was no turning back now.

"Very well, then." The ageless priestess took the crystal ball from Maisie and laid it down at their feet. She took a solid stance on the bolder, her arm wide at her side. "Witches, close the circle."

The three of them held each other's hands, Charlotte, Valerian's fierce mother, Morag, the mysterious first witch of the Celtic Isles, and Maisie, who now tremored at what was to come, but with her task kept steady in her heart.

She *would* get Val back.

"Maisie Thibodeau, witch of the coven of the White Holly," Morag Callan intoned. "Do you accept the burden of immortality? Are you prepared to pay the price required for the gift bestowed upon you? Are you willing to give your entire unending life in service of the craft, to give your soul beyond the hells and the heavens?"

"I am."

The small sphere at their feet turned at once silver and gold. It shone brighter and brighter as its shape grew bigger. Soon Maisie was facing a tall figure adorned with antlers who held a large translucent bluish globe that looked very much like Earth. *Cernunnos, The White Stag,* she recognized. The sphere in his arms shifted and transformed. A woman with a circlet of silver resting on her brow now stood within the male deity's arms. All was balance, pure and whole.

"So mote it be," Morag spoke.

A huge tide of otherworldly energy swelled through Maisie's entire body, lifting her chest and swallowing her mind. Her stomach somersaulted and her throat closed, as if all the air inside her, from the airway of her lungs to every minute part in her alveoli, were transformed into pure magical power.

The rush started at her fingertips and mounted along her arms to her shoulders. It filled her entire torso, radiated from her core to flush down her legs into the flat stone at her feet.

Her whole body vibrated in tune with an unnatural frequency but very much in unison with the two powerful witches at her side. Their gentle grips soon loosened, their images dissolved, their bodies dematerializing in swivels of white, green and gold.

The mist parted and she was left, standing and alone, in the middle of the giant pentagram of Madame Ioshta's garden. The sliver of moon shone in the exact same position as it had when she'd taken hold of the magic ball, which now lay black and empty at her feet.

She could feel her fingertips crackling with power, millions of incantations crisscrossing her brain, and she had to call on the steadier part of her mind to hold on and parse through them all.

She looked over the pond to see the seer with an expression of pure wonder on her features and Emme slumped unconscious from the energy drain in the thawing snow at her feet.

Maisie's heart went out to the blonde vampire, concerned for her newfound friend's health.

"Wake," she whispered gently in the wind.

And at the simple word, Emme stirred. She crouched on all fours. Her eyes bright, she stared at Maisie and her mouth fell open in disbelief. "Well, I'll be damned. I guess it worked after all."

CHAPTER 21

"*S*o sorry, my friend. I wish I could keep you more comfortable. But I'm afraid I sank most of my money into buying this place. Real estate is not cheap these days."

Bastard. Val strained to lift his head to get a glimpse at Collins and let it fall right back down.

He hung upside down on some sort of x-shaped cross, the blood rushing to his head, his limbs stretched to their max, every inch of his body in pain, his skin pierced with a multitude of thick needles connected to a complex network of tubes. The swishing sound of a motor echoed behind him.

It was blood, *his* blood, filling those tubes. How long before he became completely drained?

His woozy head was almost a reprieve from the breathless agony he had experienced just seconds before he'd passed out. Buried alive by the golems. He could make out the monsters now, like a giant wall of mud, standing at attention to their master.

"I wish I could sedate you." Collins was droning on again. "This has got to hurt. But I don't want ketamine inside me. That just wouldn't do."

"End this before it's too late," Val croaked, his throat parched. "We'll stop you."

"I'm just getting enough to get me started now." Collins moved before Val's vision and then disappeared behind him. "I'm afraid we have to move this whole operation out of town. Another money suck, but the private plane rental was a good call."

The pumping sound suddenly stopped, and Val felt a jolt at his arms.

"Disconnect him," Collins barked, and two heavy steps clunked toward Val.

Golems. Again.

Tubes were ripped from his flesh and Val howled in pain. His mind blurred at the torture. He gritted his teeth, catching his breath as the intense throbbing finally receded.

"Careful," Collins said to his mud giants, "he is my mentor after all." He crouched down to Val and twisted his head sideways to catch his gaze. "So sorry. I wish there had been a better way."

"You're insane," Val managed to spat at him. "Can you not see it?"

Val's mind roared. If he could just compel the man, he'd be free. But his blood loss was making his body weak. It was all he could do to focus on staying conscious.

"Insane," he huffed, laughing at himself. "An IQ of a hundred and forty-five believe it or not. Surprising for the child of a drug addict and a checkout girl. Here you are, completely under my thumb, and you still think you're better than me."

"You know nothing of immortality," Val sneered. He twisted against the cross under the bond at his extremities. Iron manacles, he realized, Collins had to know it neutralized magic.

"Get him off there!" The madman sprung up in irritation.

A series of snaps sounded in the concrete room and Val

fell with a thump on the hard floor, his left shoulder taking most of the impact.

He rubbed his wrists to get whatever was left of his blood flowing as he tried to stand. His extremities were still shackled in iron cuffs, a heavy chain between them.

Horror seized him to learn the cause of the searing pain at his forearm. Pure white rage consumed him.

Fucking hells! His mom's witch mark had been burnt off, the tattoo distorted and raw, the runes completely unreadable. He would no longer be able to call the Ice Witch's magic directly.

Adrenaline scurried through his vein. He swore he would kill Collins for this.

He tightened his fist, forced himself up and assessed his situation. His feet were bare and so was his chest, now covered in gashes and blood. His pants were torn. His limbs scattered with needle marks.

A makeshift laboratory had been set up in the warehouse. A huge lab table stretched in a corner beside the sinister blood-extracting machine sprouting with rubber tubes. Val noticed his coat wrapped over a metal crate on the floor.

GOLEMS WATCHED him with eerie round eyes of heaped mud. Over a dozen of them, tall and stone-like. No noses, mouths like a slit, but no real facial features. He shuddered with revulsion as he recalled his mother saying the very earth had to be summoned to make them.

But the ground was frozen in Montreal. Somehow the insane professor had managed to thaw it out for his evil purpose.

Behind the golems lay a gaggle of teenager vamps, some sporting countless open scars, others freshly turned with opalescent unmarred skin. They all ogled at Val and he saw the glimpse of recognition in their eyes despite their beaten composure.

With as much energy he could summon, he called to the vampiristic beast inside him.

"Vampires." He ordered their obedience with a calm commanding tone.

They came to attention, recognizing something ancient, a primeval call from their master, drawn from their very own bloodline.

"Stop," Collins barked. "They're mine."

The vamps turned to him and then back at Val, hesitant at what to do.

"Quick, hold him," the scientist shouted at the golems.

With hefty and surprisingly fast steps, two stone giants detached themselves from the mass and seized his arms to lift him up above ground between them.

The room swirled from Val's vision as he was hit by heavy nausea. His limbs were trapped, his lungs constricted.

"I contained your magic and I'm not about to let you compel anyone tonight." Careful to look at Val sideways, Collins took a cloth from his jacket and placed it across Val's eyes.

Amid his torment, Val wondered why Collins hadn't done it before. It was as if the madman wanted to show off.

"Quite a good trick, Valerian, I have to admit. You got me here with it." With one quick tug, the professor tied the blind-fold behind Val's head. "I can't wait for you to teach me how to do this."

"You won't last the night." Val bared his fangs at him, trying to get his bearing while blind.

"Oh, I know what you are thinking, friend." Collins' tone quickly shifted to a sneer as the golems eased their grip. "Your brothers will storm in, maybe with that witch of yours, and rescue you. Old Father Grégoire and your dog will bring them right here."

Val stayed absolutely still and listened to the insane voice, trying to pinpoint his location to attempt an escape.

"Sorry about your dog, by the way. Sasha is it?" Collins

had moved away from him, back to the lab table. "I like dogs. Maybe we'll get us one when we get to Yukon. They do have dogs up there, don't they? Sled dogs, no doubt."

Ignoring the man's rambling, Val focused on his situation. He was no longer upside down, that was good. His balance was coming back to him, but his arms and legs were still shackled and with the mark gone, he couldn't call on his mom's magic. Gone also were his compelling powers. And the golems were innately strong, their hold still shortening his breath.

"What is it that you truly want, Collins?" Talking to the madman might be the only thing left to do for the moment.

"I told you. I want to be like you." His tone turned earnest. "You saw the poor teens affected by the curse—you started this, didn't you? Your Emmeline bit one, then one after the other, they festered. But you, you and your bros, you're untouched. Invincible."

"No one is invincible."

"I will be. Soon. I will escape the cancer and get so much more. See, what you lack is vision. Even Professor St-Amand —oh I know all about your brother Justin's choices—he decided to study astronomy. Why?" He caught his breath. "I was more interested in DNA. And magic. I can do anything one of your Nostredame disciples can do. But I can now also alter my DNA to match yours. And soon, once I have your entire genetic makeup, I'll come back for the witches. I need to understand the biological source of their power."

"Leave the witches alone," Val growled. His body twitched with rage as he struggled against the immobile colossal grip.

"What? Worried for your mother? For that little Maisie girl? Yes, she's strong. Not many people can dispel a wraith with one word. I saw her crying her eyes out for you at the *Serpent Maudit*. Cameras. Everywhere. So easy now."

Val was livid, the blood pounding in his ear. How dare Collins violate Maisie's privacy like this? And Mag. His brother would be outraged to have his club violated.

"You know, I even re-watched that tape from my lab down under the Chemistry building. I loved to see you transform into a bat." He gushed. "Oh darn, I will be able to do that, too. Maybe I could compel your witch to be my companion? Now that's an idea!"

"Stay the fuck away from Maisie," Val roared. "You got me. That should be enough."

Despite the lack of oxygen in his lungs, every muscle in his body was coiled for action. He was done listening to the ramblings of a lunatic. As soon as they moved him somewhere, he would run.

With his echolocation abilities still fully intact, Val listened to the shuffle around him. For now, it was only Collins moving around in the makeshift lab. His voice scattered back and forth, and Val knew he was just a few meters away.

"The car ready?" Collins asked.

"Sure, boss," a teen vamp replied.

A car. They were planning an exit. Val wobbled furtively under the golems grip, testing their strength.

"I will miss this lab. Kayden, pack it all up. Bring it over to that airfield from yesterday."

"Got it, professor," another kid vampire said. "What about all of us? How do we get to Yukon?"

"Oh I don't know. Drive." There was an edge in his voice. "I can't think of everything. Don't you kids have a brain?"

"Yeah, sure. Don't worry, boss. We'll get there."

Collins was now inches from Val. He sounded edgy, distracted.

The golem holding Val shifted his weight and suddenly slightly loosened his grip.

Maybe this was his chance. Val took a slow inhale, ready to bolt and knock over Collins, roll over and make a quick exit.

"Give me that," Collins shouted at one of his underlings.

The golem shifted Val's body to his other arm.

And there it was, in a mere second, Val's moment.

He wrestled himself from the golem and lunged forward with all his might. His hand swept blindly, caught something. *Collins' jacket.*

"Whoa there," the madman called as a striking pain seized Val's throat.

Fuck! A needle had pierced his skin, followed by a burning tide of agony.

"Hold him tighter, you stone morons," Collins snarled. "Sorry, Val. But I can't have you travel fully conscious."

With his heart suddenly numb, Val's head slumped forward as the poison travelled through his veins.

"Let's roll," Collins declared.

The golems dragged Val's barely responsive body across through the rough concrete floor, his bare feet dragging along the hard steps.

"Put his jacket on him, damn idiots," Collins called from behind. "I want him alive and well when we get there."

Warm cloth covered his back, and the familiar scent of his own coat gave him hope. But the stone arms were still like vice grips under his shoulders and at his sides. The golems hands were huge and unyielding, again making him feel as if he were being buried alive in solid mud.

So that was it, he was being transported out of the province. He searched his emotions and found he had none. They were moving away. Collins wouldn't feed on Val's people in an immortal rampage. Not in his city. He wouldn't go near Maisie.

Maisie. A sharp ache knotted in his heart. Val had never apologized to her.

Regret swept him whole.

But she would be left unarmed. Likely go back to the White Holly coven. She'd be their high priestess. As she should.

Back to Berwick Hollow.

Mag wouldn't let her stay in Montreal, anyway. He liked

her but wouldn't want the influence of the Order of the Black Oak here.

Their leader, Diesel Stanford, would not be pleased, dead set against immortals stockpiling magical artifacts.

Would this mean a war between the warlocks and the St-Amand brothers? And the witches, which side would they pick? How about Madame Ioshta's clan? Would they join in the fight?

Was Val the one who managed to keep the delicate balance between them all? He had fought side by side with the Black Oak necromancer in Seattle.

Surely Malcolm Dunsmuir would appease his leader to keep the peace. Hells, his brother-in-law Evan worked at the *Serpent Maudit*. But Malcolm was now in the Daemon Realm, running his kingdom.

Val's heart sank at the idea of leaving Maisie and his brothers to deal with all this.

He trusted Maisie would see all sides and make the right political decisions.

But no! He shook himself out of his grim thoughts. She would *not* be burdened with this. Val had to attempt another exit.

Slumped between the golems, he let them continue to drag him down the flight of stairs. As long as they thought him unconscious, they wouldn't drug him again.

Each staircase step was taking forever, every one of them banging the top of his bare feet with a whack that radiated straight to his shin.

Collins was droning orders behind him, and his vampires replied, with a lot of meek, compliant "yes boss" responses.

"Careful," he suddenly yelled in Val's direction. "Lift him higher."

The stone grips raised him from the ground until he was finally thrown over the shoulder of one stone creature, jabs of uneven cement piercing his bare flesh tender from the many wounds covering his chest. But the move was good. He could feel the blood returning to his arms now.

They had talked about a car. They would go outside. Val might have a chance to break free.

Again he assessed his situation. Magic gone. His wrist and feet had maybe three feet of chain. Enough to run with, *if* he could muster the strength despite the drug.

He remained lifeless over the golem's shoulder, slowing his heartbeat even with the rage fueling him.

All he truly wanted was to shatter the golems back. Snap their colossal necks.

But he needed distance.

He needed to get far away from them before they smothered him to near-death again. Then could he attempt to free himself from the iron bonds, source whatever magic was left in him.

The buzz of an electric motor sounded, and a frigid blast hit him at once. The warehouse door was opening.

"Shove him into the back seat," Collins barked as they hustled out of the building. "You, Nina, get in the back with St-Amand."

If vamps were able to be outside safely, it had to be nighttime. Val realized he had no idea how long he'd been unconscious.

"Aren't you taking the giants with us, boss?" A female voice chimed in.

"No, dear. Their task here is done. We'll make more later," Collins replied.

Val could hear a car engine running, a sliding door opening.

This was it.

He could *not* let them put him in that vehicle. If he did, his brothers would have no way to find him. Not before all his blood was drained and Collins turned into a lunatic monster on a feeding frenzy.

And Val would never have the chance to apologize to Maisie for letting her down after they kissed.

He held on to the sweet memory of her lips on his own to embolden him with strength. He corded every single muscle in his body, everything in him ready to act as soon as the stone grasp at his back released.

"Come on hurry," Collins' voice was charged with urgency.

The golem's grip shifted.

There, finally. Val was just about to roll over and hurl himself to the ground when he heard it.

The clear female voice, filled with power and intention, roaring in the frigid night air.

"Annyenthex!

CHAPTER 22

a rumble of thunder followed her spell.

"Get your freakin' hands off him." Maisie's voice seemingly came from both outside and inside of her. It resounded unusually deep within the cloud formation she had gathered around the parking lot of the warehouse.

The streetlights dispersed dimly over the idling white minivan crowded with monsters and vamps carrying metal crates. But all she could see was him, embedded in a tower of gelatinous mud, his body inert, his coat thrown haphazardly over him, a dirty cloth blindfold secured over his eyes.

Oh heavens! Please be alive.

The golem holding Val slowly turned his head toward her and the vision of horror finally hit her.

The monster restraining the one she was willing to die for was a colossal pillar of stone. There was absolutely nothing alive inside the horrific being and the others like him behind the van. Just pure malevolence that came from the deepest part of the hell that had made them.

Shoving her disgust aside, she summoned more power from the natural elements around her, the ice and snow at her feet, the structure of the charged air around her along with the dormant life of the meager trees adjacent to the lot. The place was barren but still resonated with Earth's essence.

She called upon her lineage, upon Morag of the Callanish Coven, upon the Thibodeaus, the Beaudrys, and Aradia, herself. Their force animated every cell in her body, filling her with inconceivable power.

"Careful." Emme was right by Maisie's side, her blonde hair escaping from her thick fur hat and floating in the stormy wind Maisie had created. "Don't hurt Val."

And that, there, was Maisie's only concern.

She could blast the whole lot of them easily. But she couldn't risk hurting Val.

With Emme at her side, she slowly advanced toward them. With each step forward, the snow and ice melted at her feet while the frigid temperature around her warmed. The clouds rolled and thickened above her. The magical power hummed in unison with the land surrounding the witch and the female vampire.

The golem holding Val still stared at them. The others—the teen vamps, and what looked like about eight more golems—were now transfixed at her sight.

"You bastard!" Emmeline let out a piercing scream and gave Maisie's cloak a sharp pull. She pointed at a human figure amongst the monsters. "Maize, over there, that has to be him. Collins. The lunatic!"

The human in a plain brown parka slowly turned toward them. His eyes filled with horror, his mouth opened in shock, at the sight of the two women closing in on him. He gave himself a shake and reached for something inside his winter coat.

With her fist tight and tingling, Maisie narrowed her eyes at him. She focused on his exact location, ready for any weapon or magical device he had in store for her.

She was set to blast him to shreds.

But no! He swiftly revealed a hypodermic needle. Horror filled her as he lunged for Val.

The sequence of moves happened within nanoseconds.

Val shifted under the golem's grip. He hurled himself at the madman who then promptly jabbed him in the neck.

"Maisie!" Emme gripped her arm in hysterics.

No. No. No. Fury mounted in her, like a roaring volcano that erupted from her sternum up to her throat, grabbing her with a vigor that wouldn't let go.

Val lay unconscious at the golem's feet. Poisoned by the madman.

"*Annyenthex!*" Maisie shouted again and this time an electric blast shot straight from her skin.

It slammed into the stone giant's chest. The immense mass of mud burst in a bright flash of light. Bits of stone exploded, raining down on them all.

One down. Now onto the others. Her wrath at seeing Val defenseless knew no bound. What she really wanted was to get at the madman, but his mud giants still stood shielding him.

The minivan was still running, back open, metal crates on the snowed-in parking lot. Vamps lay stunned, blown off their feet, a few shaking the mud off their winter garbs. The other golems were absolutely still, waiting for their orders from Collins.

And Collins was staring at Maisie, a mix of fear and righteousness in his posture, while he stood uncertain by Val's unconscious body.

Without second thoughts, she crossed the distance between them.

The warm wind blasted hard around her, making her fur cloak flutter behind her body. Dark clouds hovered thick above, waiting to be called upon by her powers.

"Get the teen vampires away from him," Maisie instructed Emme.

Inert on the ice beside the van, Val was still breathing. His features were pale below the thick linen blindfold, his bare

197

chest bloody. Her pulse picked up as her heart went to him. She would get him out of there.

The madman still surveyed her, first with awe, then with his lips drawn into a viscous smirk.

Emme strode away from Maisie. Her tall boots clicked on the now dry pavement, and her deerskin coat beat with the wind. "Vampires," she called out, "hear your maker."

In unison, the teen vampires snapped to attention and looked back at the professor, their faces lost in confusion.

"Come on, little vamps." Emme's voice was now a seductive purr in the cold air. Like a siren calling to her prey.

Those standing around the van dropped their crates and ambled, entranced, in Emme's direction. The ones closer to Collins followed suit. Soon she was leading a small horde of fifteen or so teen vampires towards her, the group waiting for her orders.

The golems remained motionless by their master, their eerie lidless eyes fixed upon Maisie.

"She can have them." Collins dropped the needle now empty of poison at his feet. "I have the one I need."

With inhuman strength, he grabbed Val by the waist, opened the back door of the van and lugged him toward the back seat.

Fuckin' bastard. No you won't. Rage at Collins swallowed her whole and made her blink. She would not let him take Val from her.

"*Annyenthex!*" The spell was cast swiftly and aimed straight at the human's forehead.

Its blast torpedoed at sonic speed through the air.

Collins was thrown with force against the minivan, denting the metal. He dropped Val at his feet and fell to the ground, unconscious.

In seconds, Maisie was at Val's side. She cradled him in her arms, ripped off the blindfold.

"Wake up, honey." Her heart bounced in her chest. Her eyes welled with tears. "You have to wake up."

She was filled with dismay at witnessing the wounds on his body. What the hells had the lunatic done to him? His skin was covered in marks and wounds, blood smeared all over his chest and arms.

Val's head slowly lulled to one side. His eyelids fluttered.

"*Rhònhla!*" she called with one hand stretched out. His coat was in her grasp and she wrapped him in it, tucking the fur around his neck and the cloth around his shoulders.

Far behind her in the deserted street, Emme was subduing the teen vamps with her seductive tone.

The golems remained motionless.

Quick. Val is the only one who matters now.

"*Slihnach ayn fhuyl sao...*" She lay her palm on his thorax, right over his heart. "Come on."

And as she had done before, she found the fabric of his blood and fixed every cell and organic bond. Destroying anything that didn't belong to the immortal's true essence.

His dark gaze seized hers as his body shuddered into life. He then sat straight up and held her arms. "*Seigneur*, Maisie, I'm so sorry."

She frowned, now overtaken by the intensity in his eyes. The deep link humming strong between them. "For what?"

He glanced at their surroundings and traced her cheek with a tender touch. "I should never have left you like that after I kissed you."

She flashed him a smile as the memory of their kiss hit her full force, wanting nothing more than relive it, away from this wretched place.

"Let's get out of here." She seized his hand to brush the inside of his wrist with her lips but froze in horror instead. His mom's tattoo was a mess of burnt flesh. "Oh gods, what have they done to you?"

His expression turned grim. "Never mind. Let's go."

"The Ice Witch's mark, Val. It's gone. This means, you can't—"

"I know." He bolted to his feet and helped her up. "Let's find my brothers. Before Collins wakes."

"I can fix it," she reassured him. "No worries."

He slowly released a deep breath. "How?"

Maisie smiled, filled with joy that she had the ability to restore him fully. She gently placed her hand over the burnt flesh, and called upon Charlotte Callan, the ancient Montreal witch's aura quietly filling her.

"*Lisaquiren kolipas!*" she intoned. The spells from Valerian's mother's tradition rose inside her very own blood to mix with her legacy. A white and silver hue swirled around them as tremor of restorative magic traversed them both. She sensed Val shudder, and he looked in awe as the skin healed itself, the complex and ancient mark fully redrawn.

"How did you—"

"He's awake!" Emme warned.

Both Val and Maisie sharply turned to see the professor stirring beside the van.

"Collins," Val roared.

In seconds, he had the man by the throat, pinning him against the vehicle. The madman's face turned ashen.

"Stay," Val ordered the two teen vampires who had been sitting inside the car the whole time and had escaped Emme's compelling power.

They both froze at his command.

"Golems, kill them!" the man managed to croak before Val could squeeze his throat harder.

Hells, Maisie's mouth opened in shock.

Collins' call was all the stone monsters needed. A tremor passed along their bodies, like a pressure wave spreading through hard-packed rock.

"Maize!" Emme yelled from the middle of her horde of teen vampires. "What do we do?"

"Get the vamps out of here," Maisie called over her shoulder before turning to the mass of golems surrounding the minivan.

The scientist dangled from Val's grasp. Even killing him wouldn't slow the golems now that they had their order.

With his face by the madman's cheek, Val growled at Collins. "Stop them." His voice was so icy, even Maisie shivered. Val released his grip just enough for an answer.

The madman licked his lips. "Too late." His voice sounded almost sad.

The golems were now advancing toward them. Surrounded, there was no escape. The golems would crush anyone crossing their paths.

Val turned to Maisie, his face unreadable, but even from here she could feel his sorrow. As if he knew they would both die before anything between them had a chance to spark to life.

But as she'd told Emme earlier, only an immortal witch could destroy golems.

And Maisie was that witch.

She stood to her full height, her chin high and pointed to the sky. She now channeled everything, from the immense fuel of the charged air at the bottom of the rolling cumulonimbus clouds she had summoned, to the ancient Callanish Stones earthly peaty power that now ran inside her timeless blood legacy.

"*Strieahadhr...*" Her word was almost a whisper but the effect cataclysmic.

A huge boom echoed around them as shards and shards of lightning rained down upon the golems, each bright tentacle hitting their stone target relentlessly.

Blazing channels of light hit unnatural stone limbs, slicing and binding appendages. It carved through humongous arms, cut heavy necks, jabbed multitudes of thin lightning bolts into the lifeless round eyes.

One after one, they fell until there were only three left standing.

Their silence unnerving, the giants viewed her with dead

lidless stares, spine-chilling looks that had no emotion, but just one goal.

Kill. End life.

Then the three raced at her, their surprising speed catching her off guard.

She disappeared under the rock-solid assault.

"No!" The call came from both Emme and Val at once.

But she barely heard it. No sounds reached her as the weight of the golems clung to her body. Her chest constricted, air no longer able to reach her lungs.

Their limbs were plastered on her, and she could feel their solid shape molding against her arms and legs, melting into solid rock around her. Her head throbbed madly, seized by the incredible agony from the lack of oxygen.

Quick. She had to hurry before being buried in a torrent of solid mud.

Millions of spells flashed through her brain. She had always been fast, but this was something else. Ancient and modern incantations alike erupted in her consciousness, from languages she thought she never knew, spanning eras and continents.

And it all settled within her. *Yes, there it is.*

Fuyrich aloiys lusgadh. She repeated the conjuration inward as she gathered the power from inside the golems themselves, using them, their killing strength, their dark essence, to fold it all into one point, right there inside her pentacle digging into her skin.

And just as she had done to Emme on her very first night in Montreal, the one word echoed loudly in her brain, but this time with a power infinitely fiercer.

"Stryos!"

The blast took them all.

It gushed through their stone entities, from the black slithery system that was their blood and internal organs to the scaly carapace that served as their skin. The golems were obliterated.

"*Oh diable*, Maisie..." Shock carved deep into Valerian's features.

Her eyes were now wide open, unblinking as she looked upon the scene, the filthy black and brown snow falling all around them. She surveyed her destruction, detached.

"Kayden!" Collins croaked at an underling and the two teen vamps at the front of the minivan jumped at Val long enough for his grip to loosen on the professor's throat.

Val slammed both of them away from him like two annoying bugs, but the distraction was enough for Collins to escape Val. He leaped into the running car. Tires caught pavement and the scientist peeled out of the parking lot.

"Maisie?"

Val inched toward her. But she stood frozen among the carnage, not wanting to move, shocked by the power she had cast.

"Val, bro, are you okay?"

She vaguely noticed Mag and Justin racing down the street with Emme and the horde of teen vampires. The two kids smacked by Val scrambled to their feet and meekly joined their pack. Father Grégoire was there, too. Sasha barked and dashed to Val's side.

"Maisie." His voice was quiet now, his posture steady as he reached out to her. But his image disappeared from her sight before she could feel his touch.

Little witch.

As her reality vanished, Maisie turned to the imposing and ageless figure in the long red hair. *Morag.*

The Montreal warehouse and frozen parking lot had waned from her sight and she was in the middle of a foggy barren land, surrounded by tall crooked stones.

Maisie. The call came from inside her.

Mom?

Her mother stepped toward her from one of the gray stones, clad in her usual jeans and t-shirt.

She looked back and forth from her mother to Morag.

Maisie, another call echoed in the misty air. From the tallest and crookedest stone this time.

Nana? She frowned at the stooped figure in the familiar gauzy pastel ceremonial robe. *What are you doing here?*

Maisie? Cousin Jo was here now. Concern crossing her creaky tone, her parched small features lined with worry.

Maisie, Maisie. The Beaudry cousins. Five of them detaching themselves from the stones, shouting for Maisie who recognized them by their dark hair and crystal blue eyes. Like fairytale princesses.

Maisie, Maisie. Her name was echoed over and over upon the foreign moors and she turned to them all, one after the other. Her throat dry. Unable to focus. *Maisie, here. Maisie.*

She no longer knew where to look.

Maisie. The tone was deeper this time. Commanding. *Girl, look at me.*

The Ice Witch. Charlotte Callan. Her dark hair and eyes just like Valerian.

Yes. Val, where was he?

But she was surrounded by women, thousands of them calling her name. *Maisie, Maisie. Maisie!*

She saw them all chanting, gathering, in a huge circle, holding hands. They were full of power, and she opened her mind wide to welcome them, in her heart, her soul, they were filling her.

Circling, twirling.

Screaming.

And she saw it. The blaze.

A bonfire erected at the edge of a village. Then one in the middle of a marketplace. Another in a forest.

And she saw them all burn.

The flame licked fresh skin, dark and light, all races and ethnicities, female and male alike, their flesh bubbling under the inferno. Black smoke from their own burning bodies filling their lungs. She heard the coughing and the screams.

And she felt it. All of it. Every bit of each witch's persecution.

Their unspeakable suffering shattered her soul. Splinters of pain rippled through the very fiber of her being.

Through her unbearable torture, she saw the nooses. Hanging from trees, from executioner blocks. In the brightness of the day, under the cover of the deepest night. She witnessed with horror the people watching her torment with glee, jeering and leering, throwing rotting vegetables, rocks. And she felt every piercing shard of stone, smelt the putrid goo that slid on her skin, blood still lingering in her mouth from earlier beatings in a dank cell, her limbs recalling every blow.

Her hands bound. She was helpless. No way out. Trapped and knowing the end was near. Unable to stop it. Unable to explain why.

Lost in her visions, she swallowed with difficulty, her throat scorched as if she'd gone days without water. Why were they chanting at her death, why? What had she done to them?

They cheered as the rope tightened against her neck. At the pain that made her eyes bulge.

Little witch. The redheaded ancient high priestess was now at her side as Maisie swung dying. The First Witch shook her head with sadness at her. *It seems you were not strong enough.*

And among all that pain all that horror, she heard a faint call.

"Maisie!" From very far away, Val was calling her back. "Emme," he was roaring, "What have you done to her?"

But Morag Callan was right.

It was too late. Maisie was lost.

And Val would never reach her.

CHAPTER 23

*V*al's throat thickened, his heart shattered, as he stared at her in confusion. Her eyes were glassy and rolled inward.

"What's going on?" He turned to Emme then Father Grégoire. "One minute she's commanding a freaking storm and now she's not even here." He put his arm around Maisie's shoulder as she stood trembling and muttering nonsense.

"She's going insane." Emme tilted her head to the side and shot him an empty stare. "Madame Ioshta said she might."

"What the hell?" Val's muscles quivered in sudden anger. "What did you do to her?"

"Me, nothing." She stared at her hands, her voice broken. "She did this to herself. For you."

Horror pierced him as he was hit with the truth. "She made herself immortal."

The revelation hung in the air for a moment. Everyone was quiet. The vamp pack had their head bowed in line behind Val's brothers who all looked at him with sorrow.

Renaud was here, somehow joined in the effort to rescue him. Somber, he kept his hands tucked in the pocket of his heavy deerskin coat. Justin was polishing his glasses with a pensive frown dug at his forehead. Mag was eerily silent.

Father Grégoire was also very quiet, flipping through the pages of a small grimoire. Sasha pushed his muzzle on Maisie's leg and when she didn't respond, he sat next to her with a whimper, his entire furry body pressed hard against her thigh.

Val drew her closer to him and wrapped her heavy fur cloak tighter around her.

"Tell me exactly what happened," he asked Emme, attempting to keep his own sanity in check while his heart raced at the idea that something worse than golems could take Maisie from him.

"Not much to tell. She made herself immortal," Emme said. "We went to Madame Ioshta who knew how to do it. The ritual was pretty wild. They used me as some sort of anchor, so I missed part of it. I was out. But when I came to, there she was, a freakin' force of nature."

"She is going mad, like her cousins," he lamented. Millions of thoughts crossed his mind. He'd have to tell High Priestess Thibodeau. He had failed to protect her granddaughter. Worse, he had lost her.

He rubbed her back tenderly and tucked her deeper between his arms.

"They're burning." The frail voice against his chest was not Maisie's, but something ancient.

"*Mon ange.*" He placed both hands gently on her shoulders and looked her in the eyes. "It's okay."

But she screamed, then big tears rolled down her cheeks.

"They're killing us all." Her head snapped to the vampire pack before she turned back to Val, her eyes blank. "They're killing me."

"You're safe, *ma belle*," he told her, wiping her eyes. But no matter how much he peered into her dilated pupils, the connection between them was gone.

"No one is safe," she uttered. "All of you," her gaze shifted to Emme, "all of us."

Val held her head gently between his palms. "No one will hurt you," he promised. His heart crashed at the pain etched into her face and he brushed his lips to the top of her forehead.

"They will never stop." Her eyes widened without seeing him. Her body started to shake, and she was overcome with fierce convulsions.

He clutched her back within his arms, rested his chin on her head and stared at Father Grégoire, silently pleading with him.

"We need to get out of here. The sun's rising," Justin said. "Those vamps will disintegrate."

"True," Mag said.

But Val wasn't seeing anyone. And for the first time in centuries, the fate of cursed teen vamps didn't trouble him.

His heart pounded, his eyes narrowed with expectation on the priest who was looking back and forth from his mystical book to Maisie. The old man *had* to find something.

"An anchor," Father Grégoire finally stated. "Emme, you said you were an anchor during the spell that made Maisie immortal?"

"Yes," she answered. "You think we can reverse Madame Ioshta's spell?"

"No. I could never undo that spell. This was the doing of the First Witch. There is only one thing that could perhaps keep an immortal witch sane."

"What! Just fucking tell us." Val had difficulty breathing— his whole world was slipping away from him.

"This much power needs to be balanced. If memory serves, the Beaudry witches who survived have soulmates." Father Grégoire rummaged through his shoulder bag for another grimoire. This time a thin but ancient tome.

"What the hell does that mean?" Emme cried.

"A soulmate. Someone who gave themselves to each witch. It has to be what keeps them anchored to our reality."

"How does that work?" Val would search heavens and hells for whatever would restore Maisie. He was already missing her single-minded wit and strong energy.

"Someone needs to sacrifice themselves for her," Father Grégoire said, his tone grim.

"And if we have that anchor, we can bring her back?" Mag strode closer to Val and laid a heavy hand on his shoulder.

"Maybe. The ritual is all here." The priest shook his head as he poured over his open book. "But we need someone strong."

"I can do it," Emme proclaimed, her jaw set, her lips a thin line. "I did it already."

"Emmeline?" Justin questioned. "That's not like you."

"She's my friend, okay?"

"No, Emme," Val replied. "I'm the one."

Father Grégoire nodded with gravity. He knew. Val was always the one.

"You can't die for her." Mag grasped Val's shoulder tight.

"He won't die," the priest said. "But his life here will be over. He'll have to leave Montreal. Tie himself to the White Holly coven. Lose his free will."

Maisie was hit with another convulsion and started to intone unintelligible words against his chest.

"Let's do this." Val lifted his chin at them all. "She's getting worse."

"Wait, now?" Mag's tone was broken. He wasn't happy.

Val turned to catch his brother's eye in a meaningful look. "Yes, now. Look at her."

Maisie was shaking her head back and forth in a frantic panic and his guts tightened further in anguish.

Sasha whimpered, crouching low beside them, worried from her lack of response.

"I'm not ready to lose you." The stress in Mag's tone was palpable. "Can't we just wait?"

"We need her." Justin calmly put his clean glasses back on. "This evil man is turning into one of us as we speak. I saw what she did to those golems. She will be able to help stop him."

Val nodded. But he didn't care about Collins. He only cared about Maisie. "You'll be fine, Mag." Val told his brother before addressing Father Grégoire. "What do you need?"

"Are you sure, Valerian?" The priest cleared his throat. "You will have to leave your mission here. Join the White Holly coven, answer only to their high priestess."

"That's Marianne Thibodeau," Justin said.

"Why not Maisie?" said Emme.

"If her mind recovers," the priest said. "But there are no guarantees."

"You want to put yourself at risk of being the Thibodeau's puppet?" Mag's hands fisted, his knuckles white.

Val held tighter onto Maisie who was muttering and scraping at her own skin with her nails, drawing blood.

His heart went to her, and he pursed his lips in readiness. There were no questions in his mind. He was the one.

"You might never see your brothers again," Father Grégoire added. "It will be in High Priestess Thibodeau's hands."

"I don't fucking care." He pinched his brows. Maisie had done this to herself for him. But a twinge of regret pierced him as he rested a fond gaze upon his brother Mag. "Tell Cass and Griff I'm sorry."

"And Emme?" Mag said, his tone scathing.

Val looked at his ex-fiancée with a wavering smile and searched his soul. He had been bonded to her for so long, his heart filled with remorse every time he looked at her. His mind, his life had been consumed with righting his wrong.

But this time, something else tugged at his soul, something much, much bigger. Saving Maisie.

He had never been so sure of anything before in his life.

He would give up everything just to see her smile again. His life here, his mission. Even his beloved Sasha. Just for her.

"Let's do this, Grégoire."

"I need a space we can consecrate." The priest surveyed the bare parking lot with nothing but snow banks and a few scrawny dormant trees. "We should go back to the *Sanctuaire*."

Maisie suddenly struggled into Val's arms. Her hand waved in the air and she mumbled in a language that sounded too much like magic.

"Is she casting spells?" Emme called with alarm.

Maisie continued to moan and snuggle further into Val's arm, her cheeks flushed.

"No time." Val nodded at the building. "Inside."

He swept Maisie off her feet and crossed the warehouse's entrance, Father Grégoire and Sasha right behind him.

He flung a look over his shoulder to his brothers and Emme. "You all need to take the vamps back to the sanctuary before they burn to a crisp."

"Hells, no," Mag protested, closing the distance between them. "If you're giving yourself over to their coven, I'm not leaving your side. Not until I have to."

"Same here, *chéri*," Emme echoed right behind Mag. "I care about both of you."

"I should stay." Justin strolled to their side. "Assist Father Grégoire with the ritual."

Val paused and looked at Renaud, the features of his taciturn sibling somber under the shearling hood. "Brother," he casted a meaningful stare at his silent sibling, "I need you."

Renaud was sometimes hard to read, always stayed away from the city, preferring the woods and his wolf companions. But he had come at once to Val's rescue, the bonds between the two brothers strong.

Val stared at the group of teen vampires, confused and searching for a leader, their eyes darting from Emme, Mag, Renaud, then back at Val.

Who would take care of them now?

He let out a heavy sight. But his gaze rested on Maisie's troubled features, her cheek plastered to his chest, and again his soul cleared. She was his life now.

"I got you," Renaud finally said, his steady voice a reassuring pledge in the cold night. With one last look at Val, he gave a hand signal at the vamp horde, and they turned at once toward him.

Relief swept through Val to see Renaud leading the teens down the empty street. At vampire speed, they'd easily reach the shelter before dawn.

"Upstairs," he told the others while stepping through the warehouse loading dock.

"What do you need, Father?" Justin asked the priest.

"Time," Father Grégoire uttered. "I wish we had more time for Valerian to think this through."

"No." Val was painfully aware of Mag's grievous look upon him. His brother was not ready to let go of him by his side.

And Mag was still brooding silently when seconds later, they all stood in the center of the lab, Emme holding Sasha by the collar, and waiting for Father Grégoire to finish drawing his runes circle in dark chalk on the concrete floor.

With Maisie finally settled against his chest, Val watched his brother pace the length of Collins' hideout.

"These are yours." Mag stopped to pick up Val's boots and daggers in an open steel crate at the corner of the lab, ready to be shipped, no doubt.

He threw the boots at his brother and was about to hand him the knives when Father Grégoire looked up from his ritual circle.

"Magnovald, I will need those," he said.

"Why?" Mag frowned with a shrug.

"They're your mother's sacred daggers. The ones she carried with her during her Atlantic crossing. Just what I need to bond the two of them." He shot Val and Maisie both a pained look.

"You ain't stabbing them with it, I hope," Mag sneered.

"Actually, I will."

Mag recoiled. "What the hell?"

"I have to. Through the heart." Father Grégoire nodded firmly. "They must die together."

"You're joking." Mag was still taken aback, not at all on board with this, his skin unusually flushed, his nostrils flaring.

"I wish I was."

"No way, bro." Mag confronted Val in a fit of fury. "I won't let you do this."

Justin remained silent, but Val felt his somber brother's gravity through his bones.

"I have to." Val looked down at Maisie, his heart swollen with purpose. He recalled the first time he laid his eyes on her this summer, the deep instant connection they shared. How just beneath his consciousness there was a hum when she was near, how when they shared their passionate kiss, he could almost touch a destiny woven from the two of them.

She had risked all for him without hesitation and now he would do the same for her.

"We can take the scumbag. Renaud can turn all the vamps back against him." Mag waved his hands in the air. "We have Emme. All of us, immortals. We can find him and stop him. We can send the witch back. Her coven will take care of her."

"No." Val's tone cut through the concrete room, frigid with resolve.

"I know you're hot for her," Mag insisted. "But it's not worth losing everything for her, your whole life, for her."

"It is." Val had nothing more to say.

"You don't know what they will ask of you. You may never return here."

"I trust her."

"You will become Marianne Thibodeau's weapon, a pawn to wage against anything threatening their coven. You'll have no say in it."

"It doesn't matter to me." In fact, it did. It was *all* that mattered. He would give everything he was, just to save her.

The last time he had carried her in his arms like this, she was laughing, slightly embarrassed to be unable to manage the icy threshold of *Sortilège.* But so trusting.

And just as she had depended on him with such a slight task, he was now all she had to restore her sanity. He would let no one else step in for him. He was hers entirely. He would tie her back to this world.

"What about your existence's mission? All those vamps you've saved? The ones going to the sanctuary right now? You expect me to take over?" Mag would not let it go. He was furious and Val knew the harsh words came from the deep pain of losing him.

"The disciples will cope."

"And Emme, how will she cope? You took care of her ever since you turned her. You have been there for her. Are you saying you're willing to give her up?"

"I am." And right there, by stating it out loud to the brother he was closest to, he knew. It was time for him to move on.

Maisie had given her sanity for him. And there was nothing, not even the infinite weight of his guilt over turning Emme, that would prevent Val from saving her.

"Mag." Emme ambled to Mag's side and seized the top of his shoulder while Sasha sniffed him cautiously, understanding the levity of the moment. "We will be fine without him. He has to do this."

Relief swept over Val at Emme's words. She understood his choice.

Mag spun to her. "You agree with his decision?"

"She loves him," she told Mag. "More than you and I ever could."

"A dagger to the heart." Mag huffed and shook his head. "Mark my words, they will both die. And that is that."

"They won't die." Justin looked up from Father Grégoire's

small spell book, which he had been scrutinizing this whole time. "Mag, don't be stupid, they're both immortal."

"It's okay, Mag." Val rested his palm on his brother's shoulder. "This is what I want."

"Oh fine." Mag rolled his eyes, but his tone shifted. "I'll take care of your bloody vampire brats."

Val was immensely grateful. "Thank you."

"I still don't like it."

"I'll miss you, too," he said. And he meant it. He would so miss these repartees and the companionship only a brother could bring.

"Sure." Mag shook his head. "Grégoire, can we get on with this?"

"Valerian?" Father Grégoire bowed at him, and he knew what he needed.

With Maisie stirring in his arms, he stepped into the circle and bundled her inside the cloak. "It will be okay, sweetheart. I will bring you back."

She looked at him with a quick flash of recognition, and then shook her head in her delirium, battling her demons again. He kept her embraced as he lowered them to the ground in the middle of the alchemy circle. With her body nestled to his side, he laid his back flat against the hard floor. He turned her so that both their chests were open for what Father Grégoire would have to do.

Daggered. Bonded.

The pain was not something he worried about for himself, but he hated the idea that his familiar blade would pierce through her flesh.

"Let's do this quick."

Father Grégoire was kneeling just above their head. "*In namineh spiritac sanctuy.*" He read the language of Nostredame from his ancient prayer book. "*Ut matryem benah-fixitque.*"

Somber, Emme, Mag, and Justin stood at the edge of the sacred circle.

A golden light rose from the runes at Father Grégoire's chant. A smoky scent permeated the air while faint mist twirled around the mystical space.

Val turned his head to Maisie, steady in his love for her. Her mind had died for him. And he was ready to die countless deaths for her.

"In namineh spiritac sanctuy..."

When the time came, he did not look at the knives in Father Grégoire's hands.

As the blades struck them both, his sight was full of her. Her laugh, her touch, her soul.

Just her.

CHAPTER 24

"*You came.*" *Light-headed, Maisie blinked a few times with wonder at the vision of hope before her.*

Piercing the images of death, hushing the screams of agony, covering the stench of putrefaction with a light scent of heather and spices, there, at the far end of what looked like a hill blooming in spring, he stood.

Valerian.

The one for whom she had willingly sacrificed her sanity. The one her heart had been hungering for since she had laid her eyes on him in the clearing of the woods of Berwick Hollow.

Tall and fierce, his gaze filled with emotion, his stride purposeful as he cut through the multitude of skeletal tree branches keeping her captive within her nightmare.

"You came," she called to him again as the million thoughts in her mind cleared to be replaced by one focus only.

Him.

"Sulahs Vyenrt aheir!" He commanded an ancient spell she recognized to be drawn directly from his mother's essence and the thick fog of her horror parted. A purple halo appeared high above her to settle like a warm blanket around her limbs, chasing the darkness from every recess of her mind.

In seconds, he was with her, holding her hands, his intense gaze on her. His warmth filled her entire body down to the smallest corner of her soul.

"Did you get lost, too?" she asked, utterly disoriented, trying to distinguish between dreams and reality.

" I'm bringing you back."

"How?"

"I love you, Maisie." He was beaming and she fell deeply into his charisma.

"How?" Her chest tingled with bliss, yet she was unable to respond to his confession, unwilling to believe in this happiness.

He had come to save her. She knew it in her very bones.

But at what cost? Her heart suddenly seized. There was always a cost.

Her early relief was replaced by an incredible worry. "What price did you pay?"

"No price, Maisie. Only one thing matters. You. I'm taking you back. I need you." His voice was thick with torment.

" I love you, Val. I've always loved you. As if you were always there, within me." Apprehension was still lodged at the depth of her throat as she stroked his cheek with infinite tenderness. There had to be a cost to her rescue. This could not be.

"I love you," he said again, touching her soul.

This time, she let his words filled her. Joy suddenly flushed through her, chasing the shadows and leaving her weightless with delight. The worry would have to wait. He was here, he loved her.

"Whatever you gave up, I will pay it back for you." This she resolutely vowed. "I will not let you suffer for me."

"I told you, there is no cost." His smile carried through his entire face, his tone as warm as a late spring. "Just us."

While his words soothed her emotions, a searing physical pain struck her chest. She was seized with a fierce agony that scattered down through each of her bones. With a primal cry, she clutched the left side of her chest. She turned into him to hush her scream and gripped the hilt of a blade that was buried in her heart.

It will be okay, mon ange.

His thoughts rang through her mind, past the searing pain. She could feel and hear every one of his emotions as if they were one and the same.

"They're alive!" A clear female voice was cheering above her followed by a loud happy bark.

"Damn, bro, you gave me the scare of my immortal life."

But Val didn't reply. One hand at Maisie's dagger, the other at another blade embedded into his own torso, he stared at her with pure adoration.

His brow creased with what had to be done. He swallowed, and in one swift tug, pulled both daggers from their chests.

The acute pain receded. Their wounds closed instantly.

He discarded the blades then he drew her close. His embrace was solid and fearless as he held her tight in his arms and she buried her head against his muscular chest.

She had no idea where she was, until she remembered the battle with the golems. She let out a sharp gasp.

"Maisie." Val pushed her softly back to look at her face. "Are you okay?"

She nodded, trying to parse through her thoughts. She frowned at him, still unsure. "I think so."

"You scared me." He drew her hair back and softly kissed her on the lips. A kiss full of love, gentleness, closeness. "*Diable*, how I love you."

Still, as she took in the bare concrete room, the runes around them, and the four people standing at the edge of the circle watching them with caution, she was confused.

She turned to him again. "How did you do this? How did you find me?"

"Father Grégoire helped." Val nodded at the priest above them. "We're bonded now."

"Bonded?" Puzzled, she glanced up at the elder who grinned.

"You're my anchor?" she asked Val. Her stomach knotted

and she sat up, shocked. "Just like the life partners of my Beaudry cousins?"

"I am."

"What did you give up for this?"

"Nothing. I gained you."

"That's not true, is it?" She looked at the others around them, caught the eyes of the blonde vampire who had sort of become a friend, her face was unreadable.

"Emme, tell me, what did he give up?"

Emme shifted uncomfortably, holding tight on Sasha's collar, but did not answer. Magnovald and Justin's mouths were thin slits, their expression dark.

"I gave myself over to your coven," Val finally said, his tone flat.

"You did what?" She blinked rapidly.

"I am tied to the White Holly coven now."

"No, you can't." And as she saw his face fall, she corrected herself. "I love you, Val. So much. I want to stay here. With you. Forever. You can't leave your life here for me. You don't answer to anyone."

"I will now." Val's words were measured. "To the High Priestess of the White Holly coven."

Oh cripes. Nana. Maisie frowned and then shot him a decisive nod. She would *have* to convince her grandmother to let go of him. It was only fair. He had saved her life. No way she would have survived the torture she'd just been under.

But would her grandmother want to release him? A St-Amand Immortal in Berwick Hollow, at her beck and call. To protect the coven. It would be an alliance strong enough to curb the Black Oak Warlocks. It would be hard to part with that kind of power.

She let out an even breath. Calm settled over her entire body. "I *will* become the High Priestess. I will free you."

"That would help." He teased her with a wink of levity. "But it's okay either way."

"I *will* free you from this."

"Sweetheart, whoever is in charge, you still need me. To survive."

"I don't want to force you. No." Her brows knitted as she pondered the consequence of their union. "That's too much."

"Is it?"

Her mouth open, she had nothing to respond to that. Oh hells, here was the man she loved and who had now given everything to her. And who proclaimed his love in return. Did she have the right to keep him bonded to her like this?

"I love you, Maisie. I know you love me. I saw your entire mind."

"I do. More than anything." She nodded as she realized that none of the political alliances amongst warlocks, witches, and immortals mattered now. Only the two of them together were important. "We'll figure this out."

"We will."

"Together."

His smile was now easy, full of happiness, and with a hint of boyishness that lit his somber features with an inner glow. "Always."

"Oh gods, we're both immortal now." The implications started to sink in. Together they would watch humanity grow, witness the cycle of life around them.

"We are, *ma belle*."

"And Emme?" What would this mean for Val's ex-fiancée?

"We're good," Val said.

"Are you?" Maisie looked at the woman who had turned from a dire enemy to her closest ally in just a few days.

"He loves you." Emme smiled, her cold perfect features softened with warmth. "Our relationship was a teen infatuation. We got caught up in the drama of it all. It wasn't love. Not like what you two have."

She let go of the dog who hastened towards them, his tail frisky with happiness. Maisie was patting his furry flank when the sound of Justin's cellphone dinged.

He fished it out of his pocket and swiped the screen. "Oh shit."

"What?" Mag frowned.

"It's Renaud." Justin peered up from his phone, anger radiating from him. "Collins is at the *Sanctuaire*."

Collins. The madman. It all came back to her and she recalled the crazy scientist speeding away before she battled the golems.

"Oh flaming hells, no!" She jumped to her feet, followed by Val. If the mad professor had turned immortal with all of Val's blood, he was now free to feed on people.

And what of the human disciples at the shelter? They had to take action now.

"The golems?" she asked around, all business. The magic within her buzzed with power, enhanced by Val's essence running fierce through her veins.

"You destroyed them all." Val had laid a protective hand at her back.

"This is much worse," Justin said with an inward gaze. "He's summoned something more horrible. Mothbeasts. Flying all around the place. Ren's barely holding them off with Collins' horde of teen vampires."

"Mothbeasts?" She shivered in horror. The giant humanoid flying creatures were said to travel in swarms and multiply by the minute. A sudden fear gripped her by the throat. "Oh gods. The tortured kids in the cells."

She felt Val's dread as he pulled her closer, his entire body coiled with fury and ready for action.

He drew himself to his full height beside her. "Time to end this."

CHAPTER 25

"*J*'m not having you fight him alone." Val sighed
from the back seat of Emme's Porsche, unable to
tear his eyes from Maisie sitting at the front. She might be
looking fearless right now but he had an overwhelming need
to protect her. "You just recovered from the nightmare. In fact,
I'm not having you fight at all."

His mind was set. Let her fight the next battle.

Sasha was safely driving back with Father Grégoire. And
he wanted Maisie far from harm as well.

"That's nonsense. Do you know how to take on a horde of
mothbeasts?" She narrowed her eyes at him then returned to
scrolling her cellphone screen. "I got it all right here. Book of
Shadows, remember?" She waved her phone for emphasis.
"I'm looking it up now."

"Right." He huffed and sat back, none too happy with her
urgency to jump in the fray so soon. He'd have to come to
terms with the fact that the woman he loved was the
strongest witch north of the border. His job was to protect her
at all costs.

"I thought all the spells were in your mind now." He
wanted to know everything about her new status.

"More or less, but I still need to check the coven's records to find the beasts' weaknesses." She swiped across her phone with purpose, strands of black hair plastered on her cheek.

She was shaking her head now, biting on the knuckle of her index finger, deep in concentration. "Nana used to scare us to sleep with these creatures. Always thought they weren't real."

"Did you tell your family in Berwick Hollow?"

"About the immortality?" She looked up from the phone with an intensity that struck him down to his core. And to think that they were now bonded to each other. The warmth at his chest spread to his entire body.

"Not yet." She added with a shrug then smiled. "When this is over, I will."

"Once this is over, it will be just you and me, *mon amour*." His lips curled into a slow smile and he finally tore his eyes from her to turn to Emme. "Can't you drive faster?"

"You could have shifted and flown with Mag and Justin," the female vamp grumbled.

"And leave Maisie behind?"

"Right. You won't leave her side now," Emme teased as she switched gears and pressed on the accelerator. Her sports car slid on the snow as they took speed.

His anger at Collins grew tenfold. The professor's obsession had forced Maisie to put herself at risk. He'd captured Father Grégoire and Sasha. Two innocents caught in the middle. And now he was attacking the *Sanctuaire des Truands*, the summation of Valerian's life.

Rarely spiritual in modern time, he now found himself sending a prayer to the Almighty to keep his wards well and alive. As he silently begged for divine assistance, the Porsche turned into the narrow street leading to the old nunnery.

Nothing could have prepared him for what was before him.

"Oh shit," Emme blurted, echoing his thoughts.

The entire historical building was covered in a fibrous whitish cocoon. Layers upon layers of sticky webs made of ghastly strands clung to the stone walls of the *Sanctuaire*, sticking to the stained-glass windows and trapping everything inside. The usual warm glow from the sanctuary's windows now turned to a dull unnerving greenish light.

Buzzing eerily to protect their massive nest, giant humanoid flying beasts darted around, wide gray wings spanning the length of their bodies and ended in vicious clawed limbs. Large glassy compound eyes protruded from oddly shaped heads.

And below, at the edge of the courtyard, stood Justin, Mag and Renaud, surrounded by the confused vamp horde they had rescued earlier. His brothers looked mad as hell as they faced the entrance of the sanctuary.

Val coiled with power, each muscle tensed with fury as they got out of the Porsche.

Maisie was still focused on studying the monsters, her face illuminated by the screen of her phone, determined and attentive as she leaned against Val.

"Oh please god, no." Father Grégoire bolted out of nowhere to Val's side, his rosary clutched tight between his fingers.

The priest's despair cut right through Val's soul.

Collins stood blocking the curved entrance to the shelter, the Nostredame disciples were corralled by a gathering of mothbeasts standing on misshaped limbs.

Someone, a younger woman amongst Father Grégoire's pupils, was sobbing, her cry echoing softly in the night.

Hells no. This was Val's home, his people, his entire life's purpose. His work built in an immortal lifetime focused on creating peace and relieving suffering to those less fortunate.

He would *not* let it all be destroyed by the selfishness of a madman. He laid his palm to the middle of Maisie's back, felt her strength.

"We've been waiting for you all." Collins cackled as he surveyed the St-Amand brothers, his newly formed fangs fully extended, his eyes feverish. He nodded at the captive disciples. "Which one should I bleed first?"

His gaze rested on young Ariane. The female disciple stood proud and stared at Collins with rage, her red hair flying in the wind, her chin up and her lips tight.

"Bring her to me," Collins ordered his mothbeasts, pointing at the woman.

Val strode through the courtyard toward his enemy, Maisie right by his side, his fury fueling her as if they were one. A quick glance confirmed she felt his emotion as deeply as he did, single-minded and pure wrath.

More mothbeasts wings flapped relentlessly in the cold air, a buzz that crawled eerily through Val's bones.

"We won't let him touch her," Maisie asserted, feeling his disgust. "We'll save your disciples. Then we'll get your home back."

"We will," he said, buoyed by her calm strength.

I can destroy them all. You go after Collins. Maisie was now addressing him inside his own mind.

Her plan had merit but he was not about to let her go after the giant flying beasts alone. "We kill them first," he replied. "Then go after Collins. I'll shift."

Her eyes bright, as if she was heartened for battle, she nodded in agreement.

Mag and the other St-Amand brothers had now joined Val's side, the teen vamps hoarding behind them.

"You guys need to get inside," Val ordered Mag. "See if there are any of these mothbeasts in the *Sanctuaire*. Rescue the vampires locked in the cellar."

"Sure, bro."

"Father, stay with Sasha," Val urged the elder as he surveyed the courtyard one more time. "Make sure he's safe."

The elder nodded at his directive.

"I will get your flock back, old man." Val shot the priest a firm look. "I promise."

"I can fight alongside you," Father Grégoire said, determined.

"Not this time, old man." Val eyed the holy string of beads in the elder's hands. "But we'll need every prayer you got."

CHAPTER 26

*M*aisie watched in awe as Val's body shifted once again into a giant bat. The creature he turned into was majestic. A wide sleek animal that swerved high in the air then dived down to her level.

"*Scìreadh*!" Her hands prickled with power as she slowly rose off the icy ground. Soon, they both ascended in the cold sky above the cocoon monstrosity coating the ancient nunnery. Only the belfry of the chapel peaked through the shapeless structure covered thick with the glutinous filaments secreted by the monsters, the thin moon and street spotlight casting shadows over the humongous aberration.

She knew what Val had in mind the minute he soared upward at lighting speed. She watched him dive like a torpedo toward the entrance of the sanctuary. His momentum pierced through the thick moth fibers in a wide gap in the dreadful dome, leaving long loose strands that flowed in the wind.

He shot straight back out through the belfry in a crash of broken stained glass and was back at her side in seconds, confusing the buzzing mothbeasts and causing Collins to scream in frustration.

The immortals below charged through the opening, the

teen vamp horde behind them in a gaggle of fangs, claws, and tattered clothing. Emme's blonde hair flashed in the middle of the pack, as she brandished a thin sword she had retrieved from her thigh-high boot.

As they disappeared inside, it was Maisie's turn.

The mothbeasts had been surprised by Val's move but had recovered and now concentrated their attention toward the levitating witch and her huge bat companion. Her body glowed with power and the unnatural light was like a beacon to them.

Her muscles twitched at remembering Cousin Jo's notes on the monsters. They would slash her limb by limb, incapacitating her, before devouring her whole with her heart still beating.

Their buzzing intensified as they narrowed on her, creepy sounds that reverberated through her neck. Unlike real moths, these ones had darted wings to match the talons at their grotesque arms.

She shrugged off her fear and counted fifteen of them hovering in the sky, all of them focused on her. She knew their weaknesses, right at their soft underbelly, which covered the vulnerable organs keeping them alive.

Maisie, go! She didn't know if it was her own voice urging her on, or Val's, but she felt his strong presence right inside of her.

The wide bat took off and flew again at incredible speed, weaving in and out across the rabble of moth-like monsters flying toward Maisie, attempting to slow them down and prevent them from reaching her.

"*Lruannicth tùth.*" She mounted the magic from her ancient blood. Gathering the energy into a small solid marble between her splayed palms. "*Matronae*, Thibodeaus and Beaudrys," she called forth. "Callans of the Callanish Stones."

She visualized the circle of witches inside her as she gathered them all to raise the spell. "Aradia of the twelve secrets, I rely upon your strength, upon your power. Come to your sister."

At her intention, the sphere increased from a tiny opalescent ball to a wide glowing globe of pure light of green and gold hues.

More and more it grew until she had within her arms a giant mass of colors, swirling and shifting, a few feet long. It was so big, so powerful, she could barely contain it.

With her entire mind focused on her task, the humming sound at her ear caught her by surprise.

A sharp pain sliced right through her arm as a mothbeast whizzed past, and she screamed.

Maisie! Val roared in her head.

She almost let go of the celestial globe she had created but managed to grab it from underneath as it fell, her upper arm pulsing in agony at the muscle strain.

I'm good, she called back to Val.

The mothbeast that had sliced her flesh open was now turning around and bolting back toward her.

"*Lruannicth mysticach.*" Her pentacle grew searing hot at her throat, the pain nothing compared to her upper arms as her muscles strained to hold the sphere steady.

She was about to shout her offensive spell when Val flew right into the horrible insect, knocking it mid-flight.

Maisie snapped her attention to her side and shouted her primed curse at another flying creature shooting toward her. The power jolted directly from her pendant and hit the beast straight at its front.

The exploding belly shot out a thick yellow goo, which rained down below as the mothbeast corpse bounced over the cocoon-covered roof of the sanctuary and slid down into the snow bank.

Soon the flying monsters were all on her, zooming around and humming, as if consumed by one thought—devour her. Her cloak was smeared in acidic sludge from the explosion, the acrid scent gagging her as she balanced her immense sphere between her arms.

Another beast was snatched by Val at light speed and she shivered at its startled final screech. More flying beasts rose from the ground to line up behind their mates, the swarm multiplying by the minute. She didn't know how many more Val could destroy before he would become overpowered.

Collins below had managed to snatch the redheaded disciple and held the woman by the arm, while screaming at his underlings to come back down. But they wouldn't and dotted the sky ready to fight Maisie.

She had to act. Now.

She breathed and settled everything inside her. Once she started, she would not be able to stop. She had to trust Val could protect her if needed.

"Go," she whispered to her celestial globe.

The giant orb glided down to the nunnery like an elegant butterfly taking flight.

Its golden light cast shadows over the whole area as it settled at the tip of the belfry. Gently, like a set of falling dove feathers, it opened over the entire sanctuary, covering the gooey translucent moth substance with a gentle blanket of azure and gold energy.

The mothbeasts' fibrous sheath began to disintegrate, as if touched by a holy radiance. Soon the historic nunnery was free of the grotesque layer and gleamed with a welcoming inner brightness.

"Val, get out of the way," she called out.

I can't leave you.

"I don't want to hit you," she shouted.

She felt his understanding travel through her and watched the massive bat swoop down to the courtyard, shift midair into the dark immortal she knew so well and land a few feet from Collins.

Bordering his decisive chin, Val's fur collar bristled in the wind. The edge of his coat brushed his leather boots, his wide shoulders obscuring the madman from Maisie's view.

She held tight on her pentacle and this time, reaching deep within her own personal powers now awakened, she roared, "*Stryos!*"

Her blast shot out in a bright white aura all around her, hitting every single mothbeast with a tsunami of air pressure.

They recoiled, hit by the spell, and one by one, they fell over the nunnery's roof, their inert bodies rolling over the historical green copper slope to end in the snow piled high around the sanctuary.

Most of the disciples had scattered away, now huddled on the other side of the wall bordering the property. They were watching her, transfixed.

"Valerian, my friend," Collins called out from below. "Why attack me? We are the same now."

Drained from the spells, the injury at her shoulder burning like hell, her heart hammered like crazy as she watched her love facing off the lunatic who had created it all.

With her hand pressing on her wound, she floated down and landed right beside Val to face the mad professor. He barely resembled a human, his skin pale and gaunt, his cheeks skeletal. And in the crook of his arm, he restrained the redhead woman who had fed Justin in the forest during the immortal's ritual. A handful of disciples still remained, watching with horror their companion's peril.

Val reached over to place his hand upon Maisie's shoulder. She could feel every fiber of his body recoil in horror at witnessing Collins' fangs inches from the woman's throat.

Ariane, she heard the name in her mind. The disciple's name was Ariane. The young redhead was putting on a brave face, but Maisie could see the girl's chest heave up and down with strain under Collins' grip.

"You're hurt." Val kept his eyes on his foe but was full of concern for Maisie.

"I'll be fine." Her wound slowly close on its own accord as she healed herself.

"It's over, Collins." Val stood tall, his legs firmly planted on the icy pavement. "You can stop it right now. Let Ariane go and I'll let you walk. Go to Yukon like you wanted."

"He's an immortal now." Maisie was studying Collins' every movement, searching for weaknesses and finding none. "You can't compel him."

"Collins." Val fixated on the madman, his voice steady. And Maisie couldn't help but admire his calm exterior while she knew that inside, he wanted to rip the madman's throat out and reduce him to tatters.

She touched Val's arm as she too stared at the monster.

"Collins," Val repeated as if to touch the man living within the newly born abomination. "I know this hunger you feel."

"I have to drink them all now." The crazy scientist's voice was shrill. "Disciple's blood. That's how you do it, isn't it?"

"Not like this."

Ariane's breath grew raspier as Collins tightened his grip. She was on the verge of passing out.

The disciples gasped.

"Go," Val ordered the young monks and sisters. "Get away from here." He gestured with his hand out. "Hold on, Ariane."

"No!" Collins lifted the young woman off her feet and shouted at the last of the disciples retreating away from him. "Get back here, you morons. You serve me now!"

"No one serves anyone, Collins." Val continued to speak a calm that he did not feel. "This isn't how it works."

Maisie stayed poised, waiting for Val's cue, not wanting Ariane to get hurt while diffusing the threat.

"Gosh, I'm so hungry." Collins snarled an inhuman cry and opened his mouth wide in a horrible rictus of death. He plunged his fangs straight into Ariane's neck.

She howled in chilling agony before her body turned limp in Collins' arms.

No! The spell was on Maisie's lips, Val ready to bolt, when a dark furry form flew passed them with a fierce growl.

Sasha!

The dog went straight for Collins' throat.

The monster fell to his back. He let go of Ariane and kicked madly, trying to escape the angry animal pinning him down.

"Sasha! No," Val screamed. "Let go."

Maisie sought for the best way to protect him. *Cuidletach*—the start of a sleeping spell—was on her tongue, but Collins was faster.

With inhuman strength, he gripped Sasha with both hands and pried the animal's jaw open. In a sweeping motion, he threw the dog in the air.

Sasha! Maisie sensed Val's shock and fury as his pet landed in the icy snow with a hard thump.

Collins took this moment to bolt inside the sanctuary, the heavy wooden door shut right after him.

"We'll get him later." Maisie tugged on Val, who was torn between checking on Sasha and following Collins to destroy him for good.

They both hasted to the dog's side and kneeled by its inert body.

Val's brothers and Emme burst out from the back of the sanctuary and circled to them, the horde of teen vamp with the newly rescued ones gathered behind.

"The place is crawling with these mothbeasts," Mag said between breaths before catching sight of Sasha. "Oh shit."

"He just got away from me." Father Grégoire sprinted over to their side with a sob.

Ariane had regained consciousness and had joined them, a thick scarf pressed over her wounded neck. "Your dog saved my life, Valerian."

Maisie's eyes welled, her heart broken. Val slumped over his faithful companion lying on the snowbank, the ice melting a little at the lifeless body's warmth.

Val's pain and remorse funneled through her but as he laid his hand at the dog's chest, she felt him ease. "He's alive."

"*Merci, bon dieu,*" Father Grégoire uttered with a sign of the cross.

Thank you, Matronae. Maisie prayed with gratefulness.

The somber weight eased off the gathered crowd as Sasha shook himself up and licked Val's hand. He got up on all fours, at first a little shaky and then soon with his usual verve, his tail friskily wagging back and forth.

He sniffed Maisie's hand before giving it a quick lick, and she scratched the top of the dog's head with deep relief.

With Sasha between the two of them, Val stared at the sanctuary. The building had been restored to its natural majesty, but the fight was not over.

"He's inside." Val stood beside her, battle ready as she.

"Yes," Justin said. "And with all the monsters he conjured assisting him. Wraiths, countless mothbeasts, and a golem or two ruling the halls of the *Sanctuaire.*"

"Fucking bastard." Val shook with wrath. The thought of Collins scouring the corridor of his home made his skin crawl. She sensed it.

"You helped him." Mag cocked an eyebrow at Val in disbelief.

"I helped his dad," Val said, regret shadowing his tone. "A long time ago."

"You did your best." Justin slapped his brother on the back.

"Let's go." Mag shrugged in his leather coat, ready for another fight.

"No."

Everyone turned, surprised at Val's word but Maisie knew exactly what he felt. His mind was set on something else than a building filled with monsters.

"But this is your whole life's work," Mag protested.

Yet it wasn't.

"My legacy, my family, is here." Val was without an ounce

of hesitation. "On this courtyard. My brothers, our disciples. All the teens we saved." He bowed at Father Grégoire before adding, looking at Emme, "Friends. You, Sasha," he petted his dog with an upward curl of his lip, "and you," he said to Maisie.

And more than his words, his entire being sang at what she meant for him. That she was his everything now.

"You're all my life's work. That will never go away." He shot her poignant look. "Sweetheart, you know what to do."

"I do." She nodded gravely, reading his thoughts.

With an ache in her heart, she saw again their first meeting. Her fight with Emme and how he had looked in the courtyard, so handsome and fierce, with the gentle snow falling over him. She recollected his unconscious but still powerful body when he had fallen under Collins' poison, his motionless chest under her touch, ready to be awakened by her spell. She recalled the kindness he had held over the tortured vamps he had rescued from the madman. She remembered his dedication, his selflessness.

And filled with the essence of who he truly was, she turned away from him and strode a few steps to the entrance of the century-old nunnery.

Then she burnt the whole place down.

CHAPTER 27

*V*al picked a lone fleck of ash from Maisie's hair.

He breathed in her clean scent of lavender from Mag's guest soap as she lay in his arms in one of the master bedrooms above the *Serpent Maudit.* Dawn was rising over the city, casting the ornate room in a faint rosy glow.

She was wearing an oversized staff shirt over a set of tiny lace panties she'd found in the collection of new lingerie Mag always kept for his female guests. The thoughts of her long legs bare under the bedsheet beside him sent a tide of craving straight through his core.

He gazed at her, still in awe at how much power was contained in her slender body, forcing himself to leave her alone. For now.

He traced her cheek with tenderness. "You should sleep. You must be exhausted."

She had laid the whole nunnery on fire, from the basement cells, now emptied of his rescued teen vamps, to the sky-high attic still filled with remnants from the seventeenth century. Then she'd extinguished the blaze in a single colossal vacuum blast that obliterated the monsters.

They had found Collins unconscious and barely alive in the chapel. The blaze had stripped him of his chemically induced immortality and he remained a simple human, hurt and lost, babbling incoherently. He was now in custody of Captain Akande, charged with the murder of numerous innocent youths.

The madman would not see the light of day as a free man in this life.

The combustion had been explained to the city's fire department as being the cause of old faulty wiring. It was time to rebuild.

But not for Val. No, his life here was over.

And it was truly starting now. With her.

"I don't want to sleep right now. I want you." She grinned and cupped the back of his head. "I know you still want it, don't you?"

"Want what?" He frowned, puzzled, but entertained by her focused expression.

"Feed from me." Her eyes were lit from within.

"This is our first time alone together and you think I want to feed from you?" He was teasing her but she was not entirely wrong. A pull to know her fully tugged at his inside. He also felt her strong desire of him. A thirst that he mimicked tenfold. But he could also sense how drained she was.

"I won't break, you know." She was actually serious.

"I know," he said, acknowledging her immense power. "But you're allowed to be exhausted and take the time to recover."

"This, with a man, is not my first time." She was insistent. While she had been supremely confident in annihilating Collins and his beasts, he now detected her hesitation.

He looked down at her, his heart filled with love, his body —clad only in a pair of sweatpants and a t-shirt borrowed from his brother—was on fire. "Get some sleep, *mon ange*."

"No." A tiny frown appeared between her brows, and he recognized the look she had when she focused single-mindedly on one thought. "I've had sex before, I told you about it."

"The courier boy." He hated that someone would have taken advantage of the innocent girl she used to be.

"And two others. Boyfriends from home. I'm not new at this. But this is the first time with someone I truly love."

"You love me." He knew she did. He felt it in his soul. But he wanted to hear her say it out loud, still in awe that love was something he now had after centuries of loneliness.

"I love you," she said. "I love everything about you. The depth of your heart *and* your strength."

"Of the two of us, you may be the strongest," he jested.

"No. To overcome that guilt you felt for centuries takes someone stronger than I ever could be."

He breathed and let that thought hang there for a second. Letting go was both hard and easy. Hard in that he knew above all he was responsible for Emme and the city's vampires but also easy because of the woman who showed him he was worthy of love...her love.

"I love you too."

"Did you love Emmeline?" Again that single-mindedness that endeared her to him returned, wanting to wrap her mind around it all, about what he and she were, not willing to leave anything unexplained.

"I don't know," he started, "Probably not. And I never slept with her."

"But weren't you lovers?"

"Sixteen eighty-eight. She was a proper young lady. I would never have gone near her before marriage."

"You never touched her?" She widened her eyes in surprise.

"A few kisses." His lips curled into an easy smile.

"That's it?"

"That was a lot back then."

"Have you never made love to someone?" She covered her mouth with her hand. "Truly?"

"I had sex." He shrugged, recalling the meaningless encounters he had over the centuries. "Love, no."

"A first for both of us." She ran her fingers down the nape of his neck.

He took a deep meaningful inhale. "It will be."

"Now," she urged, reaching for the buckle of his belt. Her features were pinched with attention.

"Now?"

"Uh-huh." She fumbled with the buckle, trying to undo it.

"You're not tired?" He gently captured her hands. "Even after all that?"

"No."

He kissed her knuckles. Her green gaze sparkled with need. The curve of her lips called him with undeniable temptation.

He let out a measured breath. "Then we'll do it right." He shifted his weight over her, slowly drawing her hands high above her head to gently pin them on the pillow.

"What do you mean by right?" She relaxed into his grip with a tantalizing smile.

"Slow, long, with every bit of you on fire." Her excitement prickled through his veins and he suddenly wondered if he would be able to contain himself long enough to please her just as she deserved.

With her hands trapped, she arched her hips into him, and her lips parted to summon a kiss.

"Will you feed from me," she whispered and the image she conjured in his mind drove him wild. "Like vampires do?"

"You bet." His voice was hoarse as he attempted to hide his intense blood craving while he hardened against her navel.

But there would be no hiding from her.

He crushed her lips with his, his whole weight pressing down on her as he continued to keep her hands firmly in his.

He felt the purr deep inside her throat as she twisted with content under him, the blankets between them preventing her from moving freely against him.

The predator in him roared with dominance at her captive to his mercy.

"*Ma belle*," he growled. He lifted part of his weight off her and, releasing her, steadied himself on one elbow at her side.

She slid her arm around his waist while he traced her lips now plump from his kiss. He let his touch linger on her temple, dug into the mane of her hair as he tried his damnedest to slow himself down.

But his erection pressed uncomfortably against his pants. All he wanted was for both of them to be out of these clothes, their two naked body rubbing against each other freely.

"I want to feel you against me, too." Her voice was small but filled with fever, and determination.

And he knew then that he would take the time, all night if needed, to make her bristle under his touch and cry his name for more. She was not one of Mag's waitresses, or even the shopkeeper's daughter Emmeline.

No. She was *the one*.

The one he had been awaiting for centuries. The one that would make his immortal life worth living. Beyond atonement. Beyond redemption. The one whose thoughts merged with his.

He would not rush this. And if she wanted it now, he would fulfill her wishes but on his own terms. So that before he took her, her lust for him would be a perfect match for his intense desire of her. So that their first time together felt as long as the centuries he'd spent waiting for her. He wanted her to feel every emotion, every craving he now experienced for her. Draw it all on her bare flesh, and deep within her.

"Oh Maisie. You have no idea..."

"I can feel it."

"Not yet." He smirked and lowered his lips to the crook of her neck. "There's so much I want for you..."

He nibbled at the tender skin of her throat, inhaled her feminine scent, and felt her quiver under him. As he kissed the curve of her shoulder above the loose collar of her t-shirt, he freed her from the blankets trapping her.

She kicked off the bedsheets and reached behind his neck, pulling him closer.

He captured one breast, right over the *Serpent Maudit* logo of the oversized shirt. He opened his palm wide and trailed it slowly across her nipple through the cotton fabric. The tender bud stiffened and he moved his hand again and again until it was a solid pebble under his skin.

"Val," was all she could say, before letting out a cry of pleasure. He rolled the taut bud between his thumb and forefinger, each nip bringing a feverish sigh from her, and then tugged at it gently. He could feel her every sliver of desire run straight through him.

He had no idea when they bonded that he'd experience her carnal appetite within his own body. The deepened craving drove him wild. He no longer knew where he began and where she ended. They were both adrift in such intense need for each other, that time had no meaning.

Maisie dug her fingers deeper into the back of his neck, wanting more of his touch, more of his weight, more of his breath mixing with hers.

Her whole body was a deep rush of cravings and she didn't know where to start with all that pent-up lust. She wanted to rip his pants off, crush his body on top of her, feel his erection against her and more. She wanted him to dig his fangs, right there where he had kissed her, at the crook of her neck. She had no idea where the thirst for his bite had come from, but it was there, among a thousand things she wanted him to do to her.

She wrapped a bare leg around him, his sweatpants rough against her aroused skin, and shifted to her side to face him on the bed.

He gently pushed her back, his palm now fully gripping her breast. "Not yet."

She gasped, deliciously waiting for all he had for her,

wanting at once to lay there and take it all, while also dying to flip him over and rip off his clothes until he was stark naked beneath her.

She settled for sliding her palm under his shirt, sampling his warmth and delighting in contouring the planes of his muscles with her touch. He groaned and then inhaled sharply as she sensed his desire for her rush through his groin. He wanted her, she knew it, but he also wanted to enjoy every moment.

He finally gripped the border of her shirt and lifted it slowly above her chest, making sure that the fabric slid diabolically against her tight nipples. The motion was so slow that by the time he pulled her shirt completely off, both her breasts were ready, her nipples erect and sensitive, hungering for attention.

"*Seigneur*," he said, his voice hoarse, taking the time to trail his gaze all over her chest while she lay hungering for more, catching her breath under his inspection and waiting. Waiting for his move. She bit her bottom lip, and he shook his head as if in disbelief.

Finally, after what felt like an eternity of holding back under his contemplation, he lowered his lips on one of her needy nipples. The shard of pleasure shot straight through her core.

"More," she called out involuntarily.

He licked the tender tip of her breast and, while supporting himself above her with one arm, tweaked her other nipple between his fingers.

She moaned at the intensity of the sensation and let out a genuine cry of ecstasy as he grazed the bud with one of his fangs, taking a gentle bite.

Her insides burned, everything was on fire, pretty much just as he'd promised.

He continued to play with her—occasionally leaving a breast to tease her navel and the tender skin just above her panties—for what felt like hours. She was so taken by his touch that all she could do was to contour his firm butt between her hands, yearning for him to finally take her while also wishing for this to go on forever.

When he reached between her legs with a demanding touch, she cracked. She could not wait any longer. "Val, please. I want you. Now."

He cupped her entire crotch with his hand, over the lacy fabric of her panties now damp from her need, and watched her, his face just above her breasts. His expression was feverish, his fangs fully out, love, bloodlust and carnal hunger for her warred in his features, one and all the same.

"Mine." His hands seized her further, parting her intimately through the thin silk. "All of you is mine, now."

"Yes, I am," she replied simply. Knowing that right then and there, she would take all that he offered, meet all his needs with similar thirst.

"Take me," she ordered him. "I want you inside."

And again he shook his head, denying her what she craved to make her burn even further for him.

He slid his hand inside her panties, finding the tender spot tense with need and brushed the pad of his index right over it.

She gasped at the sizzling touch.

"Like this?" he asked with a devilish grin.

She could only nod, her breath caught in her throat at the intense stimulation.

"You like it, *ma belle*."

She could only respond by parting her legs wide and press up against his fingers. But despite how much she urged him on for more, more pressure, more rhythm, he continued to keep her on the edge of climax, with tender small strokes, just enough to make her burn but not enough to provide full release.

"Now," she commanded, desperately wanting him. "Please?"

He wanted her burning and pleading for it, and she felt

his satisfaction at knowing he had taken her there, to that point where nothing mattered and where she was willing to submit to his needs, to his demands, just to find that sweet climax under his touch. A complete surrender to his love.

Please, Val. She sent the request mentally, touching his very soul, and she sensed his joy, his delight, to have broken through her last barrier. They were so close she could feel his emotions and all she saw in him was love, bliss, and a desire to make her happy, make her whole.

He growled and finally ripped off her panties. He stood from the bed, his eyes unable to tear themselves from her spent and needy naked body waiting for him to return.

"I wanted to do so much more, *mon amour*," he professed, standing there so wide and tall in the lavish bedroom. "But I don't think I can."

"Take me now, Val." She held her breath, facing him straight on.

He stretched behind his neck to take off his shirt, and she purred at the sight of his muscular chest glistening in the glow of the dawn coming through the gauzy shades of the tall narrow window.

His lips curled into a half smile, and she recognized the confident immortal she had seen at the entrance of the sanctuary when she had first landed in Montreal. The one that had made her crush hard in the forest of Berwick Hollow.

He swiftly slid his pants down. "You're burning for it, I can tell." His amused tone lightened the gravity of the moment.

"Like hell I am!" she retorted. But her desire intensified at the sight of his cock, solid and thick and so ready for her.

Nearly over the edge, she got to her knees and grabbed him by his broad shoulders. She toppled him over her and positioned him right where she wanted him, with her legs parted wide and wrapped around his hips.

"Our first time with love." The teasing smile was gone. He was completely serious now.

"For the two of us. First time for love," she repeated.

And when he took her, full and hard, deep inside her, all she cared about was the strong connection between them. His need was hers, her longing his, and they both became lost into each other as he thrust in and out of her with intensity.

"Bite me," she urged him.

And just like that, he did.

His teeth sank into her neck while he also reached between their joined bodies to stroke her intimately in time with his thrusts, and in unison with each of his pulls of her blood at her throat.

She was gripping him tight, her nails dug into his back when she unconsciously called out the incantation that would take their passion beyond the human experience.

Ist gahzem kesharan...

And for an eternity they remained, right there at the cusp of desire and ecstasy, in pure love for each other, enhanced by the witch's spell and the vampire blood trance.

Finally, their orgasm shattered them both. Together, they fell on the bed side by side, looking up at the rose-gold bed canopy, exhausted, smiling, laughing, like two kids who had discovered something incredible, something no one could ever know about. Motionless, they held hands, catching their breath, not daring to say a word.

Maisie was the first to hear the scratch at the door. "Sasha!"

"He probably feels a little neglected."

"Go get him," she said with a smile. "Poor doggy."

She admired Val's muscular butt as he strode across the room completely naked and without self-consciousness. The strong body so sexy as every one of his muscles flexed with each of his move. He was hers, all of him. Her anchor. For eternity.

"Come on, Sash." She patted the mattress as the animal barged through the door, his tail batting madly.

Val returned to bed with Sasha jumping right after him. "Not sure who he is jealous of, you or me."

"No one." She tucked herself under the blanket by Val's naked body and tapped the mattress again to call Sasha to her. "We both love him."

Val had her in his arms. He drew the comforter over them while Sasha nudged himself closer, somehow finding himself positioned right between them.

"But he is sneaky, isn't he?"

"Let him." She laughed, snuggling into safety with the dog's weight over her leg and Val's strong hold around her. "I think he deserves a little affection."

"He does." Val patted Sasha's head then tightened his embrace around her as she finally felt sleep catching up with her. "We all do."

EPILOGUE

"*I* am the high priestess now." Maisie pocketed her phone and stared at the sign welcoming them to the US. She flashed a smile at Val, her lover at the wheel of his Jeep as he drove them back to her home. "Just needs to be formalized at Samhain."

Sasha slept on the back seat, surrounded by a collection of fluffy toys bought by his new doggy-mom.

"They accepted you? You talked to your grandmother?"

"Yes. She texted to confirm that the other witches have agreed to her choice now that I'm immortal and have you by my side." She nodded and tilted her head back with confidence. "I'm strong enough to convince the whole supernatural council if they ever deny me."

"I'll face them with you if it comes to that," he told her with a grin.

"They won't deny me. My coven is behind me."

"Even the Elder Beaudry? She won't go against you?"

"Likely not. I am bonded to you. The Ice Witch's son." She beamed at him. "And who *is* your birth father anyway?"

"We're still looking."

"Your brother Griffon."

"Yeah, Griff," Val shook his head. "His obsession."

"I haven't met Cassiodore either yet. Your mom mentioned him during my vision."

"Oh right, better not turn starstruck on me when you do."

"Never." Her playful tone turned thoughtful. "Will Magnovald be okay? He cares about you."

Val let out a small laugh. "Mag only cares about one thing. His club, enjoying his night life. He doesn't think much about our parents or the consequences of his feeding on the staff. He just is."

"You'll miss him."

"Yeah." He rubbed a hand over his forehead.

"We'll be back, honey." Of that she was certain. She would not let him sacrifice his family for her. "After we deal with everything in Berwick Hollow, and maybe meet with the warlocks in Seaport."

He let go of the wheel to settle his hand on her thigh. His smile was bright. "I'm with you all the way."

"I may have this power," she said, "but you have the true strength. Without you, I'll get lost again."

"You won't."

"Magic always has its price."

"But balance has a way of restoring itself. We found each other."

"We've always been connected," she reminded him. "Your lineage and mine. They come from an ancient coven, magical sisters."

"My mother?" He slowly raised an eyebrow, curious.

"Yes, and the First Witch. I saw them both when I became immortal."

"I don't need visions to know we belong together." He gave her thigh a gentle squeeze. "I want to make this official, when you're ready."

"A handfasting?" She gasped. "Is this a proposal?"

"I was really thinking of a church wedding but handfasting will do." A twinkle appeared in his eye. "As long as it's public."

"Both." She clasped his hand beneath her own with glee.

"You think?"

She nodded eagerly. "Handfasting in Berwick Hollow, church wedding in Montreal."

"Anything you want, *ma belle*. As big as you want it." His joy carried right through her as his lips curled into a half smile. "The guest list is sure to be interesting."

Dear reader,

Montreal is the city of my birth. While I grew up in Québec City a few hours north of Montreal and I call Seattle home, it is still dear to my heart and is where most of my family lives.

My father received his Geology degrees from the University of Montreal, my mother studied nursing at the Hotel-Dieu Hospital, one of the oldest hospitals in North America and which was the inspiration behind the Sanctuaire des Truands *shelter. And I received my Physics degree from McGill University and loved my time there as a student.*

My son recently visited the city and called me from the Café Campus nightclub, which was founded in 1967 and still exist to this day. It warmed my heart to learn that he was enjoying his night at a place where both his mother and his grandparents (as well as multiple cousins, aunts and uncles) went for a night out during the last fifty years.

The cold I describe is real. A Québec winter night is nothing like I ever experienced anywhere else, and it really chills you to the bone. It was really fun to put Maisie through the experience for this book.

Thank you so much, lovely reader, for sharing this story with me. Your own support means the world to me. If you want to be part of my writing process, see how my own heritage has a way of seeping into my writing, and discover which new tortured hero will finally find his true love, I invite you to join my Secret Circle where you will receive about two emails a month (usually on Mondays) with my latest progress, small giveaways and freebie reads.

You can join me here: www.subscribepage.com/mcbourque and as a thank you gift for your lovely support, you will receive your own exclusive copy of my American Title winner novel Ancient Whispers, where the elusive First Witch Morag Callan first makes her appearance into my world.

A true soulmate story and inspired by the ply of Acadians and Cajuns in North America, this award-winning novel, currently unavailable anywhere, will touch your soul, I promise.

Trust your heart…

Marie-Claude xoxo

PS: If you're like me, you might be super curious to see if Val's brothers also meet the love of their life. Read on because I am treating you to a sneak peek into **Book 2 of the Vampires of the Black Oak Series** with Magnovald's quest for love.

He's about to meet his match with Nyssa Vlahos, a Montreal real estate magnate who is not easily swayed by his devilish charm.

Keep reading to see them together…

A VAMPIRE'S SIN

An Enemies to Lovers Slow-Burn Paranormal Romance

Son of an ancient vampire and a legendary French witch, Mont-Royal Immortal Magnovald St-Amand has lived for so long that nothing matters except his ruling over the Montreal's sultry nightlife.
But when he chooses to help an ambitious real estate tycoon rescue her kid sister from a pack of daemons, he finds deep yearnings in his soul that he thought were buried forever.

Read on for a taste of *A Vampire's Sin*...

"Mr. St-Amand," Nyssa drove right to the point with a curt nod, "I need your help."

He raised an inquisitive brow then the cocky smile returned. "Mag."

She frowned and leaned back on her heels with her arms crossed at her chest.

"I've told you before, *poupée*." An impossibly dark twinkle appeared in his eyes. "Call me Mag."

"Fine." She shook her head and took a decisive step forward. "Mag, I need your help."

"Now that's interesting," He lazily stretched his long leg under the table as he watched her with a slight tilt of his head. "No new offer for my club today?"

She nodded at the finance paperwork scattered on the table in front of him, momentarily distracted from her current purpose. "You're not up to code, Mag. It's just a matter of time before the city board forces you to comply."

She surveyed the the exposed wires alongside the mirrored wall behind the bar. The steps leading to the stage by the dance floor were crooked and old pipes were exposed just over the DJ area. The place was an opulent den at night under the colored strobe lights, but the day exposed its potentially harmful flaws.

"I can offer you more money than you can spend in a lifetime," she added.

"A lifetime, really?" he snorted. "You'd be surprised about that."

"Look, I'm not here for your club." Her current quest was so much more important than making him another generous offer for the premises. She just had to go for it. Ask him for his help. Now.

"Then you came for me." His features lightened. A crinkle appeared at the corner of his eye. "About time. Want to go upstairs right away? Or you want romance first, maybe dinner?"

"No." She brushed his banter aside with a wave of her hand. There were no chances in hell she'd ever go out with him.

Perhaps it was her own assumptions, but everything seemed a joke to him, from the casual banter he constantly used on her to the laid-back way he ran his business. Life was no laughing matter. Hers had been a challenge which she had met head on at every turn.

But all that was not important right now. She eyed him hard. "I need you to give me access to Moreno."

"Ennio?" He chuckled and slid his tall body back farther. "What happened? Are you late with your protection payment? I thought you'd be the type to go straight to the police."

"Mr. St-Amand." She huffed, correcting herself. "Mag." She grabbed a chair to sit across him. Her back stiff, she leaned in towards him. She had no time to beat around the bush. "It's about my little sister. Stepsister, actually. She's missing."

He shook his head and his expression changed. His forehead creased with gravity for the first time since she'd walked in. "Missing?"

"She ran away with her boyfriend. He's much older than she is. Some rapper named Oliver LaChance. My sources say he's connected. She's only thirteen." Nyssa swallowed, her mouth parched. "Mr. Moreno might know where to find her."

"A kid. *Sacrament.*" Mag leisurely ran a hand through his

hair and bent forward, unease warring upon his features. "Not sure I can help you, though."

With her heart racing, she pushed her shoulders back. Her gaze was unwavering. "I'm willing to trade for your help."

A VAMPIRE'S SIN is available on all storefronts.
—find it on your favorite store today at
www.marieclaudebourque/a-vampires-sin

A FREE STORY FOR YOU...

Enjoyed A Vampire's Spell? Not ready to stop reading yet? A copy of *A VAMPIRE'S HEART*, the story of Val and Maisie's first meeting, is yours to download as a thank you for joining my Secret Circle.

Get your download code at:
marieclaudebourque.com/a-vampires-heart

A VAMPIRE'S HEART

A Witch-Vampire Meet Cute Paranormal Romance Prequel

To prove her worth as a leader to her coven, awkward witch Maisie Thibodeau must battle a horrible monster in front of the whole supernatural community. But the White Holly sorceresses are not the only ones watching.

Immortal Valerian St-Amand can't tear his eyes from the small but powerful witch as she battles a dangerous troll set on her small mystic town.

While he had vowed not to interfere in witches' business, his unexpected fear for her life makes it impossible for him to keep his distance.

Read on for a taste of *A Vampire's Heart*…

"Hey, it's her!" Mag elbowed him as the pub's door opened, letting some fresh air in.

"Who?" Val frowned as he continued to scan the room, casting a brief nod at the waitress bringing them their drinks.

"The girl from the shop," Mag explained with eagerness.

Val reluctantly looked to see what made his brother so enthusiastic. The young witch from the craft store stood there, a small figure in an anime logoed t-shirt, plain jeans, and faded sneakers. Her poker-straight black hair fanned against her cheek and down to her chest.

A little geeky, but yes, there was something about her. He felt a kinship in her awkwardness. She, too, didn't seem to want to be there.

She perused the crowd, waved at a few people, before settling her eyes on him.

His breath remained caught in his throat as her gaze of the deepest jade connected with his own. The contact disturbed something in him that had been dormant for centuries.

Seigneur!

The strange force stirring within him had gone straight to his core. His heartbeat pounded madly as a flush of warmth spread down to his groin.

Oh damn. Val instinctively searched for Sasha, who was vigorously lapping water from his bowl at his feet. He couldn't remember ever feeling anything so intense before. He shook himself as he sunk his fingers into the fur of his loyal companion. This could mean trouble.

"I wonder if I should hit on her," Mag was saying.

Val moved his head bleakly as she broke their connection to survey the bar with her head held high before waving with animation at a group of women at the back.

"Sure, why not." He let out a slow exhale, his pulse now steadier, and leaned further back in his chair. He forced himself to look away from her and continue to study the patrons. But he couldn't shake the feeling that this young witch was something else.

And with his entire being, he strongly prayed that Mag would leave this one girl alone.

A VAMPIRE'S HEART, the prequel to *A VAMPIRE'S SPELL*, is available at low cost on all storefronts…
and FREE in eBook formal to all
Secret Circle Subscribers.

Get your copy today at
www.marieclaudebourque.com/a-vampires-heart

*You probably wonder about some of the characters you met here…
such as Diesel Stanford, Malcolm Dunsmuir and Harper Grant—as
well as what happens to Val's five brothers and Emmeline Dubois.*

*Here is the list of books current and to-be-released in the Black
Oak world:*

~ Vampires of the Black Oak ~

A Vampire's Heart (Val and Maisie's first meet cute): In this
prequel to A Vampire's Spell, awkward witch Maisie
Thibodeau must prove her worth as leader to her coven by
battling a horrible monster in front of the whole supernatural
community.

A Vampire's Spell (Val and Maisie): Guilt-ridden legacy
vampire Valerian St-Amand teams with powerful witch
Maisie Thibodeau to protect his city from a crazed scientist
seeking immortality.

A Vampire's Sin (Mag and Nyssa): Immortal Montreal
vampire Mag St-Amand teams up with ambitious real estate
tycoon Nyssa Vlahos to rescue her kid sister from a child-traf-
ficking ring run by a pack of daemons.

A Vampire's Soul (Emme and Justin): When female vampire
Emmeline Dubois teams up with faithful immortal friend
Justin St-Amand to escape a vicious hunter set to kill her, the

centuries-old friendship turns into so much more than she'd anticipated.

A Vampire's Fate (Ren and Rosalie): When female wolf-shifter Rosalie Gauthier returns to her town to take on the leadership of her pack after her father's illness, her birthright is challenged by a tyrannic rival and marriage to powerful vampire Ren St-Amand is her only option to save her family's legacy.

A Vampire's Star (Cass and Tilly) Can an immortal truly father a child? That's what rock star Cass St-Amand finds out when Tilly Davenport, a strong-headed music producer banshee, shows up backstage at his latest concert claiming to be carrying his child.

A Vampire's Blood (Griff and Isabelle) Can you fall in love with your lifelong enemy? Griff St-Amand has his hands full when he finds himself having to rescue French supernatural hunter Isabelle LeGall despite her hatred for his family.

~ Warlocks of the Black Oak ~

A Warlock's Kiss (Diesel and Kera): Stoic warlock leader Diesel Stanford must convince his panther-shifter ex-girl-friend Kerala Clarke to return the only magical artifact that can cure his sister from a terrible hex.

A Sorcerer's Night (Sin and Celeste): Protective panther-shifter sorcerer Sinclair Clarke battles a powerful demon who holds hostage his fiancee, legacy witch Celeste Stanford.

An Alchemist's Desire (Thorn and Raven): Recluse alchemist Thornwood Huntington must help talented violinist Raven Giancola unlock the magic of her enchanted violin despite his vow to keep all things magic away from non-sorcerers.

An Archmage's Destiny (Knight and Bryce):
With her reputation on the line, steadfast attorney Bryce
Jackson must convince daredevil warlock Knightley Morgan
to return to the folds of his powerful New England family or
apply the devastating consequences herself.

A Spellbinder's Denial (Duke and Sloane):
Riddled with guilt after his unleashed powers wrecked lives
decades ago, billionaire warlock Duke Morgan still refuses to
unlock his powers to make amends, but when savvy banshee
Sloane Davenport crosses his path again, even his fortune
won't be enough to protect her.

A Necromancer's Love (Mal and Harper):
When vampires descend on his city, Seattle necromancer
Malcolm Dunsmuir can no longer hide from the darkness of
his demon side, especially when the enticing life-loving
human Harper Grant tries her very best to bring him to the
light.

A Warlock's Storm (Rey and Saira): Stranded on a boat in a
haunted New England harbor, rugged warlock Rey Stanford
and sassy female panther-shifter Saira Varma battle sea-
monsters and revenants as they try to survive the night.

CAST OF MAIN CHARACTERS

Vampires:

Valerian (Val) St-Amand: Mount-Royal Immortal and founder of the *Sanctuaire des Truands* shelter in Montreal. Brother to Mag, Justin, Ren, Cass and Griff.

Magnovald (Mag) St-Amand: Mount-Royal Immortal and owner of the *Serpent Maudit* night club in Montreal. Brother to Val, Justin, Ren, Cass and Griff.

Professor Justinien (Justin) St-Amand: Mount-Royal Immortal and professor of Astronomy at McDougall College in Montreal. Brother to Val, Mag, Ren, Cass and Griff

Renaud (Ren) St-Amand: Mount-Royal Immortal and honorary member of the Domaine-Lassale Wolf Pack.

Cassiodore (Cass) St-Amand: Mount-Royal Immortal and brother to Val, Mag, Justin, Ren and Griff.

Griffon (Griff) St-Amand: Mount-Royal Immortal and brother to Val, Mag, Justin, Ren and Cass.

Emmeline (Emme) Dubois: Montreal immortal vampire and former fiancée of Val St-Amand. Friend to the St-Amand brothers.

Evan Grant: cursed Montreal vampire, sister to the Daemon Queen Harper Grant, and bouncer to Mag St-Amand. Was saved from blood addiction by Val St-Amand and the *Sanctuaire des Truands* shelter.

Witches:

Maisie Thibodeau: Witch of the White Holly Coven in Berwick Hollow

Madame Lakota Ioshta: Eclectic Witch of the Mohawks of Kahnawá:ke clan and close friend to Charlotte Callan.

Charlotte Callan (aka The Ice Witch): Ancient witch of the Callanish tradition and mother of the Mount-Royal Immortals.

Morag Callan (aka The First Witch): Ancient coven sister of Charlotte Callan and High Priestess of the Callanish Coven, consort of Alchemyst Iain Callan of the Celtic Isles.

High Priestess Marianne Thibodeau: High Priestess of the While Holly Coven in Berwick Hollow and grandmother to Maisie Thibodeau

The Elder Agatha Beaudry: Elder of the White Holy Coven and distant relative to the Thibodeaus in Berwick Hollow

Warlock:

Diesel Stanford: Warlock and leader of the Order of the Black Oak. Resides in Seaport with his wife panther-shifter Kerala Clarke and their young son Sai Stanford.

Disciples of Nostredame:

Father Grégoire: Oldest disciple of Nostredame, living at the *Sanctuaire des Truands* in Montreal and assigned to Val St-Amand

Ariane: Young female disciple of Nostredame, living at the *Sanctuaire des Truands* and assigned to Justin St-Amand.

Faithful Companion:

Sasha: Chocolate Labrador dog and devoted companion to Val St-Amand

Daemons:

King Malcolm (Mal) Dunsmuir: Warlock of the Black Oak, Necromancer and King of the Daemon Realm. Consort to Harper Grant.

Queen Harper Grant: Queen of the Daemon Realm, consort to Mal Dunsmuir and sister to cursed vampire Evan Grant.

Humans:

Collins: scientist and Chemistry professor at a local Montreal university. His father was saved from blood addiction in the 1980s by Val St-Amand and the *Sanctuaire des Truands* shelter.
Captain Akande: Female police officer and Captain of the Sureté du Québec provincial police. Mag St-Amand's loyal friend.
Sandrine: Waitress at *Serpent Maudit* night-club and loyal friend to Mag St-Amand.

FRENCH-ENGLISH GLOSSARY

Sanctuaire des Truands - Sanctuary of the Miscreants
p'tite fille - little girl
sorcière - *witch*
Mademoiselle - *Miss*
seigneur - *lord (common French Canadian curse)*
Serpent Maudit - *Cursed Serpent*
merde - *shit (common French curse)*
diable - *devil (old-fashioned French curse)*
Rituel du Sang - *Blood Ritual*
chéri - dear
mon amour - *my love*
fille - *girl*
merci - *thank you*
poupée - *doll*
Fille du Roy - *Daughter of the King*
la Sorcière des Glaces - *the Ice Witch*
Oh mon dieu, mon chéri - *Oh my god, my love*
sacrament - *sacrament, as in the Christian rite. (common French Canadian curse)*
ma chère - *my dear*
sortilège - *spell*
mon doux Jesus - *sweet Jesus*
une sorcière blanche - *a white witch*
mon père - *father*
Immortels du Mont-Royal - *Mont-Royal Immortal*
en cette nuit du douze décembre - *in this night of the twelfth of december*
loup-garous - *werewolves*
bonsoir, ma p'tite sorcière - *good evening, little witch*
ma belle - *beautiful*

mon ange - *my angel*

printemps du jour, printemps de la nuit - *daytime Spring, night-time Spring*

pour cette cérémonie, viens à moi aujourd'hui - *for this ceremony, come to me in this day*

ACKNOWLEDGEMENTS

I want to thank all the readers who have followed me through the Order of the Black Oak journey. Thank you all. Your support means the world to me.

I am also very grateful to talented romance author, friend and my amazing editor Jenn Bray-Webber who helped so much with this book. Thank you also to Em Petrova for her eagle-eye proofreading and Frauke Spanuth for a great set of covers.

And last but not least, deepest thanks to my lovely readers Reena, Evelyn, Cheryl, Rain, Cathy, Pauline, Shirl and Mary for their help in naming Val's trustworthy companion Sasha.

Marie-Claude Bourque is an author of gothic paranormal romance and the winner of the American Title V award with her first novel ANCIENT WHISPERS.

Her writing features modern-day fantasy skillfully weaved into infinitely romantic stories between smart strong women and complex passionate heroes.
Happily Ever After always absolutely guaranteed!
Find more at www.marieclaudebourque.com

To be first to hear about her latest book, win free copies and more, subscribe to
Marie-Claude's Secret Circle at
www.marieclaudebourque.com/secret-circle

Or connect directly with her at
www.facebook.com/mcbourque

facebook.com/mcbourque

twitter.com/mcbourque

amazon.com/author/marieclaudebourque

goodreads.com/mcbourque

bookbub.com/profile/marie-claude-bourque

instagram.com/marie.claude.now

r